'Powerful and poignant, honest and he window on some painful human experi
Jeff Lucas, author, broadcaster, speaker

'To say life has its ups and downs is really a bit of an ... Every day brings joys and sorrows. Life's learning is about how we do the journey and engage in the reality of life and death. This book brings us a story that gives us insight into how our mind, body and spirit try to deal with these "ups and downs" and how family and community don't just matter, but are essential to moving on.'
Ruth Dearnley, OBE, CEO, STOP THE TRAFFIK

'Weaving stories of a dysfunctional past with the present repercussions, the writer movingly leads the reader through the eyes of each player to a place of forgiveness and restoration.'
Nola Leach, Chief Executive, CARE

'*At Therapy's End* is the gentle, at times movingly raw, story of a family's struggle to overcome tragedy. Susie Flashman Jarvis manages to capture the rhythms of daily life and intertwine them with moments of genuine depth. Her rich understanding of human nature fills every page, and the characters portrayed are accurate and perceptive. The realism of Katie in particular made me smile. There are some descriptive nuggets that are simply beautiful, bringing the story to life (I loved, "nursing our pain like a newborn baby, not wanting to share it with anyone"), and I was intrigued from the first page to find out what had happened to this family. Honest, insightful and enriching, it flowed naturally to a conclusion that was satisfying and thought-provoking at the same time.'
Beth Moran, writer, speaker, church leader and trustee of the women's network Free Range Chicks

'This book calls forth a range of powerful emotions as it mines the painful familiarity of "real" family life and relationships; the long reach of childhood trauma; the horror of domestic abuse; the complications of family dynamics and the long journey into safe harbours. Susie Flashman Jarvis has told a remarkable story.'
Justyn Rees Larcombe, speaker and author of Tails You Lose

'*At Therapy's End* is a brave story about a brave woman who continues to discover the depth of her bravery in her willingness to uncover her past. All of us are invited to journey through the everyday life of a strong and capable woman as she makes a decision to live in the shallow or to choose the deep. Because she is brave and strong on the inside as well as the out, she chooses the deep. And in the uncovering of the unspeakable past, of wounds that go well beyond the skin and bones and cut straight through the heart, this woman chooses light and life. And this light and life set her free.

'For me as someone who walks with survivors of trauma every day, this novel is a gift. It's a familiar tale but with an essentially different ending.

'How do you continue to live while you process and heal from uncovered pain?

'How do you bring your past into the light and have it illuminate a new way rather than drag you into an old one?

'How do survivors break habits and patterns of thought and behaviour?

'These questions and many more are both asked and answered through this novel in a way that is not pushy but is absolutely true. People choose freedom. This choice by the woman in this book is the most important choice all of us ever make – it is the choice to say no to the loudest voices that suggest freedom is found in denial. And it is the choice to say yes to the small voice that keeps whispering to our own soul that the only way out is through – and that's the way to freedom.

'And it is. It is perhaps the only way to be free. To live in the light.

'I'd recommend a strong cup of tea and the willingness to journey to the deeper places inside your own story as you read this one. I'd recommend you hear the invitation that is in its pages as one for yourself. I'd recommend you listen for the whisper of God who longs for you to uncover the dark places to bring in a beautiful light. I'd recommend you read and be reminded that you are loved and that love can change everything.

'This novel is a beautiful example of how a brave life can invite others to be brave too. I hope I can live as bravely as the invitation asks.'

Danielle Strickland, Major, the Salvation Army, Edmonton Canada

'I have not been able to put this book down as I have walked with Simon and Sophie and their family as their story came alive through the pages of this book. I have laughed and wept as their story unfolded and yet throughout was very aware of love and hope threaded through every page. Sophie and Simon's story has been written with such compassion and tenderness and yet does not gloss over the harsh realities of life, offering to the reader both wisdom and insights not only for themselves but for others too. I highly recommend it.'
Dilys Threshie, spiritual director

'*At Therapy's End* is a heart-warming novel. The story reveals itself in an intriguing way and manages to give an honest insight into the effects of domestic violence and finishes by showing the redemptive power found through a Christian faith.'
Cornelia Chalke

'I found Susie's book both engaging and moving and at times it brought me to tears.

'I have worked for many years in a women's refuge setting and come across many traumatised children in that time. Susie's book gives a real insight as to how these children might be feeling about the abuse that they have witnessed and experienced and the long-term effects of this for them.

'Alongside that the main storyline kept me wanting to read on and not put this book down.'
Yvette Hazelden, Contract Manager, Look Ahead Care and Support

'This afternoon I've come to the end of your book. Wow, what a writer. I just couldn't put it down. I am an emotional person and at times had to stop and remind myself that it was a story because it was as if it was someone's testimony. I must say I got totally lost in what I was reading. It has been gripping, emotional, exciting, happy, sad and just beautiful.

'I shall now go and empty my bucket of tissues.'
Sharon Brooks, Befriending and supported house coordinator, Jericho Road Project

'Normal family life has its ups and downs. But perhaps the hardest thing that any parent can face is the death of one of their children – it goes against the natural order of life, and the shape of their family is changed forever. Traumatic experiences earlier in life can make loss even harder to deal with, so suppressing grief may sometimes seem the easiest option. *At Therapy's End* is a really well-written story about a family that has experienced that worst loss, but is unable to deal with it. Professional counselling enables Sophie and Katie to regain some strength, but the real turning point for the family comes when Simon is able to talk to another bereaved dad. That understanding support from someone else who has "been there" can make a massive difference to a bereaved dad or mum, and in this case it enables Simon to lead his family into a place where they are able to revisit memories and recognise Jakey as an ongoing part of their family.

'Written by a professional counsellor, this book gives a good insight into a bereaved family's struggle towards finding a new normality in their life together. The characters are very real and, although it is written as a novel, it could easily be part of your story or mine.'
Mike Coulson, Bereaved Parent Support Coordinator, Care for the Family

'Domestic abuse is an issue that needs to be highlighted and the emotional fallout recognised as something that needs to be dealt with. With *At Therapy's End*, Susie expertly weaves characters' lives and story lines of domestic abuse, depicting how the ripples of the behaviour can spread far and wide and can lay hidden for years before coming to the surface. Despite dealing with gritty subjects of abuse and death and coping with emotional trauma, Susie scatters seeds of hope throughout the novel showing how sharing and reaching out to others can provide comfort and support so all experiences, however harrowing, can be used for good. Susie also manages to bring her faith into the novel in a gentle and questioning but very real way, that many people will be able to identify. To me, *At Therapy's End* is more than just a novel; it is Susie suggesting and encouraging others to find ways, whether that be through counselling, writing things down or sharing with others, to work through terrible events that may be thrown up through life's journey with the final result being a triumphant message of hope.'
Libby Sutcliffe, BBC radio presenter, online journalist newsreader and founder of Slavery Free UK

At Therapy's End

Susie Flashman Jarvis

instant
apostle

First published in Great Britain in 2015

Instant Apostle

The Barn
1 Watford House Lane
Watford
Herts
WD17 1BJ

British Library Cataloguing-in-Publication Data

A catalogue record for this book is available from the British Library

This book and all other Instant Apostle books are available from Instant Apostle:

Website: www.instantapostle.com

E-mail: info@instantapostle.com

ISBN 978-1-909728-30-1

Printed in Great Britain

Acknowledgements

Writing a novel has been one of the biggest challenges that I have ever undertaken. My autobiography was hard enough, but this novel required me sitting with my imagination alone, and drawing the characters from within myself. It meant me walking with them and discovering what was happening in their lives and then sharing it with you. It has brought me tears and joy as I have stood in their shoes; and it has taught me that only the brave choose to risk all and love.

I have always loved to write, but in order for my dream to come true I have needed support from many, so thank you to each one of you:

Lyndsay Dodd, for your initial reading of the rudimentary draft and your gentle edit and direction.

Nigel Freeman, who has always championed my writing, for loving this book from the outset and for patiently dealing with my many grammatical struggles.

Kath and Mike Coulson, bereaved parent support coordinators, from Care for the Family, who have offered me so much advice and encouragement on this journey.

Mark Whitehead, who had to manage me on the end of the phone as I queried his corrections.

Nicki Copeland, who copy edited with such finesse and care.

To Bonnie, my eldest daughter who decided that shoes showed family life and then took the cover photograph, and Millie for the illustration.

To the many friends who have prayed for me.

To all those who agreed to read and review it, I am humbled and thrilled that you love this story as much as I do.

My publisher Manoj Raithatha who, with such wisdom, has shown me the way forward.

And last, but in no way least, thank you to my amazing husband and children who have enabled me to work with the broken for so many years.

I dedicate this to all the men, women and children who have given me the honour of allowing me to walk with them, in and through their pain.

Prologue

1st November
Friday

Simon poured everyone a drink, looked at each face as he handed them their glass, and then he spoke. 'Today I realised how close I came to losing you. So I brought you here so you would be a captive audience.'

He paused and drew breath. 'First I want to say how much I love you, how much I have always loved you. Nothing that has happened has *ever* changed how I feel about you.'

They visibly stiffened and appeared to steel themselves; then he raised his glass.

'To my amazing family: Sophie, Kate, Alfie and Jakey, who was so full of life we could not contain him.'

Chapter one

Three weeks earlier: 12th October
Saturday
6.30am

Sophie

She smiled, hugging her dressing gown around her waist with one arm and dipped her Earl Grey tea bag in and out of the boiling water. The required colour achieved, she was set. The dogs sat at her feet in expectation but lowered their heads as she wagged her finger in dismissal: she needed this hour, early and alone, to start the project.

Pulling the kitchen door shut behind her, she held her breath; stock-still, she listened for sounds of life, and then moved into the room.

The early morning light struggled to break through the drawn blinds that striped the room to elegant effect, the room that was full of evidence that betrayed the identity of the inhabitants. The light of the dawn was too feeble to bring into sharp focus the clutter of the room, but Sophie, familiar in the terrain of fallen toys and discarded shoes, moved with ease.

The sofa sighed as she settled into position. 'Right, let's do it.' She spoke aloud to the room.

Her laptop sat shining in the light of the lamp that was now illuminating the room in all its messy glory. She briefly took in the vista then hurriedly turned her attention to the task in hand.

Just a few short weeks ago she found herself drawing in breath as she faced her therapist for the last time. It had been a long journey. As she had looked at the face with which she had become so familiar, she had nodded in agreement: she was ready. It was time to end, time to write her story, alone, to complete the healing.

Her muscles flickered as she smiled to herself. Tentatively she slid the catch to one side and opened the laptop. Simon had given it to her last night as they sat side by side. She had leaned against him, aware of her smile, and now today she was still smiling.

She stroked her hand across the keys as the sound of the waking laptop filled the room.

'No, no, shoosh,' she whispered as she searched for the volume switch. She held her breath again to silence the air, and waited. A murmur filtered down through the ceiling and a clonk of something hitting the floor assured her that she was no longer the only one awake, but if she was quick could she do some damage limitation and have just one of them up.

She quickly swigged a mouthful of tea and left her laptop there. 'I'll be back in a minute,' she promised it. Pulling her dressing gown around her, she muttered to herself about needing to find the cord and breaking her neck if she wasn't careful, and legged it as quietly as she could up the stairs and into Alfie's bedroom.

He stood there, resplendent in his Babygro, chubby fingers clutching the side of his cot. The soft glow of the night light was just enough to make out his round features beaming at her in delight.

'Hello darling,' she whispered. 'Did you have a good sleep? Let's go and get a drink and a clean nappy, shall we?' The need for the latter hit her nostrils with a force that was eye watering. 'My goodness – dinner certainly didn't hang about, did it?' she said quietly, as another smile split her face.

She bent to gather up her precious son, feeling his warm, fresh-from-sleep body next to hers, and his arms wrapped around her neck. The love that she felt, that warm glow of motherhood, almost diminished the odour of the nappy and a frequent prowling memory that lurked, threatening to overwhelm, but not quite. Struggling to compose herself she whispered, 'Come on, let's go downstairs. Shh, don't wake Daddy and Katie.'

As she reached the kitchen, Maisie, her most indignant Labrador, and Sid, black and square, clattered around on the kitchen tiles as if to say, about time too!

'Oh please, be quiet, you two – you'll wake the house.'

13

A few steps across the kitchen and she was at the still-warm kettle. If she was quick, she'd be able to make up a bottle with what was left and get back to her laptop.

Adjusting Alfie on her hip, she reached for his bottle and milk powder. Deftly she scooped and flattened the correct amount of powder before adding water: so far so good. The sudden awareness of a warm sensation on her right hip put a halt to her plan.

'Oh no, Alfie, that is so disgusting.' Lifting him away from her body, she spied the spreading stain that seemed to have a life of its own as it worked its way down his legs and, as she turned him she saw also, up his back! There was no option: writing would have to wait. A bath was definitely required to limit any further damage. Her mind was still in full flow, though – adjectives and similes, metaphors and the like jostled for position. 'No,' she said to herself, 'hold fire: one thing at a time.'

Chapter two

The bathroom heater buzzed as the bar slowly started to glow, fighting the chill that ran freely around the large room. Pulling the plastic changing mat out from behind the cupboard, she placed her now wriggling son onto it, only to have him roll over and immediately crawl away in the direction of his bucket of toys.

'Hey, you, come here,' she laughed half-heartedly.

Checking the door to ensure that the escape route was blocked, she turned on the tap, feeling the water temperature as she showered out the previous night's bath residue. While the bath was filling, she turned to capture her errant son, who was quietly chewing a soft yellow duck, unaware of the disaster in his nether regions.

'Come on, you.' Grasping his wriggling form, she pinned him down and started the grand unwrapping. The aroma that filled the room threatened to overwhelm her, but she was not going to be defeated. Not today of all days, she thought. With the skill of one who was obviously well used to brown matter – or even green – she quickly lifted up his writhing form until just his shoulders rested on the mat. Surely it can't have gone any further? she pondered, but yes, there it was, lurking around the neck of his vest!

Finally he lay there, clean and glorious in his nakedness, laughing as he lifted his legs and a warm stream of urine sprang from his body and sprinkled over her dressing gown. Throwing it off and flinging it to one side, Sophie felt over the side of the bath. The room was now warming as the electric bar chased the cold away; the water was warm enough, just, for her to get in too. Slipping off her pyjamas she picked up her laughing boy and stepped into the warm water. Alfie's delight lifted the early morning light of the day with a new radiance, and once again she smiled.

She had hurriedly clipped her hair back, although a few strands fell around her face. With a flick of her wrist she pushed them aside, grabbed an old towel from the windowsill behind her and leaned back, wedging it under her hair clip as a makeshift pillow.

Alfie laughed, sitting between her outstretched legs, patting her skin that shone with water droplets. His outstretched palms created a thwack against the skin of water, and bubbles flicked upwards. He caught her eye and she reflected his surprise, widening her eyes even more to accentuate his response. A deep gurgle released itself through his cherubic ruby lips.

'You are my saving joy,' called her inner voice as flashbacks threatened to overwhelm her.

Settling back against the enamel of the old bath, she regarded her leg, stretched out in its fullness, her toes wrapped around the old brass tap. She loved the quirky design, embraced its history. She had chosen not to update. Things almost held memories of their own, and they had seen things that time could not wipe away. How many people had lain in this bath? The idea did not repulse her as it would many a modern woman. She could name quite a few who had enjoyed the full length of it, and some too painful to name. As Alfie splashed and gurgled, she let her mind wander to safer ground.

Chapter three

Simon had been thrilled, and the interest he took in her changing body and his growing child overshadowed her concerns about the accidental nature of the event. They had shared the news with her mum and stepfather but her hope that the baby would bring a new start for them all had come to nothing. Antenatal classes were shared times, and as she pondered the memory of the first scan she was pulled back into the present as Alfie started to bang his squeaky duck on her leg. She reached for his sponge, and he watched as it became heavy with the warm water. As she slowly lifted it over his dark head, he followed her movements, tilting his head back to receive the full torrent in his face.

'Steady there, you'll choke!' she laughed as he spluttered underneath the flow. 'It's for your hair, Alfie.' His eyes, now surrounded by wet, dark lashes, creased into a smile that was the image of his father's.

Sophie continued to wash his hair and then lathered up his body and her own, the fragrance of baby products filling the now steamy room as they enjoyed the moment of intimacy.

Pulling herself to her feet, while still supporting his slippery form, she reached for the towel she had placed on the back of the chair. Together they stood naked, mother and son, flesh on flesh, his chubby legs kicking against her body as she wrapped the towel around them both. 'Hey, you, what are you up to?' she muttered, her lips against his cheek as he pulled her close.

The bathroom activities were brought to an abrupt halt by a rap on the door. 'What are you doing, Mum? I need to get in there.' The familiar yet unexpected voice of Katie reverberated through the door. She sounded irate. It wasn't a college or work day so why was she up now? Sophie wondered.

'What are you doing out of bed at this time? It's Saturday.'

'I'm going out. Hurry up, Mum.'

Pulling Alfie to her, Sophie whispered, 'Come on, you. Let's go and get dressed. Katie is getting cross.'

The sound of water emptying through the old Victorian plumbing filled the room as Sophie opened the door to reveal irate but beautiful 17-year-old Katie – or Kate, as she liked to be called these days. Her angry face, with its delicate nose piercing, still showed the remains of last night's eye make-up, giving her an unhealthy ghoul-like quality. How did she manage to still look beautiful nonetheless?

'Hurry up, Mum. I need to get in here. Hey Alfie, kiss me.'

As she squeezed past she thrust her face towards her young brother. He made a grab for her face, catching her sparkling nose piercing, which resulted in her screaming in early morning rage.

'He didn't mean it, Katie,' Sophie interrupted, pulling Alfie to one side. He was now letting out an indignant scream of his own. 'Why are you so angry? You weren't late for bed last night, by any chance?' Sophie spoke with attitude.

The slam of the door was the only answer.

'Let's get a drink, kiddo.'

Sophie made her way downstairs. On her way she peeked round the door of her bedroom to check that Simon was still asleep. His head was buried under the duvet and the stillness of his form revealed that either he was determined to portray that he was asleep in spite of the racket that had been unleashed outside the door, or he was truly still exhausted from his trip. Whatever, he did not want to be disturbed. Silently closing the door, her finger pressed against her lips, she crept in an exaggerated fashion downstairs. Alfie's eyes, bright with recently shed tears, smiled in delight.

Less than ten minutes later they were ensconced on the sofa together. Not yet dressed, they leaned in their post-bath warmth and drank their individual drinks, heads bent towards each other in shared enjoyment of the moment.

'What's it like having a mummy who is 40, eh, honey?' mused Sophie. Sipping her second cup of tea she luxuriated in the sublime moment, just her and her son. 'You, my wonderful boy, are my treasure,' she smiled. Holding one of his feet, she leaned forward and kissed his toes causing him to yell in delight.

'What shall we do today?' she giggled, tickling his tummy and planting loud raspberries on his bare midriff as he wriggled with joy.

The thought of moving did not really appeal. The laptop still needed exploring and the urge to write was increasing. The front room seemed to embrace the two of them, inviting a day of calm. Alfie would be happy playing and she was not expecting anyone around as everyone had been over the day before. Simon would be having an ill-advised sleep – not the best way to deal with jet lag, in her opinion, but it did mean that she could doss, and if she really fancied it not even bother to get dressed.

'Let's get breakfast first, pickle. And you need some clothes on.'

Sophie reached across to where she had left a folded pile of clothes. She didn't like to waste time ironing so everything was leaned on and placed in piles belonging to each person. Alfie's pile had not made it upstairs yet – sleepsuits, denim trousers and chunky jumpers, vests and socks, and t-shirts. She loved dressing him; she could buy him lovely clothes now life was not such a struggle: no jumble sale clothes for him! She pulled out a pair of trousers and a jumper that had 'Baby' emblazoned across the chest, socks and a vest. Cute boy, she thought. She held them up for Alfie's approval. 'Shall we put these on, gorgeous?'

He laughed, the teat of his bottle still in his mouth. Milk leaked out of his smile and ran down his cheek to the crease in his neck. Grabbing a muslin cloth, Sophie quickly cleaned him up and kissed his head. She just loved the smell of him and could never get enough – his smile, his laugh, and his life – her boy. Her guilty pleasure still held the percussion of distant pain, so she quickly sorted him out and they moved into the kitchen.

The heating had kicked in now and the room was warm, welcoming and messy. Last night's celebration crockery was still in evidence. Most of it had been loaded in the dishwasher but there were still a few things out of place – not that she was particularly tidy, but she did like some order.

Pulling out Alfie's high chair, she sat him in it and secured his reins to ensure he did not climb out. As soon as the high chair was put into position, two silent companions appeared, with begging eyes and wet noses. They were furry piranhas that would wolf down a crust, soggy or not, in seconds. If no scoop bib was in position, Maisie was particularly partial to lap food too.

She passed him his plastic spoon and started to gather the items needed for breakfast. A croissant left from yesterday was put in the oven to warm. Warmed milk was poured over his cereal.

Once everything was ready she pulled up a chair. 'Here we go – posh breakfast just for us.'

She handed him a torn-off piece of her croissant, then put some apricot jam on her plate and ate some herself. The taste took her back, her thoughts rampaging: holidays in France, days long ago; days before the children with their pleasure and pain; before Simon too. Life had appeared to be full then. But now, this life, with unspeakable pain and her now re-emerging from it, was surely much fuller? Maybe the book would bring healing for everyone; not just for her.

Her musings were interrupted by Katie who had suddenly appeared in the doorway. 'Hi, hon, do you want some breakfast? Alfie and I are having posh breakfast. There aren't any more croissants but there is toast. Fancy some?'

'I'm not hungry. Do I look ok?' She was wearing skinny jeans with a tight blue top that was cut low across her breasts. They had seemed to grow overnight and it was difficult to see the little girl she had once been, looking as provocative as she did now. Sophie paused: she had to be careful, aware that her daughter could read her expression all too well. Remember they all dress like that, she told herself.

'You look fine, hon.'

But Katie had not missed the pause. 'You don't like it, do you? The top, I mean?'

'It's ok; I just think it's a bit low. Where are you going?'

'Into town to meet some friends! No one else's mum says anything.' Irritation laced her words.

'They probably don't ask,' was Sophie's quick retort.

Too late the words were out of her mouth. The eye roll happened before she had time to retrieve the situation.

And so it began the all-too-familiar diatribe. 'You always say I look awful. Why can't you just say you like it?'

'I didn't say I didn't like it. I just said the top was low. Please don't let's argue today. Have some breakfast with us. We'd like that, wouldn't we, Alfie?' Sophie hated the way she pleaded with her daughter, but desperation for peace meant she often withheld her true feelings.

Alfie had succeeded in wiping his croissant around his face and was in the process of mashing the chewed remains into his freshly washed hair. Distractedly, Sophie prised the leftover croissant from his fingers and started to spoon his cereal into his mouth. Her mind started; 'stay, Katie, stay...' She looked up and smiled at her angry child.

'I'm not hungry.' And with that she walked out of the room and stomped off upstairs.

Sophie sighed, picking up her coffee with its freshly frothed milk and wondered at the ability of a 17-year-old to totally change the atmosphere in a room, and to turn her lovely breakfast into a mundane procedure of fuelling her body as opposed to a delicious, albeit reheated, delight.

Alfie shouted next to her.

'Sorry, little man. I should just enjoy you, shouldn't I?'

They finished their breakfast and she cleared away the rest of the clutter, fed the leftovers to the dogs and, still leaving last night's remnants, took her refilled coffee cup and son back through to the lounge to continue on her early morning plan.

Chapter four

She had always loved this room, particularly first thing in the morning. The strengthening sun now shone brighter through the gaps in the blinds, the muslin curtains diffusing the light but still setting dust motes dancing. Alfie lifted his fingers to play with the light, and as Sophie pulled the curtains wide the thin striped streams of light became a torrent and the room was bathed in a warming glow.

She flicked up Alfie's mat with a magician's flourish and something that looked like biscuit crumbs flew into the air. She put Alfie down, and he turned and crawled towards his favourite squeaky part. Now sitting comfortably on his padded bottom he turned and smiled at his mother. She arranged other toys around him – buckets of bricks and animals, soft toys and larger ones too, and then sat back on the sofa which once again breathed its welcome. The retrieved laptop released it start-up sound and caught the attention of her son, who crawled towards her.

'Play with your bricks, hon,' she tried as a means of distraction, but he was not so easily sidetracked. He pulled himself up to a wobbly standing position, and tapped the back of the screen.

'This is Mummy's,' she said. 'No, you can't have it,' she stated as he attempted to turn it towards himself.

'Ok, come up here then,' she relented, and hauled him up along with the mat that she lay enticingly over his lap.

Life feels different, she thought as she watched the screen fire up. I feel calm, like the rush is over and there is all the time in the world. When did that happen? Even Katie with all her hormones did not distress her too much at the moment – well, at least for the time being.

Still the distant gunfire of memory vied for attention.

Alfie laughed as the screensaver was revealed. There in all their glory were Maisie and Sid. Alfie loved them. He would crawl after them and they seemed to know what his next move would be and either avoided him or complied with his wishes. Simon had been very careful to make sure they knew their place and would often get on his hands and knees, nudge them out the way and pretend to take their food as they were eating. 'We're in charge of them, so they need to know their place,' he would mutter in response to her grimace.

When Katie was younger and had more time for them, Simon would get her to sit with him and take their food and give it to them piece by piece. And it had worked – the dogs loved the children and Sophie had never worried.

The dogs had not arrived together. Sid had been first, a small black bundle of scruffy cuddles that was just right to hug when times were hard. He didn't argue or complain; in fact, he was partial to hugs, and if he did not get one he would seek it out for himself. Katie had been ten at the time and had been through the worst of times. She had chosen him with Sophie, a small dog for a then small girl. He was a distraction as well as a companion, needing walking and brushing.

A smile flickered over Sophie's face as she remembered the day Katie had played 'dog parlour' and gave Sid her own version of a trim. She had walked into the front room where silence had been reigning for rather a long time to find Sid standing amidst a sea of black hair. He looked as though his legs had suddenly extended and become very thin: the hovercraft effect that Scotties have with fur that trails the ground had disappeared, to be replaced by something that looked like a different breed of dog. She had not reacted at the time, no laughter or even anger: her responses to the normal – or abnormal, for that matter – were lost behind the wall that trauma had created in its wake.

Alfie's banging on the screen brought her back to the present. 'No, you can't do that. I tell you what, let's make a tower, eh?'

The pair of them slid unceremoniously onto the floor. She pulled a bucket of bricks towards her, a mishmash of old and new. Pulling out an old, chewed, green brick, she was tripped back in time again. Katie had always loved bricks. When she was a little girl, before everything happened, they would build intricate towers that would then be knocked down to the accompanying shrieks of delight. They would have their heads bent together in a secret language that only they were privy to, and had seemed to move with a synchronicity, mirroring each other without words. The memory was sharp and a sigh released itself from her lips, and she looked up to see Alfie looking at her.

'Gorgeous, gorgeous you,' she smiled, pulling him to her so that he struggled to be released. 'Where's the big dinosaur? He wants his breakfast.'

The discovered beast attacked the pile of bricks. 'Roar, roar.'

Alfie squealed with delight, grabbing the dinosaur and making him eat more bricks as he mimicked his mother. Leaning back on the sofa, she basked in the moment.

The door was nosed open by Maisie, who crept in, followed by the not-so-subtle Sid, who walked straight over to Alfie and licked his face. 'Hey, get off the mat, Sid,' muttered Sophie as Alfie jumped with surprise, and then clambered after Sid for more of the same.

Sophie lost no time in restoring herself to the sofa, pulling her laptop onto her lap. She tapped the keys, all the while keeping an eye on her errant son and dog. Simon had set up some files for her to use. She was ready to write her story, but even now she wasn't totally sure if she had it in her.

Her therapist had spent many a session helping her to access her inner strength, strength that had evaporated years ago when it had happened. The journey had been long and tortuous, full of dead ends and wrong turns, but she had finally arrived in an open space, with time and air and sunshine on more days than she had been used to in a while. Alfie had brought with his birth an invitation to engage once again with life. But it had taken so long.

The trouble with writing was that she really didn't know where to begin. The idea had been to access the 'budding young writer' who had been lost in her youth and to give her a voice, the voice she had discovered in her sessions. Therapy had been so hard, yet she had grown to really love her counsellor. It was strange how a person who only saw her for one hour a week could read her so well; also how she could hold her pain and apprehension yet not sink under it. Ending her sessions with her had been very scary. She still missed her, but then it had only been a few weeks. The laptop was a plan that had been hatched in the therapy room.

Casting her eyes behind the sofa, Sophie watched Alfie pull himself to a standing position while holding on to Maisie, who seemed to know it was best not to move, even though her collar was tightening under his determined grip. Leaping to both their rescue, Sophie quickly moved to resolve the situation. 'Come on, let's give Maisie and Sid their food.'

Hauling Alfie onto her hip, she moved to the kitchen and fed the dogs, then reheated her coffee which had now gone cold. It was still only 9.00 in the morning: the day lay before them, free and sunny. It would be cold outside but it would be beautiful nonetheless. Maybe a walk with the dogs and then perhaps Alfie would sleep and then she could write?

She decided on her plan and crept back upstairs to see if Katie would keep hold of Alfie while she grabbed some clothes. Tentatively she knocked on her door and carefully pushed it open. The mess that she tried to avoid these days greeted her: clothes strewn across the carpet, left where Katie had stepped out of them. This was not the time to comment; the possibility of a continuation of the breakfast confrontation was too great.

'Can you have Alfie for a moment while I get dressed, please?'

Katie turned from her mirror, her eye make-up applied with the perfection of an artist. She sighed but then relented when she looked at her much-loved little brother. 'Come here, little squidge,' she said as she put out her arms. Alfie reached out to his sister. Once seated on her lap, he watched his own face in the mirror.

Sophie moved out to the hallway and pushed open her bedroom door. Simon's sleeping form released the steady rhythmic breathing of a deep sleeper. She moved stealthily in the limited light to the chair as she gathered her clothes together, opening drawers with her holding breath technique again. Finding the correct footwear was even more of a challenge; she rummaged under her chair, feeling for them. Eventually she found what she was looking for and, holding everything together against her chest, she crept out again.

'What time is it?' Simon's muffled voice rose from under the duvet.

'Sorry, darling, it's 9.00. Go back to sleep. I didn't mean to wake you. I'm going to take Alfie and the dogs out.'

'Mm, ok.'

Pulling the door to, Sophie moved into the bathroom and pulled on her clothes. She didn't feel like rushing but Katie might not want to look after Alfie for too long, and her room was full of temptation for a young child. She quickly moved back to her son and daughter, opening the door to find Katie teaching her brother facial features in her mirror.

'Nose, nose,' she said as she pointed to her nose and then touched his.

Sophie's heart seemed to move up to her throat and she fought to check it. She spied her daughter watching her in the mirror and smiled a weak smile. Katie reciprocated with one of her own.

'Look Alfie, it's Mummy. Where's Mummy's nose?'

Katie stood, moved towards her mother and handed over her brother. The slight touch of her hand discreetly allowed a transaction of affection that was so minute that the giver almost missed it herself; the recipient was not so easily fooled.

'Thanks, hon. I'm going to walk the dogs. When are you going out? Do you want a lift?'

'Yeah, that would be great. Can we pick up Ella on the way?' The response confirmed that the storm was over; normality was restored.

'Ok. I'm just going to get Alfie's bag then I'll be going.'

Sophie moved downstairs to the kitchen. Maisie and Sid looked up, expectation written all over their faces. She was always amazed at the way they knew when they were going out.

She found Alfie's all-in-one and lay him on the table to put it on him, but not before sniffing his dreaded nether regions. He was so cute: the suit had ears on it and he looked like a teddy bear, just right for an autumn walk in the woods.

Katie appeared and grabbed some bread, quickly putting it in the toaster. Sophie's relief at seeing her eat prevented her from commenting. She had often wondered if Katie ate enough. Her fixation with her body sometimes caused Sophie great anxiety, but she tried to keep her worries inside as Katie just got mad at her when she mentioned it. So out of the corner of her eye she enjoyed surreptitiously watching her eat.

Dogs leads found and nappy bag ready, Sophie went out the front door, put Alfie in his car seat and the dogs in the back of the car. Katie, last piece of toast clutched in her hand, plonked herself on the front seat. 'I'm ready.'

Sophie dashed back to the house and grabbed the nappy bag, and at the last minute remembered to take some bread for the ducks.

Chapter five

Ella was waiting on the corner near her house. Sophie was struck by how similar they all looked – they were all so thin. Was I ever like that? she wondered. Ella clambered in next to Alfie, who banged a toy towards her in a wild burst of energy.

'Hey, baby boy, how are you?' He squeaked his approval as she stroked his cheek. 'Hi, Sophie. Thanks for the lift.'

'No problem; how's your mum?'

'Oh, ok I suppose.' Ella's voice was quiet and low with emotion.

'Don't talk about depressing stuff, Mum!' Katie's irate voice filled the car.

'Sorry, Sophie, it's all a bit much at the moment.' Ella voice almost counteracted Katie's rudeness, but not quite. She leaned her head against Alfie's car seat. Alfie reciprocated with a mirrored move.

'There's always space for you with us if you need to stay,' Sophie said.

'Thanks,' Ella replied.

Sophie joined the traffic as she drove towards the town. Out of the corner of her eye she could see Katie's steely expression. She wished she hadn't said anything.

Once in town, the two girls dropped off, she turned towards the park. The dogs seemed to know where they were going and started to whine quietly.

Large wrought iron gates welcomed them into a wide expanse, a lovely childhood idyll with a myriad of trees – some fantastic for climbing and some for hiding in. Grass spread out like a carpet; dogs ran and people strolled across it.

The dogs were now barking wildly. As she lifted the back door they leapt out and dashed across the green. 'Hey, wait!' Sophie shouted as she hauled out the buggy and fixed Alfie in place. She pulled up his hood against the cold of the day, and followed quickly after the dogs.

The wind was biting under a brilliant autumnal sky. Breathing in deeply, Sophie allowed the season to touch her soul deeply. This was a place of memories poignant and strong, as well as newer ones that were bright and full of colour. It was the first time in an age that she had been aware of the Creator; she felt the familiar warmth and inner peace that she thought had been lost forever. A kite, yes, that's what I need: Alfie would love that, she thought.

'Would you like a kite, darling?' He kicked his legs in agreement and shouted sounds that were indecipherable but showed the joy he felt at being out.

The dogs returned and ran around them. They were so funny: Sid chasing after Maisie, whose long legs sometimes looked as though they would cause them to fall on top of each other. They never did, though. Sophie tried to fool Maisie by pretending to throw a ball for her, but to no avail: they didn't run off until they saw another dog to chase.

She pushed the buggy on the gravel path towards the lake. It took them through the trees, evergreen alongside deciduous, greens against gold and bronze, oranges and citrus yellow, a feast for the eyes. She allowed herself to bathe in her surroundings, the voices of children from the past slipping into the present: Katie dressed in a tartan hat and woollen coat hiding behind trees and collecting acorns and saying that the empty little cups were fairy cups. And chestnuts held between booted feet, revealing their rich bounty. Katie would try to pick them up gingerly in her gloved hands: those spines would always get through to her little fingers, but she would keep trying nonetheless.

Alfie shouted in delight as the lake appeared in view, stopping Sophie from being overwhelmed by the past. He had an uncanny way of doing that – her gift, her boy.

'Dogs! Maisie, Sid, come here!' she shouted against the wind. The dogs were put on their leads in the nick of time as a swan floated into view. 'Look, honey, look at the swan. Shall we feed it?'

Alfie kicked his legs and shouted. The picnic tables near the lake were perfect for tying the dogs: they could bark, but at least they wouldn't be able to chase the ducks.

Swinging Alfie onto her hip, Sophie moved to the waters' edge. The birds flocked nearer the platform as Sophie squatted down, allowing her son to stand and throw bread into the water. He had trouble releasing the bread to the birds; his fingers full of dough pushed towards his open mouth. Sophie lifted her head and laughed in free pleasure, the beauty of the day, of the moment, was not lost on her one bit. The blueness of the sky coloured the water as the wind lifted it into little rivulets that danced across the expanse. Alfie's eyes creased in delight, his mouthed stuffed full.

'Shall we throw some to the ducks, Alfie?' She planted affectionate kisses on her son's cheek as he laughed, and reaching into the bag, she threw the rest of the bread into the melee of ducks. The resulting scrum released a cacophony of sound that startled Alfie and made him gasp. Sophie lifted him up quickly so he could watch from a better vantage point – his mother's shoulders. She held his ankles as he screamed again and again with delight. Only Sophie's tight grip prevented him tumbling backwards.

The dogs' barks summoned them both back, and once Alfie was firmly ensconced in the buggy again, they moved back towards the trees so that the dogs could run free again. It was not long before they were on the open grassland and the dogs ran and ran.

The wind built in volume and was now causing Sophie's eyes to stream. She checked her son for the chill factor and decided that hot chocolate at home was needed sooner rather than later.

Chapter six

The warm milk was whisked to froth; they had peeled off their coats and had that fizzing thing going on that happens when the warmth of your home meets the chill of your skin. It reminded her of days long ago when, having peeled off her mittens that were caked with snow, she would sit in front of the fire, watching as the snow cracked and dripped. Hugging her warm drink to her lips she would feel her face warm as the cold red of her cheeks was thawed. It was a good memory, and there were not that many.

Sophie took herself and Alfie into the front room and settled with their respective drinks on the sofa. The sound of contentment filled the room; the aftermath of a lovely morning. She closed her eyes, leaned back and let her mind relax; she really didn't want to cater to anyone else's needs today. Rumblings of anger flickered around the edges of her mind. Not now, she decided.

Alfie's body relaxed against her as he dropped into sleep. Holding him carefully, she moved so that she could lay him down next to her. He looked so long, and in fact he took up so much room that she moved across to another chair. She could watch him from where she sat, and as she gazed at his face she remembered the day of his birth: the fear and the joy.

Simon had sobbed without holding back as he beheld his son's face. If she let herself she could smell the hospital; she could see her husband's tears as they ran fast down his face and dripped onto Alfie's closed eyes. He had held him to him and smelt him, looked closely at his features, kissed his head and counted his toes; his little fingers had wrapped around his own as he gazed in wonder. She herself had gasped as she had allowed herself the experience, one she never thought she would see again.

Alfie sighed and stretched, stopping Sophie mid thought. He did not wake, though, so she grasped her laptop and gingerly opened it again. Sophie's book; her raised heartbeat could mean two things she remembered: excitement or anxiety.

She clicked on the icon and an empty white page appeared. So white, so empty, so scary. Holding her breath, she closed her eyes. I am ready; I can do this now; I am an adult, 40-year-old woman; I am a wife and a mother.

She remembered the day she had brought Alfie home. Katie had been with her in the car, along with Simon. She had sat on the back seat, looking at him as he slept, a little miracle.

Kate was 16 when she had first been told that they were going to have another child, and she had been rather disgusted. That means you have sex, was the underlying message written all over her face. But she had no idea how hard it had been for Sophie to allow herself to feel sexual desire again; the letting down of her wall meant that she was more conscious of pain as well as pleasure. It had been worth the risk, though. Still, it was hard to see her daughter's confusion: would it be ok to have another child; would she feel left out; what would it be like; would it be a boy or a girl? And yet the joy, the immediate love Katie had felt for this small person had pushed her fears to one side, and in the first few months she had stayed close to him, engrossed by his every move. She had wanted to bathe him, to change his nappy, to feed him once he started taking a bottle. For her he was absorbing and a wonder and she part owned him as she pushed him along in a pram. 'Alfie is my baby boy,' she would chorus. In fact, she called him that so often that her friends also called him 'baby boy', and the name had stuck.

The first seventeenth birthday in the family had heralded big changes. Katie suddenly appeared to think that she could do whatever she wanted, and overnight she had started to present a new, angrier version of herself. She would flout rules, and timekeeping was a thing of the long distant past. Attention to Alfie diminished to a barely tolerant smile on occasions: Simon and Sophie had discussed it; they had no idea what was the matter with her. Did she feel left out; was she looking for attention, a reaction? The day she had come home with her nose pierced still stood out clearly in Sophie's mind.

Sophie had been in the kitchen, making cakes; it had been too long since she had done any baking. Maybe it would cheer Katie up and she could help her decorate them. She had come in that evening, on time for a change. The routine recently had become, go to college and then pop into town and not come home until the shops shut. When Sophie asked how she managed to stay there without money, she was given short shrift. As least she wasn't coming home drunk and she wasn't suddenly appearing with lots of new clothes that she had managed to 'acquire' somewhere. So, on the whole, she wasn't too bad, considering what a lot of teenagers got up to. Sophie was starting to realise that she had missed her – the hugs, the smiles that would pass between them; the opportunities that would have been there had all evaporated into thin air, and it had been her responsibility, but now, there she was, home on time, much to Sophie's delight.

'Hi, hon, I've made cakes. Do you want to decorate them with me?'

'Ok,' she had replied, to Sophie's surprise, and had sat down opposite her. As Sophie had looked up she had seen the piercing, and her daughter's defiant eyes challenged her soundlessly.

Sophie made an instant decision: she would say nothing. 'What colour icing shall we make?' she had said, struggling to keep the emotion out of her voice.

Katie had blazed her eyes at her and had stormed out of the kitchen. As she left, Sophie had dropped her head into her hands and wept silent tears. What was happening? The relationship they had once had was gone, and she was scared it was forever.

The blank page once again caught her attention as she pondered where to start. She had looked at this issue with her counsellor: the past, the distant past and the not-so-distant past. If she were to go back to when she was young she would avoid the present stuff of life, but then on the other hand, anything she wrote would need a good background for anyone who happened to read it to understand her.

She lifted her fingers and in trepidation wrote the words, *When I was young...*

What shall I tell them: the truth or a version of the truth? she wondered. As quick as a flash she realised that she would only be able to tell a version of the truth: some of the people concerned were still alive and did not know the truth themselves.

I could write about my teenage years and then work backwards and forwards and explain why I was the way I was and why I am the way I am today. Her thoughts traipsed back and forth as she attempted a decision.

32

It suddenly seemed like such hard work, just thinking about it. She closed the lid of the laptop and crept past Alfie and into the kitchen. She looked around and found what she was looking for – her present from Katie: a new book, lovely. The dogs only lifted their eyes to look at her, so that was good – they wouldn't make a noise and wake Alfie.

Curled up on her chair, she opened the book and passed her son's morning sleep in a world of fiction.

Chapter seven

12.00 noon

The two males in Sophie's life woke in unison.

Simon managed to have a shower without her even realising it and now, clean and freshly shaven, he stood grinning in the doorway. He moved across the room towards her and stooped to kiss her full on the lips. Absence definitely makes the heart grow fonder, she thought as her body responded to his touch.

'Your timing is not very good,' she said as his hand lingered on her. Alfie wriggled on the sofa, confirming her words. Suddenly, two excited hounds appeared, leaping and barking in joy. Sid writhed around Simon's legs while Maisie jumped up, unable to contain herself. 'Make her get down, hon,' said Sophie. 'She keeps doing that, and I live in fear of her knocking someone over.'

'Ok. Maisie, get down.' He squatted down and both dogs leaned their heads on him as he ruffled their coats. Alfie's face shone as he smiled across the room at his dad.

'Hello, Alfie.' Simon crawled over and put his head on his son's tummy. Grabbing his head with both arms, Alfie writhed in pleasure, lifting up his legs to enfold his father's head.

Sophie soaked up the moment, enjoying the scene – her two favourite guys together – and she stumbled slightly in her mind. 'Do you want a drink?' she asked, as she countered her thoughts as usual.

'Mm, that would be good. How is my 40-year-old woman this morning? Managed to start writing yet?'

'I've tried. It's hard with Alfie around, and really I've no idea where to start, or even how.' Hearing the defeat in her voice, she solved it with a familiar solution: 'I'm going to make lunch now. Do you want some?'

She moved past them into the kitchen. The need to feed children on a regular basis made food, which never used to be a priority, part of the routine, a necessity, she thought. And she'd still not been able to get rid of her post-baby tummy, or the legs and bum, for that matter. Memories of her mother and slimmer's crackers tripped soundlessly into her mind. Mum always worried about her weight. I still think it was Dad's fault that she never felt good enough. What's hip size to do with who a person is, for goodness sake? she wondered. Yet on a bad day she still measured her own worth by stones and inches. Was that the reason she struggled to find another route for comfort? She could feel that old demon, rage, starting to surface. She had forgiven him so many times, and yet when she thought about her mum she was mad again. Mad at her and mad at him, the curse of a rescuing child.

She opened up the bread bin and pulled out some slices. Then she opened the fridge and, before she had even thought about it, she stuffed a couple of pieces of chocolate into her mouth before grabbing the ham and pickle. Still munching on the chocolate, she put her head round the lounge door. 'What do you fancy to eat – a sandwich, or are you on breakfast time still?'

Simon smiled at her, picked up Alfie and came into the kitchen. 'I don't know what I fancy. What are you making?'

'Ham and pickle sandwiches.'

'That sounds fine, thanks.'

Sophie loved the way he didn't fuss about food; he was easy, most of the time. The scrape of the chair behind her informed her that they were sitting there watching her. She loved these moments when all was well with the world and momentarily time stood still, and only the present mattered, not the past or the future.

'Did you enjoy last night?' Simon asked. 'I couldn't believe the flight was delayed for so long, I'm so sorry. Need to make it up to you, eh?' His conspiratorial smile lit up his face.

The realisation that they had not really spoken about why he had been delayed dawned on her. The party, or rather the gathering, had overtaken everything, and her disappointment had been allayed when he had finally walked into the room. He had looked exhausted, but she had missed him so much. She hated his trips away.

'You know what, I did enjoy it. Katie was in a good mood and made the start of the day lovely. She even took Alfie while I had a bath; she

35

hasn't done that for ages. She bought me the new Anita Shreve book and then let me read it!' Sophie smiled as she recalled her birthday with her daughter. Katie had really tried to make up for the fact that Simon was still away – and she had succeeded.

'What was going on this morning? She didn't sound very happy,' Simon asked.

'She's tired and grumpy. I should have realised. I keep trying to be calm with her, but her rudeness winds me up.'

'I know; no chance she would take up the therapy?'

'No, I asked again the other day.'

Sophie put the sandwiches on a plate, made coffee and frothed up some milk. Once everything was on the table she sat down, taking another mental snapshot as she looked at them.

'Here you go.' She handed Alfie's food to Simon and gave another spoon to Alfie. 'Watch out – it's a bit runny, more soup than stew.'

Taking the bowl, Simon pretended to eat the food himself, making loud slurping noises. Alfie's face creased into a smile.

Sophie cupped her coffee in her hands as she watched them together. As she sipped she pondered on father and son, and as her smile moved across her face, Simon met her eyes and smiled back. 'It's so good to be home. I really missed you. I missed you too, terror.' He reached under the tray of the high chair and squeezed Alfie's knee, causing him to jump in surprise.

To Simon's delight Alfie chimed, 'Dada!'

'You are so clever, my son, aren't you? I hate missing even a day with him, Sophie.'

Sophie watched Simon breathe in deeply. 'Soon he's going to be one; what shall we do? Shall I speak to Katie to see what she thinks?' he asked.

Sophie could feel a distant memory stirring; unspoken words echoed around the room for a fraction of a second until Alfie distracted her again, and she nodded.

The sandwich tasted delicious for some reason. Does good company make ordinary food even tastier? she pondered. Her mum used to make sandwiches that fell apart as you ate them. They were packed full of everything; nothing was chopped finely but they tasted so good. It had been a while since she had tasted one, she realised.

Simon was assisting the now very messy Alfie who had succeeded in putting food in his hair as well as all over the tray of his high chair. The game of the spoon aeroplane going into the tunnel mouth still worked to a degree; he was just pleased to see his dad.

'Why don't you have a go at writing? I'll amuse this one,' Simon offered.

'That would be great. Do you fancy a trip to the shops? I'm almost out of soap powder and I bet you've got a load of washing.'

'Sure. What do you think, Alfie – fancy a stroll to the shops? Hey, how about an Indian later? I could murder one!'

'Oh yes, lovely. A bottle of red, too? Why don't you text Katie and see if she wants to meet you, but then you'd have to drive: I dropped her and Ella in town.'

'What's happening round there, by the way? Is Ella ok?'

'She wasn't too happy today, but Katie was angry with me for asking, so I didn't like to pursue it.'

'Ok, I'll text her and then decide.'

Sophie cleared away the remains of lunch and sorted out Alfie while Simon found his phone and texted Katie. When he returned to the room, he said, 'She asked if Ella could stay. I said yes. Is that ok?'

'I did tell her she could this morning.'

'I know, but we were heading towards a cosy night together.'

'It's fine, don't worry.' She wrapped her arms around him. He still made her feel so secure even after all these years. They stood still together, their small son in view, watching them both.

Simon lifted her face, his hand under her chin, and looked at her intently for a moment without saying anything. It had become their way, a silent language between the two of them. Sophie nodded and lowered her head and eyes, then leaned in against him, gaining strength again.

'Alfie, I can see you,' Sophie eventually chimed in her sing-song voice.

He grinned at her, sucking his fingers and slurping on his own dribble.

'You go and discover that laptop. We're going out, aren't we, Alfie?'

Chapter eight

Silence reigned as Sophie settled on the sofa. She paused before opening the laptop. Was this the right time? She knew she had planned this but there never seemed to be a good time. Space and time was at a premium, literally, and also emotionally. She wanted to do this, but was it right to do it now?

She once again wondered where she could start. Her life had so many different strands, and there were many difficult periods as well as days of absolute blessing.

Blessings: that word took her to a hospital ward where she lay looking into the eyes of her firstborn: Katie.

Sophie breathed air in slowly through her nose and blew out through her mouth. Her 'here I go' sigh tightened her bra around her rib cage as she refused to let the memories have room to flood her being. The tidal waves had become smaller during the time with her therapist, but now she was alone monitoring their strength, and that in itself was overwhelming.

Closing her eyes, she wondered at her daughter. How could she help her? Would writing like this help her? She really wasn't sure.

So with a concerned heart she opened up her Word document. Now was the time to face the truth and be honest.

Katie: the beginning.

Simon was a good-looking man; I could see that even through the fog of alcohol that had penetrated my grey matter.

I had been invited to the party with the express intention of meeting him. My friends had seen me dumped and alone for long enough – not that I knew that at the time. We were both walking wounded and suspicious of new relationships: I had been hurt by betrayal and he had not met anyone he could trust either – being good-looking was a problem. The old saying of wanting someone for 'one thing' really applied, and we immediately had something in common – the feeling of being used.

The music rose in volume as the hour got later. Eventually we found ourselves doing that strange dance that happens when the drink has run low and the music has that 'blast from the past' air to it. We went our separate ways; but that was just the start.

We were again both invited out, this time to see a band in London. I can't remember who. What I do remember was the look we gave each other when we simultaneously realised that we had been set up – the old 'Oh I get it!' look.

Still, we started to talk before we went to see 'whoever they were'. I found out that he had finished university where he had studied law, and now he was working for a company doing I'm not sure what. The long and the short of it was that we agreed to meet up again.

A week later found us sitting in a restaurant doing what was to become a habit for years to come – eating Indian food. We hit it off straight away, in more ways than one.

She sat back in her chair and realised that she would have to explain to Katie why she had behaved the way she did, especially when she didn't want her to do the same. Her only defence was that she was not living out her faith at that time.

There was something about Simon that made me throw caution to the wind. He was solid and calm, and he seemed unflappable. That appealed to me: I had not encountered any man like that before, and if the truth be known, the fact that he was so different to my dad was part of the attraction.

The discovery that I was pregnant was a surprise, to say the least.

Sitting there now, a woman of 40, she wondered at her own naivety. It was ridiculous. How she could have been so stupid? Leaning back she pondered her behaviour: why had she acted so carelessly; why didn't she care if she got pregnant? Her silent words seemed to reverberate off the walls. Pushing the laptop to one side, she went out to the kitchen. The washing machine let out a beep, signalling that it had finished. Still pondering her unintentional pregnancy, she opened the door and pulled out the clothes in a huge armful, setting them on the table to sort. Katie's once tiny clothes had changed into long tight jeans and pyjamas with legs as long as her own. Gone were the days when Sophie chose what she would wear. She sighed as she recalled the morning's outburst over a top. Sorting out clothes that would go in the dryer and clothes that would shrink, she remembered that she had not had a dryer when Katie was little, and life had been very different.

Deciding against the distraction of the washing she grabbed a glass of squash, which was the reason she had gone into the kitchen in the first place, and returned to her laptop.

> *The pregnancy caused great surges of anxiety that were so unpleasant that I did not know how to handle it. I couldn't speak to my mum, as she was involved in her new relationship with the man who was to become my stepfather.*

Sophie paused in her writing. This was going to be harder than she thought, and it was going to involve writing about issues that she had not realised were so important to the story, but the dad thing definitely was. She typed a sub heading:

Dad: growing up
When I was little my dad was really scary.

She suddenly felt exhausted as a memory assailed her senses. It came from out of the blue. She thought she had forgotten about it, but there it was, full in her face.

As the full colour of the moment hit her, she almost flinched. She held on to her hands, each one in the care of the other, until her tremor finally subsided. Gritting her teeth, she banged out the words on the keyboard with a determination that was fuelled by her adult anger.

My dad used to hurt my mum a lot.

There. She had said it. Now that felt weird. A kind of smug half-smile played about her face as she read the words. Adding bold to her font, she added:

40

My dad hurt my mum.

And she added:

I didn't stop him.

A sob finally released itself from her diaphragm. Her head dropped forward as the tears sprung out of a deep-seated pool within her body. 'No,' she said to the room, 'I can't.'

Once again the laptop was discarded and she headed for the kitchen, the solace zone. The fridge was flung open to reveal its treasure: cake from yesterday, cold sausages, bags of goodies tied up in sandwich bags. She grabbed a dinner plate and put the assorted goodies on it, then, seated at the table she started to devour them. She did not have an order, just an insatiable desire to stop whatever was happening in her head. Finally satiated, she stood, her frenzy ended. Moving with slow deliberation she refilled the kettle and leaned on the work surface, her body heavy as she waited for the water to boil.

Tea made, she moved slowly to the sofa again. The cards from yesterday were on display, and from where she sat she could read plainly the one which said, 'To my special mummy'. It was written by hand and the letters rested across the print of Alfie's hand. Katie had made it with her brother. The sight of the love token flicked up one corner of her mouth, and she allowed the moment to obliterate the events in the kitchen and the memory that had forced that frantic feeding.

The tea was scalding hot, and as she sipped it she allowed its heat to diminish the flavours still in her mouth. It travelled hot down her throat and purged her from the guilt of the outburst. This is ridiculous, she thought. This has got to stop. Why do I keep eating too much? He is dead, for heavens' sake. Memories of eating alone, the secrets snacks given to her by her mother, leaked into her awareness. Days, long ago, when the only way her mother was allowed to show her love was through a plate of food.

Once again she pulled her laptop towards her and pressed the key to reveal the already typed words:

I didn't stop him.

Lifting her fingers, she wrote:

I couldn't stop him: he was too big.

She could almost feel the smile of her therapist reaching across to her. There, I said it.

I was little; he was big.

'Well done me.' Before she was even aware of her actions, her arms were wrapped around herself in a self-congratulatory hug. Back to the keyboard, she continued.

My dad was a bully. He scared me and Mum. Sometimes he was really nice to me, though, and if he gave me presents, I felt bad for my mum.

The confusion of that time creased her brow. She had examined the games he played already, but as she continued to write she almost heard her younger self speak: 'Why does he do that? Why is he so unkind? He says he loves Mum but he makes her so afraid.'

Shaking herself she regained her adult self and was reminded of what her therapist had told her about how domestic abuse played out in families and how terrible it was for the children.

Glancing up once again she scanned the cards. Simon's was large: 'To my wife' was emblazoned in red. He knew she loved being called his wife. She could not believe she had ended up with a good guy. Her kids never needed to worry about their dad – how good was that?

Chapter nine

The slam of the door heralded the arrival of the troops. The door was pushed open and into the room fell her man and various children.

'It's freezing out there, Mum. Let's have a fire!' Katie shouted. Ruddy with cold, Katie came over and flung herself next to her mum in her typical unpredictable fashion. 'Sit here, Ella,' she said, patting the seat next to her. Katie leaned against Sophie and put her cold hands in her mother's.

'You're freezing, hon. Where have you girls been?'

'Just down town. I'm so glad Dad picked us up – it's too cold to walk. I forgot my coat too.' Katie turned and pulled a throw around her shoulders.

Simon was standing in the doorway pulling off Alfie's suit, holding him with one arm as he wriggled his body out of the confines. 'I'll make a fire. I fancy some cosy family time, with you as well, Ella. Girls, can you get some wood in?'

'Oh, Dad,' whined Katie, 'that's not fair. I have a friend round.'

'Ella doesn't count. You know what I mean, don't you, Ella?' he said with a grin.

Ella smiled. 'Sure, Simon.'

'You girls get the logs, then I can make a fire, and if we smile nicely at your mum she might make us all a hot chocolate.' Simon made a begging look at Sophie and whimpered with an annoying puppy whine.

'Alright you lot, I can see that my peace has come to an end. I'm glad you're staying, Ella. Are you sleeping here tonight, too?' Sophie posed the question with a permissive air.

'Do you mind, Sophie? I know Simon is only just back. But it's all kicking off at home. I never know whether it's better if I go out or not.'

Ella looked at Sophie with an expression of helplessness. She reminded Sophie of herself sometimes, and this was one of those occasions.

Katie had let slip a long time ago about problems with Ella's dad which had resulted in Sophie checking on her welfare, much to Katie's dismay. Sophie had actually called Ella's mum to make sure she was alright. She had blustered a denial of the situation down the phone but had realised that her daughter had spilled the family secrets. Sophie remembered the caught sob in Ella's mum's throat: it had triggered too many memories for her and she had been unable to stop herself from saying, 'Let's have coffee together. I know what you're going through. Are you able to get out at all?'

Tracy had been taken aback by the offer of friendship. She had later told Sophie that it was very unusual, to say the least, for someone to want to get to know her, let alone when they had not even met her. A tentative friendship had been struck up that day, but it had been difficult to maintain because of the circumstances, so the next best thing Sophie could do for Tracy was to provide a bolt-hole for Ella, her eldest child.

'You're welcome here any time – you know that – and your mum will know you're safe. Give her a ring if you want, to let her know and to check on things. Is your dad about? It's Saturday so might he be down the pub?' Sophie raised her eyebrows to Ella to indicate that it might be a good time to ring.

'Yeah, ok, I'll call now.' Ella pulled out her mobile and went out to the hall, shutting the door behind her.

'Thanks, Mum.' Katie snuggled against her mum in a rare moment of solidarity. 'She was so upset today. He was awful last night, and went crazy.'

'Is Tracy ok? What about the twins? Do I need to go round?'

'She said her mum went to A&E and told them she had slipped down the stairs. She was back before we picked Ella up this morning; that's why she could come out. The twins were really upset, though.'

'This is so awful. We should really call the police.'

They had not heard the door open and Ella reappear. 'No,' she muttered in a low tone that was more suited to a grown woman than a teenage girl. 'He'll really hurt her if he knows I've spoken to you. Promise me, Sophie – please don't.' Her eyes pleaded with Sophie from the doorway. 'Maybe I should go home just in case. Mum sounded ok. In fact, she sounded kind of relieved that I was staying here. That's a bit weird.'

'No, stay here. Your mum knows where you are. Where's your dad, did she say?'

'She didn't know but probably up the pub. There's been a game today.'

'Look, stay here. I won't say anything, I promise.' Sophie patted the sofa. 'Sit down with Alfie while I make hot chocolate.' Ella moved with a reluctant acceptance, almost as if she was Sophie's own daughter.

Exiting to the kitchen, hiding her anxiety, Sophie closed the door behind her. She knew all too well what might happen if his team lost the match. Rummaging through her handbag she finally found her phone and quickly went upstairs and tapped open her contacts list. Tracy answered the phone straight away.

'It's me, Sophie. Are you ok? Ella said he was watching football somewhere. Is he coming home soon?'

'I don't know, Sophie,' came Tracy's strained reply. 'I think they lost. I've been trying to find out. I think I might go to Mum's, but don't tell Ella. I don't want her coming here.'

There was silence until Sophie broke it. 'Are you still there? Tracy?'

'He... he really hurt me last night,' came the whispered response. 'I might leave this time. Sophie, I'm so afraid, though. What if he finds out?' She left the words hanging in space.

'Look, Ella can stay here. She's safe here. Simon is home too so we're all ok. Won't he come to your mum's, though?'

'My mum will call the police if he goes there. I'm going to get in touch with a refuge, I think. The trouble is...' her voice broke as she started to cry, 'we'll have to move away unless I can get him to leave us alone, and he won't, will he? What about Ella? She won't want to but she won't be safe either.' Tracy sobbed inconsolably.

Sophie did not know what to say. It was all true, but at least they would be alive.

'Listen, Tracy, you've got to protect yourself and the kids. I'll come and see you wherever you go. I'm so sorry.'

Slowly the conversation calmed and a plan was made. They would speak tomorrow and see what the new day would bring.

Slipping her phone into her pocket, Sophie went down to the kitchen. She could hear the voices of everyone in the front room and the sound of Simon making a fire. The washing powder he had bought earlier was on the table alongside a bottle of red wine. He was so lovely. Poor Tracy. Giving herself a shake, she prepared the hot chocolate, moving around the dogs that were looking at her with those 'isn't it dinner time?' eyes.

'Oh, come on, you two.' She opened the back door, letting in a gust of cold air as she made a dash for their bowls. Lack of space meant using the garden for storage. They just had to watch out for rats though, who were able to gnaw through many containers and loved dog food. 'It's freezing!' she moaned as she put out their food.

The milk was ready for the chocolate; she whisked it before she poured its frothiness over the chocolate mixture to produce the special drinks. A feeder cup for Alfie too. 'Let's see how he gets on with this,' she muttered. He had been very reluctant to move from breast to bottle, and now she was having the same trouble moving him from bottle to beaker. Putting everything on a tray, she pulled out the remains of the cake – there was not much left after her earlier episode. Cutting it up into small pieces, she put it out among some biscuits to disguise the small amount.

She smiled as she entered the room. Everyone was lounging in relaxed fashion watching Simon play with the fire. 'Here you go,' she announced 'Ta-da! Hot chocolate!' She put the tray on the footstool and everyone grabbed a mug.

'Squidge up, you three.' Sophie wriggled into a corner next to Alfie and pulled him onto her lap. 'Look what I have for you – a special cup with a teddy on it. Hot chocolate for Alfie too. Mm, yummy.'

Taking the beaker in both hands, Alfie leaned back and, glancing sideways at the girls, started to imitate them. 'Mm.'

'Yummy, baby boy, isn't it?' Katie reached up to his face. 'You are so clever.'

The fire hissed and spat behind the guard, making them jump and Alfie splutter over his drink.

Simon and Sophie's eyes met for a brief moment, 'This is good hot chocolate, Soph, eh Alfie? Yummy, isn't Mummy clever?' Alfie kicked his legs in agreement.

Holding up a small square of cake, Katie asked if there was any more. 'I didn't have much last night. It's really good, too.'

Simon glanced across at Sophie, eyebrows raised, as she replied, 'No, that's all there is, sorry.' She was not going to admit to the earlier event.

Chapter ten

4.30pm

It was so good to be all together once again. Her mind settled as she took in the room, glancing from one to another. Katie had moved nearer to her again, her head resting on her mother's shoulder. Ella, a little more relaxed, sat next to her, but a pensive look was still visible across her forehead as she stared into the fire. Simon sat on the floor in front of the fire. He had moved backwards to lean against Sophie's legs. The intimacy of the room descended like a blanket as the quiet calm wrapped them all up in the moment.

'I wish we had a fire at home. It makes it so cosy.' Ella mumbled her appreciation, her chin resting in her hand.

'Yeah, it's great, isn't it? Did I see a bowl of chestnuts in the kitchen, Soph? I really fancy some. What do you reckon, girls?' Simon's pleasure at being home was apparent for all to see.

'We got some the other day, didn't we, Alfie? They're on the table. If you get some foil and a knife we can pierce them in here.'

Simon re-entered the room with everything required; the bowl was full of large chestnuts – round shiny globes bursting with potential flavour. Alfie was moved to one side as Sophie started the preparation, splitting the skins slightly to prevent them bursting, then putting them in foil and handing them to Simon.

'It's nearly Alfie's birthday. What shall we do?' Sophie cautiously pondered aloud. The silence in the room seemed to expand, taking with it all the available oxygen. Breaths were suspended as the outcome was anticipated.

'Let's enjoy yours first.' Simon spoke wisdom, and oxygen entered the room once again. 'Who wants a game of Uno? I fancy thrashing you lot.' He threw the words into the replenished air.

'I'll play,' Ella offered. 'Come on, Kate – we can beat him. What about you, Sophie?'

Sophie looked at her daughter, realising that she was again facing one of those moments when things could go either way.

'Oh, alright. Come on, Mum.'

Sophie breathed a sigh of relief and recognised her close shave. More care would be needed to broach the subject of Alfie's birthday, that was for sure.

A good half hour was passed playing cards, with intervals where with blackened fingers they prised open the hot chestnuts, so hot they hopped them between their fingers to prevent burning, and then revealed their softened centres. They relished the autumn fruits. Even Alfie was able to enjoy the pleasure of a first taste, sucking on the small amounts of crumbs that were deposited on his tongue. He smacked his lips together in approval and continued to sit there like a little bird waiting to be fed, mouth open.

Ella was right – they did beat him. Sophie's mind was elsewhere and Simon was suffering a surge of jet lag. Using the excuse of needing to prepare a meal for Alfie, Sophie retreated to the kitchen. She had always loved this room – what it represented as well as what she could do in it. The kitchen had been one of the places where it had been safe for her mum to be free to be herself if they were home alone.

Sophie pulled out a mixing bowl. Her mum had given it to her, and she still remembered wiping out cake mixture with her fingers, the feel of the yellow gritty substance that would transform itself into her Mum's lopsided cakes. The white icing would run over the mounds of the individual cakes, filling the cases in an uneven fashion. Even when they were slightly blackened they were delicious.

Placing the bowl on the table she pondered her different life now. It was God's provision that she had met Simon; she had honestly thought she would never be at peace. That was her language now, her adult language, but when she was young she had thought in her rage that men were to be feared and avoided or challenged and run from. Simon was like a breath of fresh air – she had had no idea that men like him existed. He was an oxymoron, a kind man – you couldn't have them both, as far as she had been concerned.

The urge to write overcame her, and quickly and quietly she retrieved her laptop, placing it on the table next to the mixing bowl.

'I must write my thoughts down as they happen; then I won't forget anything,' she said aloud to the empty room. The thought that it would be easier that way moved around her mind; maybe it would be less traumatic, too.

Weighing out the ingredients with the aplomb of a practised cake-maker, she pulled out the mixer that had also belonged to her childhood days. It gave off a strange smell as the motor turned: she had no idea why; it was like it contained an old engine within its casing that puffed and panted with effort as the blades turned. The ingredients, once mixed, were put in an uneven, careless fashion into her old cake trays to make her famous sponge cake. Once they were in the oven, she turned to the screen, poised for action.

Scanning her previous writing, she wondered about just putting down her thoughts.

God and me, me and God.
Why does He love me?

She had often wondered about that. It had seemed like a miracle when she found out about Him. She had no idea that He would or could love her; in fact, she had not given Him a second thought until she met Ruth. Now she couldn't imagine life without faith, although she had so nearly lost it along with Jake.

Sophie had wanted her new faith to obliterate her memories, but it didn't work like that. Her memories had become things to work through, and that involved forgiveness, which often felt impossible. Still, she had persevered, and now her main struggle was with her rage which surfaced regularly, a hang-on from before. Her justice-warrior teenage self had thought it was a justifiable feeling, until the day she had felt God challenge her.

Leaning back on her chair, her eyes wandered around her kitchen. It was a mishmash of styles but it suited her. Sometimes she yearned to be different, tidier, more houseproud, with everything neat. She pondered briefly what her house said about her state of mind, but threw the thought away before it took root. She knew she would be unable to maintain complete order, and really it was because other things took priority. She sighed and let contentment fill her being.

The timer beeped. See, life distracts, she thought to herself. Cakes, kids, friends – even dogs, for that matter, she was reminded, as a black nose was placed on her lap. She stroked its owner with an absent-minded affection, once again realising that the dogs, too, were a blessing from God, and one which she had not been allowed when she was young.

Chapter eleven

When I was little it was like I was invisible.

The difference with the past and present struck her with force. Pondering on her life today revealed a contrast to her past and provided a secure framework, a viewing platform from where she could look back safely. Joanna had said the same thing about therapy: the safety of the therapeutic relationship had enabled her to look back and not be overwhelmed.

No one in school had seemed to notice that she was afraid to go home. She hid it well, but nonetheless you would have thought someone would have been aware of the little kid who didn't smile much. She was invisible at home when her dad was around – or rather, she was supposed to be, for her own good – and thus she must have been invisible at school, too.

The door was pushed open gingerly to reveal Simon and Alfie. 'We can smell cake, Mummy, can't we, Alfie?'

Looking at the two of them, she acknowledged the similarities in their features – dark hair over dark eyes and wide, wide smiles that melted even the most virulent rage into a trickle – well, most of the time, anyway.

'Been writing? How's it going? Make sure it's saved, won't you?' A gush of advice flowed from Simon.

She loved his care; it was one of the things that attracted her – his nature to protect and provide without meanness. He seemed to derive pleasure from it. And so she felt loved.

'Yes, I made a cake, but I haven't made your dinner yet, kiddo,' she said. 'Let's see what's in the fridge, then you can have cake for pudding, eh?'

Closing her laptop, she was once again aware that space and time were going to be difficult to find. Remember your blessings, she said to herself.

Vegetables were retrieved and heated and one hungry son was fed. Simon was dripping icing over the cake as instructed under the beady eye of Alfie, who watched fascinated by the drip of the icing as it fell off the spoon in globules, only to run down the surface of the still-warm cake like slow-moving lava.

'Do you want to put the kettle on, Soph? This cake isn't gonna last long either.' Sophie turned to the tap, aware of his invitation to confess to the suspected eating frenzy, but she decided against it. It had been a while since she had succumbed to one, and it was a one-off, she hoped.

He came round the table and deposited the icing spoon in the sink, wrapping his arms around her waist in the process. She leaned against him. 'I'm so glad you're here,' she mumbled, her voice full of emotion.

He turned her towards him and looked at her face before hugging her close. Still in their hug they both turned and looked at their son, realising that he had been quiet for far too long. He sat there with a look of mischief written all over his face, and looking down they could see the nose of Maisie stuck in his lap and the black body of Sid filling his face with the food that had been silently dropped on the floor beneath Alfie's chair.

'What are you doing?' they said almost in unison.

Alfie laughed, 'Wow wow.'

'Yes, we know, naughty wow wows,' Sophie laughed back.

The girls' voices and laughter could be heard from the lounge as they raced each other in some game.

'I really want to write. Are you in the mood to get Alfie sorted? I reckon he needs a nappy change. I'm sure you missed all your fatherly duties, eh?' She smiled her winning smile, still encircled in his arms. 'Do you really want cake now?'

'Absolutely. It's a masterpiece,' he grinned.

Hot tea and sweet cake can always be squeezed in, Sophie thought as she licked the stickiness off her finger. That's the second lot of the day. How can I change my thoughts around food? I eat to celebrate, to comfort myself, to buck me up and to vent my anger.

She was still living in the days of privilege that result from a big birthday when there is permission to play with new toys, so Sophie took advantage of it and once again opened up her new laptop.

Invisibility is a strange phenomenon for a child; you would think I would be able do anything because no one would notice. But no, it wasn't like that; it was like being a robot. I was there but I was not allowed any feelings. I had to be a silent, invisible presence. I had come to believe that Mum really thought I could manage everything that was going on, but the truth was, I couldn't.

There had been a fall-out in my education. It was hard, failure after failure, and in the end I believed I was stupid, but it is said that you only need one person to believe in you, and that person was my English teacher who championed my corner. I loved to write, and he encouraged me. He was a tall, lanky man who, in all honesty, had probably not been out of university that long, but he thought I was great, and it was nectar to a starving child.

She went back to the beginning, an unplanned pregnancy and a man who, for some crazy reason, loved her.

The door slammed open. Ella stood there, shaking with what looked like rage.

'What's the matter, Ella? Come here, hon.'

Ella flung herself down on a chair. 'The hospital called me. It looks like he's broken her jaw.' The tremor in her voice indicated that she was either going to punch the table or break down in tears.

'Oh no. I'm so sorry, hon. I know, it's so hard.' Sophie tentatively put her arm around Ella's shoulder.

Ella's violent reaction took her by surprise as she shoved Sophie's arm off her shoulder and moved like a threatened animal to the corner of the kitchen.

'Oh really, Sophie, what would you know? You've been to my home and I've stayed in yours. We're from different worlds.' Ella's tears ran freefall in her sarcasm and desperate anger, and as she slammed out of the door Sophie was left gasping for air.

***

Katie was shouting in her face. 'Mum, she's gone! What shall we do?'

The shaking of her arms violently brought Sophie into the present. Katie's face peered at her. 'Mum, what shall we do?' Katie's voice filtered through to her as if down a long tunnel. 'Mum! Mum!'

Sophie felt like she had been dragged from her bed in the middle of the night. She shook her head, snapping herself out of a dream and looked at a very distressed Katie.

'Where's she gone? Mum, Ella's gone!'

'I don't know. She was shouting at me. Her mum's been really hurt.' Sophie's words stammered out. Shaking herself, she spoke. 'Ok, get your dad. Where is he?'

'I don't know.' Katie stormed from the room, the door reverberating as she vacated the space. Hanging her head, Sophie shook herself again, realising that she had found it difficult to keep herself emotionally separate from Ella and had dissociated. She hadn't done that for a while. Dissociation was a word she had become familiar with in therapy. The technique was usually perfected in childhood. In the face of trauma, a child's mind would enable them to survive the unspeakable by taking them out of the situation, almost as if they hovered above it. It was a perfect safety mechanism.

Simon appeared and shrugged his hands in a sign of hopelessness. Katie appeared under his arm. 'Are we going to find her or what?' Her words challenged her parents.

Simon looked at Sophie with a quizzical expression. 'What do you think, Sophie?'

'You'd better go. Take Katie with you. I'll stay here with Alfie.'

'Ok. Get your coat, Katie. Alfie is asleep. I'll call you when I find out what's happening.' He came and quickly kissed his lips hard against hers, and then he left.

Silence settled in the room, and she cried.

Chapter twelve

On rare occasions when she was under pressure, apart from when she would eat, Sophie would clean. The kitchen was always in need of attention, and she became a whirling dervish, cleaning surfaces that had ingrained jams and gravy on them; she was not even sure how they got there. Just the moving of jars left a trace of their presence – just like us, we leave trails where we go; some beautiful, some not, she thought. Today had revealed the trail of a dangerous man and the turmoil left in his wake.

Her phone vibrated. They had found Ella and were on their way to the hospital, thank goodness. Sipping more tea she moved her laptop towards her. Alfie's steady breathing through the monitor filled the room. She pulled herself back to the task at hand: *Katie*.

Discovering my pregnancy was a joy and a worry. The love affair between me and Simon was full steam ahead, but that did not mean marriage at that stage. We agreed to live together at first. Simon had secured a place as a trainee solicitor and I had been doing various odd jobs, having come home from travelling with my former boyfriend, but I could turn my hand to most things, and jobs at that time were not difficult to get.

Feeling unable to seek support from my mother had maybe done us a favour: it had thrown us together. The fun of finding a flat was rosy-eyed as the full force of the situation had not really hit home yet. It wasn't even that I was that young – at the age of 23 I thought I was fairly mature, but really I was a wounded young woman who had no idea what a normal, healthy relationship looked like. Still, we bumbled along; I worked through my pregnancy at a publisher and was enjoying my changing body, as was Simon.

It was her first pregnancy, and she reminisced about how her body was young and able to manage the rigours involved, unlike later. Hugging herself, she imagined the stretch marks that lay across her stomach like a network of railway lines witnessing the carriage of babies. The swelling of her belly had finally resulted in the repeated tearing of skin tissues until mending the tears had become impossible and her body had been changed forever.

> *I felt so well and so happy then. It had been risky loving Simon, but he was worth the risk. It was strange how I was attracted to someone who I would not have normally gone for. Oh, he was good-looking, but his predictability would have been a no-go. I had always gone for the naughty ones who could harm me; it was what I thought was normal at the time – how terrible is that? And my pregnancy was almost a subconscious sabotage: do you love me enough for this? An invitation to be rejected again; it was what I thought I deserved.*

It was not until she entered therapy that she had discovered these truths about herself. Absent-mindedly she lifted her top to reveal her bulging tummy, still extended from her pregnancy. She traced her fingers over the white lines that criss-crossed the expanse. A sudden shudder shook her as she realised she could not hear Alfie. She held her breath – one, two, three – then she heard him cry quietly in his sleep, more like a whimper, really, and she exhaled, wrapping her arms around her flesh.

Her mind blank again, she stared at the screen; the baby monitor's tone steadied her and she gained present time once more.

A bottle of red wine stood where Simon had left it. Moments later some of its rich contents were dancing and sparkling in her glass. Sipping deeply, she realised that she was drinking alone – again. Not a good thing: I'm like some sad old housewife.

She took her glass into the front room. The fire in the grate did not need much persuasion to leap into life, sparking and spitting as the logs were consumed with hungry gusto. It was comforting to space out and stare into its flames. The glass of wine warmed in her grasp, releasing its hedonistic flavours to their full extent as she sipped the ruby contents. She was not alone technically, she thought, as the steady rhythm of Alfie's breathing continued to fill the room. Thoughts of Ella and her mum invaded her temporary peace: how bad were things? Where was Simon?

The pounding on the door started her heart racing within her chest; she suddenly felt very alone. Maisie and Sid barked furiously as his voice hurtled through the letter box, and she was very afraid. Did he know she was in? Her mind ricocheted as her hand covered her mouth to silence her scream. He only had to look through the front room window to see the fire and know!

A vibrating from the kitchen echoed loudly as her phone announced to the world and his wife the arrival of a text.

'Ella! I know you're in there. Open the door.'

Sophie crept across the room to the window and tried to lower the blinds. His face suddenly appeared on the other side of the glass, startling her as she stumbled backwards and released a scream.

'Where's Ella?' Ella's father shouted, his face as red as the wine she had been drinking. Rage had pinched it into a contorted grimace.

'She's not here. Please go away – you will wake my baby.' Sophie's voice sounded robotic as she reached deep within herself to find it. The absurdity of using Alfie as a means of release from her paralysis surprised her. As her body was flooded with adrenalin, bringing with it a distant, vaguely familiar feeling, she battled to stay in control. The dogs were now around her legs, still barking their displeasure.

Alfie's snuffles increased in volume and had a disjointed sound to them, as if his dream world was being invaded by something. Outside the window, he pushed his face against the glass as he mouthed, 'Where is she?'

'I don't know. They went out. I'm not sure.'

By now Alfie was starting to whine, and in some way this gave Sophie the courage she lacked for just herself. 'Look, my baby has woken up. She is not here. Please go now.' She sounded more in control than she thought, she realised with sudden clarity.

He appeared to glance around the room. 'You'd better be telling the truth,' he shouted, and was gone.

Blinds down, curtains pulled and windows secured, Sophie grabbed the phone and summoned her surprised and delighted hounds to come upstairs to the bedroom where Alfie was now crying.

An hour later Simon returned, clutching a curry, to find his wife and child asleep with the two dogs on the big bed that they shared. He told Sophie later that he was really shaken up to find them there, and for one moment his heart had stopped for fear of them being dead.

Sophie roused as she heard her name being spoken. For a brief moment she was terrified and clutched her son to her, much to his surprise.

'Sophie, what's the matter? Why are you up here?'

'Why were you so long?' she accused her husband. 'Ella's father came round here; he was so angry.'

'He did what?' Simon's face twisted with an outraged expression that was very unfamiliar to Sophie.

She relayed the story, sobbing between her sentences. Simon's shirt began to slowly turn colour as her tears soaked into the fabric.

'I'm so sorry.' He repeated time and time again.

Eventually they went downstairs, Alfie safely back in his own bed with the monitor on. They sat in front of the fire and ate curry off bended knees and drank warm red wine. Simon recounted the events of the evening.

They had eventually found a very cold Ella by the bus stop, trying to hitch a ride as she waited for a bus into town. Sophie could not believe how close she had come to being discovered by her father. They had arrived at the hospital to find Tracy unable to speak without a grimace. She had a bruise that had spread across her nose and under her eyes, making her look like a masked villain. He had punched her, and this time she was going to press charges – or so she said; they had been here before.

Simon had been shocked by her appearance and had a quiet tremor to his voice as he recalled the scene. Sophie moved closer to him, wanting to give him the strength that he usually gave her.

Ella had broken down, full of remorse that she had not been there to protect her mum, only to move rapidly to the rage that she wore like a uniform. Her dad – how could he? She had shouted at her mum, demanding that she leave the evil man who had fathered her 17 years previously.

Simon recounted how her young cries and shouts had reverberated around the hospital and how security had arrived to calm her down. They had had some success: the girls were allowed to stay. He was told that Tracy would be admitted for probable surgery and because there were questionable injuries that might have caused internal problems. Katie had wanted to stay with Ella and so a plan was hatched. Simon had allowed her to stay, with some conditions.

Sophie lay back on the cushions and surveyed her husband. The firelight lit up his face as he smiled at her. She could not imagine her life without this man of strength.

She woke a while later to a hot cup of tea and Katie lying next to her. She smiled at her. 'You ok, hon?'

'Sorry, Mum.' Katie leaned over and wrapped her arms around her mum. They lay back on the same cushion. Sophie was aware of unspoken words of love and security and once again was grateful for the love in their home. Turning towards her daughter, Sophie looked into her exhausted eyes and recalled the first glimpse of her daughter all those years ago. She wrote later:

> *Giving birth was an unknown quantity; I had no idea what I was doing but my body took over. After a long labour, Katie arrived, and we lay on the bed looking into each other's eyes.*

And here they were now, those same eyes looking back at her, hungry to soak up the safety of her home that she so often took for granted.

'Mum?'

'Mm, what is it? You look so tired. What happened at the hospital?'

Katie answered with a question that Sophie had known would come: 'What happened when Ella had a go at you? You looked really strange, like you didn't know where you were.'

Sophie shrugged, unable to speak. She didn't want to go there. She had not spoken to Katie about her father before. It was all too much.

'Can we talk about that later? Tell me what happened at the hospital. How did you get home?'

Katie started to look disgruntled, then appeared to gather herself and put her misgivings to one side. 'Tracy has to stay in and have scans or maybe an operation or something. The police want to talk to her but she can't really speak at the moment, so they're going to go back later. She looks so awful. Ella's gone to a friend of her mum's who's looking after the other kids – the dad came and collected her and dropped me off here. I don't know how Ella copes. I love my family, Mum.' Tears came into her eyes and fell in languid drops down her beautiful face.

'Lovely girl, I love you so much, to the moon and back.' She pulled her daughter closer into her arms and they lay there, Katie with her head on her mother's chest, reminiscent of 17 years previously. The fire sparked as Simon bent over his wife and child and replenished the grate.

'My beautiful girls.' He pulled another cushion into place, wedged himself next to Sophie and leaned over to stroke his firstborn's cheek, as Alfie's monitored rhythmic breathing continued to fill the room.

Chapter thirteen

13th October
Sunday

The strong, heady aroma of the morning coffee punctuated the air. Sundays were often full on, with church and lunch and a general busyness, but last night Sophie and Simon had decided to try to have a day out together, if Katie would come. Such days were few and far between since she had refused to go to church or believe any more.

Simon and Sophie had trudged on through the darkest times, turning up at church nearly every week, apart from when it was impossible. It was almost like church held the oxygen tank to keep them afloat, and it became more than faith; the routine marked the days and weeks and gave structure to an otherwise chaotic time. In fact, it was almost as if faith did not come into it any more, especially for Simon: it was just a clinging to some sense of purpose and vague normality.

Alfie had slept through, which was fantastic, but that had meant an early wakening for Sophie. Now, as she chopped onions and carrots, he sat on the floor with a wooden spoon and saucepan as his noisy entertainment. This is where I am content, she thought, with all my family together – asleep or awake, but in the house.

Alfie steadied himself against her legs, gripping her trousers with a steely determination. 'Mama.'

As he let go with one hand to reach up towards her, he spun round in an ungainly pirouette and deposited himself on his padded bottom.

'Oops-a-daisy, what are you up to?' Sophie soothed his troubled face, then lifted him up and deposited him on the work surface next to her. He was surprised by his sudden elevation, and a delighted look spread across his face.

'Now don't touch anything,' she said, knowing the futility of her words, and giving him more spoons to bang.

Her skill as a practised mother once again to the fore, she threw together a chicken hotpot, grabbed her son and her replenished coffee mug and retreated to the lounge. She had never really wanted a playpen for Alfie, although now she had a moment of wishing she could imprison her son to keep him safe while she grabbed her laptop for a bit. She resorted to her other pet hate, the 'television babysitter'. Still, it works, and if it gives a mother a moment's peace, then what the heck, she thought.

Scanning back over her writing she added some thoughts to those of the previous day: *Katie's birth*. She was definitely recalling the times through rose-tinted spectacles, she realised.

> *Her arrival, although delightful, still brought with it some troubles. For Simon and me, living together had been a steep curve as we got used to each other's idiosyncrasies.*

A sudden random memory was carried into the present, with the word 'toothpaste'.

> *How crazy – I remember my dad going berserk if we squeezed the tube from the middle, and yet I didn't like it either, and it did annoy me that Simon didn't care about things like that.*

Funny irritations, although not so funny at the time, invaded her mind, along with the realisation that it had actually been quite a difficult time for them all.

She leaned back and surveyed the room once again. The dogs lolled against each other and eyed her in the hopeful expectation of a walk. Alfie was still engrossed in the bright-coloured creatures that were moving across the television screen. The floor above her creaked as someone started to move and so she quickly turned back to her screen, the pressure of time forcing her to focus.

> *Money was tight then, and jumble sales were a real excitement for me. I got to know the good ones to go to, the ones in posh areas where wealthy people got rid of a shocking amount of really good*

things. Although I hated the scrum of people pushing and shoving, I did get rather good at finding clothes for us all.

Her irritation with dealers who thronged to those events like greedy piranhas still surfaced at times, she realised.

Katie had awoken before her father and came into the room hugging a mug of tea. She plonked herself on the opposite seat, much to the delight of Alfie, who immediately clambered over the floor towards her.

'No, Alfie, I have hot tea. HOT.' She exaggerated the word, making a warning sucking sound. But there was no deterring him as he proudly hauled himself to standing position in front of her.

'He loves you, hon.' Sophie's placating tone reached across to her. Raising her eyebrows, Katie made space for her little brother, lifting him up to settle in the crook of her arm. She sipped her tea under Sophie's watchful eye while Alfie was distracted with a book.

Sophie realised how grown up her daughter had become; she was totally able to look after her brother. Some teenagers became mothers at her age and had to manage all alone. That was certainly food for thought. How had her Katie got this far without her noticing? Had she failed her in some way?

Katie: what I missed. The words stood out on the page before she minimised the screen.

'So, do you fancy a day out at the seaside, Kate?' She deliberately used the name, playing with the abbreviation like a sweet rolling around her mouth, testing the texture.

Katie's surprise was written all over her face. Such a small concession for such a large reward, her mother thought.

'Well, I kind of do, but where are we going and what are we going to do?' she replied. 'What about Ella?'

'I rang and spoke to the hospital when I got up. Apparently she's going to be there with her mum. I got the impression that Tracy really wanted her there otherwise I would have asked her to come too, but you could always double-check if you want. We're planning on going to Whitstable.'

'Oh, its ages since we went there. I remember having a milkshake there in some old-fashioned place; they had those thick glasses like the

64

Knickerbocker Glory glasses we used to get at Gran's. What happened to them, by the way? I really liked them.'

'I don't know, but we could see if we could find the place, couldn't we? Maybe Alfie would like a milkshake, eh Alfie?'

'When will we be back? I wanted to meet up with some friends tonight, and maybe I could see Ella too. I'll text her to see if she wants to stay. You don't mind, do you?'

'We won't be too late, I shouldn't think, and no I don't mind. Once your dad is up and has had breakfast we can go. I've made us dinner for later, so we can have that when we get back tonight. I'm desperate for a family stroll along the beach; it's going to be beautiful today. Do you remember the fish market and harbour? There are a few stalls there too so we could shop.'

'Ok. Come on, Alfie. Sorry, I have to get up.' Katie scooted him to one side and, after checking his safety, Sophie noted, disappeared out of the room.

The journey to the sea had always been a treat. It really didn't matter what it was like weather-wise; there was still the expectation of getting there. The sight of the sea always brought a shout of, 'I can see the sea', no matter whether they were adults or children. The sun had brought out the crowds en masse, along with their accompanying dogs. Sophie felt a momentary pang of guilt – she had left Maisie and Sid behind, wanting to wander down the lanes without two filthy, wet mutts knocking into people.

The buggy made the usual train-track noise as they moved along the boardwalk just in front of the unique little seaside houses. Sophie had often fancied a therapeutic retreat by the sea, and the walk was punctuated with, 'Oh look at that one, Simon,' and, 'That's so lovely.' Even Katie had an opinion, and discussion about which one was the best filled the air.

They stopped at a breakwater for Katie and her mum to touch the water. The sea looked like an inland lake – uncannily still with no ripples, and their reflections were perfect in the still glassiness.

They turned, mother and daughter, and surveyed the boys: Alfie was sitting on top of the round post of a breakwater while his dad held on to his legs. His arms were waving like a windmill as Simon pointed towards them.

'Alfie, look,' Katie shouted as she held a wet shiny piece of seaweed aloft; the more she waved it the more he waved. She ran off up the beach to show him her wares, leaving Sophie standing alone.

Sophie turned and stared out to sea, watching the gulls taking off and landing on another breakwater. I love the sea, she mused, as her thoughts came thick and fast. She sent up a silent prayer; she had found prayer difficult recently – it had become a lost language, one she was slowly trying to discover again. Nature had always been where she had accessed her Creator, and now she tried to find Him again. The peace of the water almost obliterated her concerns, but not quite.

Simon was suddenly standing next to her. She felt like she had woken from a dream, like that guy in *The Matrix*. What was his name? She couldn't remember. Nemo? Nero? Oh well, it didn't matter really.

'You were miles away.' Simon put his arms around her shoulders.

'I was trying to pray. I know He hasn't gone away but it seems like ages since I heard His voice.'

'I don't think I've ever heard His voice.' His dulled tones caught her attention.

'But we talked about this before. I really think our relationships with God are unique to us, and I'm a talker and a listener, and I expect to hear Him.' Her voice took on an urgent quality. 'I'm excited that I'm starting to expect it again; it's been so long.'

'I know; my hotline-to-God woman,' he said as he spun her round and enfolded her in his arms.

They stood there together until cries of 'Get a room!' reached them. Katie stood with Alfie waving wildly on her shoulders. 'We want a milkshake, don't we, Alfie?' sounded down the beach.

The crunch of wet pebbles accompanied their return, and the foursome continued their walk. Tour guide commentary once more filled the air as homes were appraised.

The fish market greeted them long before their arrival. The pungent aroma took some getting used to and almost meant a change of direction, but the thought of a fresh pot of cockles and prawns kept them focused, and the taste was immense, with sweet shallot vinegar sprinkled on top. Katie was itching to find the stalls, and so mother and daughter went off to explore. Sophie's heart filled as Katie linked arms with her.

The market comprised an assorted arrangement of little black huts, from which individual traders hawked their wares. Home-made jewellery, decorations, old furniture reminiscent of childhoods gone by caused hilarity as Sophie realised she had grown up with many of the items that now fetched a tidy price.

Comments such as, 'Mum, I didn't realise you were so old,' united the two of them in mother–daughter jokes; the trying-on of strange hats and other clothing led to heads bowed in hysterical laughter.

A puppet stall elicited a cry. 'Oh Mum, we must get this for Alfie for his birthday,' rang out before Katie was able to process her thoughts.

She was standing stock still in realisation, and quickly Sophie linked her arm through hers, 'Good idea, hon. Which one did you mean?'

It was too late, though, and Katie had retreated again. 'Oh, I don't know.' She shrugged her release from her mother's grip and walked away. Silently, Sophie shadowed her as she moved back towards her dad and brother.

'Can I have a cup of tea, Dad?' her voice, sounding younger than her years, reached Sophie, who was shrugging out of sight at Simon.

'Sure. Do you want one, Sophie?'

She nodded her assent before moving into position between her two children. 'Did you see the boats, Alfie?' Her voice sounded brighter than she intended as she tried to counter the mood around the table.

Katie went to stand with her dad, who had gone to buy the tea, and allowed him the intimacy of an arm around her waist. Sophie's pain stuck in her throat like a gobstopper that she was unable to swallow. Breathe, breathe, she said to herself. Alfie looked at her with moist, quizzical eyes, and in an instant Sophie realised that his curiosity could quickly dissolve into fear, and so with that gift that mothers so often possess, she managed to stifle her feelings. The gobstopper disappeared and the regain of control was instant. And Alfie smiled. Being unexpectedly caught up in his mother's arms delighted him and banished his alarm.

'Here you go.' Simon looked at her with concern as Katie remained a distance from the table on the pretence of looking at the boats.

'I'll tell you later,' Sophie whispered. 'Have a cuddle?' she quickly handed Simon his son as she sipped her much-needed tea.

The streets of Whitstable were awash with people. Shoppers, strollers, those out for lunch, people just out of church, buggies and walking sticks all jostled for position on the narrow pavements. But Sophie was not disappointed; the pace of life was slower here, and it delighted her. People, in the main, seemed to have time; shopkeepers spoke with interest and concern about what you were looking for. It had an old-fashioned deliciousness about it that delighted even Katie, and appeared to help her regain her equilibrium.

What's Up Cupcake? was a lovely unique cake shop that enthralled both Katie and her mum; it was a treasure trove of ornaments, cups and teapots. Little sayings on glass decorated the walls, and brightly ornate cupcakes, like something out of a romantic novel, were displayed under glass with fancy names like 'Ella's Bella's'. Their swirling creamy tops enticed the passers-by and the boys were forced to stand on the pavement as more people squeezed into the space. Katie, totally distracted at last, looked like a young girl again as she laughed and pointed out the funny quotations.

The prized cakes were boxed and placed carefully under the buggy for later consumption, and their wanderings continued.

'There's the cafe,' Katie called as she spied the old exterior of the tea house. Sophie and Simon walked arm in arm as Katie pushed Alfie's buggy. Simon squeezed her arm as they watched their daughter bend over the buggy to speak to him.

'Hey, baby boy, how about a milkshake?' He kicked his legs in response; he was putty in her hands most of the time, and was thrilled to be noticed again.

The froth of the milkshake clung to her top lip like a strawberry moustache; she had deliberately left it there, to Alfie's delight. Sophie smiled tentatively at her child and was rewarded with a full-on smile that told her the crisis was really over. Coffee and cake tasted so much better when there was peace.

The ride home was uneventful. Alfie slept and Katie plugged in her headphones and appeared to doze too, but not quite enough for the adults to feel secure to talk – that would have to wait until they were home.

Chapter fourteen

14th October
Monday

Sophie surveyed her friends. It had been ages since they had met: six women, a mishmash of personalities with the common thread of God in their lives. They had journeyed together through the years, and had met regularly for a while when the children were little. It had been a juggling act to ignore the chatter of kids as they struggled to share and 'play nicely', but somehow it had worked, and hopes and dreams, troubles huge and insignificant, had been worked on and dealt with. Prayers had been sent up with cries and pleas, and in later years as the children had grown and circumstances had changed, as the pressures of life had evolved and more money was needed, so everyone worked and time was limited.

Sophie sat and wondered how that had happened. Time had become a commodity that had increased in value because of its rarity. Still, these women all knew her so well; they knew each other's difficulties, both personal and public. They had walked intimately together, almost as if they were third parties in each other's marriages. How weird was that?

Laughter splashed around the room as someone retold a tale, and kindred spirits merged together in harmony acknowledging commonality.

There were areas where they were all sensitive not to go – losses too painful to speak about, marriages too rocky, children too troubled – those were kept for when they met in ones and twos, but nonetheless, Sophie thought, I don't think there are any real secrets. Sometimes she could see the small asides that were made to one or the other that indicated additional time spent together, but that meant it was still in the group in some way.

Today they spent time discussing the book they had been reading and made plans to go and see the film of the book; it was a special time.

Sophie had planned to talk about Alfie's birthday, but the words had stuck in her throat and, just like when she was young, anxiety had banged on her chest wall so badly she thought it could be seen. If she could not talk about it here, where could she talk about it? The trouble was that here there was permission to cry, and if she started she really did not know if she would be able to stop. The atmosphere changed and she realised they were all looking at her with concerned expectation. Had she inadvertently said something aloud? she wondered.

'How are things, Sophie? How's Katie?'

The whoosh of air as she exhaled launched her vocal cords into action. 'She's not too good; in fact, she seems to be building up the nearer it gets to Alfie's birthday. We knew it would be bad, but I had been hoping that because it's been so long she might be ok.'

The tremor in her voice had increased, she realised, and she was now shaking as her friends gathered around her. The silence was a blessing as they held her in solidarity.

Women, it was later discussed, are plagued with the need to protect their children, and as they get older it makes no difference – they still want to, and in fact, it sometimes gets worse. Children make decisions that they know will break their hearts, and they cannot stop them. So they have to accompany them in silence without commenting and wait for them to come to their senses, or just pick them up from where they fall.

Mondays were often spent clearing up the mess of the weekend, but after coffee with the group, a walk in the woods was far more appealing. The dogs ran to and fro, manically chasing each other round and round trees, like children playing It in the playground.

Sophie linked arms with Tash as they walked their dogs together, and Alfie banged his feet methodically against her ribs as he sat in the backpack. 'It's getting harder now. I really wish Katie would talk to someone. She seems like a volcano about to erupt.' The words hung in the air like the few leaves that still hung on the branches, reluctant to fall.

'What does Simon think?'

'He's as stuck as me. We kind of pussyfoot around, afraid to release an outburst. It's awful, Tash; she totally changes in front of my eyes.'

Tash looked at her and said gently, 'You change too, Soph. It's like you go off somewhere and no one can reach you. Where do you go? Maybe you can help her.'

'It's weird: I find myself in the place that I created for myself in therapy. When it was all too much I used to go there a lot, but I find I'm going there without thinking at the moment, like something is building in me, too.'

They stopped and looked down the slope of trees to the stream. The three dogs were frantic, heads down in the water, running up and down; they were full of joy anyway.

'I've started to hear God again sometimes when I walk here. I almost feel loved again. How can I help Katie feel that too? She wants nothing to do with God; she's so angry.'

'Isn't it normal for teenagers to challenge their faith? So it's probably her age as well as everything else.' Tash's wisdom once again normalised the situation.

Tash lifted Alfie out of the carrier and between them they held his little hands and walked and swung him as he laughed and laughed. The two women fell silent, and the only sound was of Alfie's laugher and the crunch of their footsteps.

Chapter fifteen

Sophie called her therapist and got through to her voicemail. She decided not to leave a message and opened up her laptop. Simon would be home soon, Katie was upstairs watching something with Ella, who had come home from college with her today, and Alfie was playing on the floor. It was strange how crises came and went, but Alfie's birthday was in two weeks and there was no alternative but to face it. I want to enjoy it, she thought, surprised.

Katie: what I missed. The words flashed on the screen,

What have I missed? My 10-year-old child seems to have metamorphosed into a 17-year-old young woman. She pondered her ever-changing, unpredictable daughter, the similarities to her younger self causing a wry smile to play about her face.

Mum. Mum was not able to keep home a safe place for me.

Her sympathy swelled uncharacteristically as she thought about having a child to manage in such unstable surroundings. The memory of Ella's dad at the window deepened her breathing. She had spent so much time trying to steady her breathing that it was not until her therapist commented on her breath-holding technique that it had 'come into her awareness'. She loved that phrase.

There were days when I would hide in my room. Secondary school definitely meant growing up for me. I had been invisible in primary, but by then I had perfected a mask of anger and humour that disguised very effectively the confused feelings that lurked beneath the surface. The quiet little girl who could not save her mum from her father had changed into a rage-filled young woman who was full of opinions, especially on the subject of men.

Alfie's voice distracted her, but not before she saw, once again, the similarity between her and Katie. Things that happen as you are growing and changing affect how you develop and deal with life, she thought.

She had always thought that men were a waste of space, until she met Simon.

But at least Katie can't think like that about her father, she pondered.

My dad is dead, but he still makes me mad.

She started to write haphazard phrases across the screen.

My dad is dead.
He has been gone a long time.
Dead.
DEAD.

Alfie stood swaying in front of her, a proud grin displayed across his face. 'Look at you; are you going to walk soon?'

Simon's return was heralded by the barking of the dogs; the sound of the thwack of tails against chairs escaped through the kitchen door as they greeted him with enthusiasm.

'Who is it, Alfie? Is it Daddy?' He jigged up and down, eyes pinned on the door. He loves his dad – no fear here, Sophie thought.

The smell of dinner filled the kitchen as she walked in and set eyes on her husband.

'Smells good, Soph. How was today? What have you two been up to?' He reached out and took his outstretched son.

'It's been good. I went to women's group. I couldn't believe it had been so long. Then we went to the woods with Aunty Tash, didn't we, Alfie? Then just the usual – preparing a feast for my husband, cleaning his house. What happened at work? Was it ok?' As Sophie served dinner and called the kids, they caught up on the day.

Ella and Katie appeared in full make-up; they had been having another styling session. 'Wow, look at you two,' Simon commented with exaggerated appreciation in his voice. 'How's your mum, Ella?'

'She's getting better. Still looks terrible, mind. She took out a restraining order on Dad so he can't come near the house. Hope it works – we haven't gone back there yet.'

The silence settled with the appreciation of food. Once again Sophie took a mental snapshot – everyone she loved around the table, here, secure and well.

Glances across the table unleashed a fit of giggles from the girls. 'What's up with you two?'

'Nothing. It's just so quiet and when you're not meant to laugh you just have to, like in maths today. Mrs Jackson had her trousers tucked in her socks; she looked so weird.'

'How embarrassing! Poor her – I bet she rides a bike to college. I remember leaving my skirt tucked in my knickers and walking about for a bit before someone took pity on me.' Shrieks of laughter surrounded the table. 'And I had walked across an airport concourse!'

Mid-mouthful Sophie suddenly remembered that she was due to be weighed that night. 'Oh bum; I've eaten now.'

'What's wrong with that?'

'I haven't been weighed, and I bet what I've just eaten weighs a lot.'

'Don't be mad. You look lovely. Don't go tonight.' Simon squeezed her waist as she writhed out of his grip.

'I need to get rid of this.' She squeezed her own fat. 'I've had this since you were born.' Sophie waved a finger towards her son who laughed at her wiggling digit. 'Anyway, you know what, I like to go – women together supporting each other.'

The occupants of the room all looked at her as if she was crazy, shrugging their shoulders in hopeless agreement.

Ella pitched in, too. 'You could be too skinny, like my mum, and that's not nice. I think you look great, Soph.'

The room was full of women; the queue always seemed longer as Christmas came nearer, or at the start of summer. The thought startled Sophie as she realised that she had been on this treadmill for far too many years, and that really Alfie had nothing to do with her body mass index.

'Hey, Sophie!' called the leader. Jade was a lovely lady who had supported her ever since she had plucked up the courage to come. They both knew that Sophie didn't lose weight because she didn't want it enough, but they still went through the same comments in order to work out the plateau she had become stuck on.

Simon's comment stayed with her, as did Ella's, but still she couldn't let it go. If I don't come I may get even bigger, and I don't want to become content with this, was her answering thought.

They all gathered, the women of discontent and attainment discussing what they could change and why they didn't. Some were very overweight and some looked to be the size that Sophie would like to be. Now that was weird – why were they not content? There must be something else, surely?

The rows of chairs were suffocated with hips and bottoms and the chatter swelled up and down like waves on a slightly turbulent sea. Stickers of reward were handed out. Nothing like a sticker to put a grown woman in a good mood, Sophie smiled to herself.

'So how was it tonight?' Simon greeted her on her return.

'I stayed the same.' Sophie sighed. 'Better than putting any on though, I suppose.'

'Why don't you do something fun instead of going there? I just don't get it.' Simon's face betrayed his thoughts – it was a waste of money.

'I know, but I don't want to get any bigger. Let's have a drink, eh?' She laughed as she fell onto the sofa next to him. 'Alfie went off ok, then?' The soft, rhythmic breathing could be heard through the monitor. 'Where's Katie?' Sophie wrapped her arms around Simon and lay with her head on his chest.

'Upstairs with Ella. It's much better when they are together – for her and us.' He hugged her suggestively. 'It's so hard to relax when they're around. Do you remember what our life was like before, when we'd get naked in front of the fire?'

Chapter sixteen

15th October
Tuesday

Tash arrived as planned at ten the next morning. Coffee sat in red mugs as they looked across the table at each other.

'I love your kitchen, Sophie; it's always so warm and inviting.'

'You mean it's messy and cluttered,' Sophie smiled.

'I don't, I really love it. I love your style, honestly,' Tash said earnestly.

The words that needed to be spoken hung in the air as they paused.

'Ok, let's do it, Tash.' Sophie drew in her breath as she readied herself. 'What do you think we should do? Simon and I are stuck, and we have to get through the next two weeks somehow.'

'Why don't you just do nothing? It's the first one, and no one expects anything from you.'

Sophie stared at the table, noticing the places that she had missed regularly when cleaning. The layers of what looked like dried-on Weetabix enticed her to touch it. Her fingernail filled rapidly with the sticky detritus of months of 'slack Alice' cleaning, as she raised her eyes to meet Tash's.

'You're right, Tash. Alfie doesn't even know he's going to be one, but it feels like he's being hard done-by and he deserves more.' She paused, feeling momentarily relieved. 'Look what I found under the table.' She thrust her fingernails towards her friend. 'I need a cleaner; it must have been there for months.'

'What is it?' Their two heads bent together in conspiratorial fascination. 'Is it alive?' Tash giggled.

Tears ran down their respective faces as they bent forward and laughed, and pent-up emotions were finally released after the pain of constrained control. Sophie loved her friend who was so tidy, and who never appeared to judge her lack of commitment to domestic goddess prowess. They knew each other well, and learned from the differences each saw in the other. The years had seen them share ideas and behaviours as they discovered better ways to live and to be, and so, because of that, they would tolerate suggestions that they maybe would not have managed from anyone else.

'Do you remember the kipper?' Tash asked. The tears and howls flowed around the kitchen table as they reminisced.

Alfie banged his spoon on his high chair, like a little judge bringing the room to order.

'You are such a good boy, Alfie, listening to us go on and on. Are we being silly, eh?' Tash lifted her godson up and hugged him. Sophie looked up at her friend; she was so grateful for all that she was. 'Do you want to do some writing? I could take him to collect Naomi from nursery if you like. We could even have lunch together, couldn't we, Alf?'

Sophie felt her face split wide open with delight; the thought of guilty space filled her eyes to overflowing.

'Don't cry. It's meant to be something good, you wally. No cleaning, though, and no hunting about for more special stuff under the table,' Tash teased.

Her one-armed hug lifted Sophie to her feet as Tash wrapped her arms around them all.

The emptiness of the house settled into the sound that silence makes, a kind of tinnitus that sounds in the absence of anything else. Sophie had opened her laptop and, with another recharged coffee cup, was ready to resume her writing. The screen revealed her chaotic approach: Katie, her dad, Simon, her childhood; all areas that had been touched to varying degrees, and she truly didn't know how to bring order. Everything led with inevitability towards pain, and she still wasn't quite ready – not yet.

Jake. She had always loved that name. A shudder rent its way through her like a freight train. No, not yet.

Dad was so strange; he was so encouraging on the one hand and so cruel on the other. It was definitely weird, the way he would manipulate us.

She had spent so much time looking at those moments in therapy that she thought she might be repeating herself on the screen.

I remember Dad telling me that Mum was having a breakdown, and believing him as well.

She felt a surge of guilt as she recalled being mean to her mum; laughing at her for not getting their little joke. How come I fell for it? I was so naive, so young. She chided herself with typical but unnecessary self-criticism and closed her eyes as she was transported to a scene in the kitchen. She began to write.

Red Formica table – no Weetabix on that surface, no way; that would not have been tolerated, would it? Pyrex dishes, blue and white, filled with shepherd's pie, the classic dish, and baked beans.

How come they don't taste so good now? We were the 'Beanz Meanz Heinz' generation, she recalled, and everything was new.

No big supermarkets then; proper shops where people knew your name, and greengrocers and bakers who drove round in large vans selling their wares door to door. That brought more problems, she recalled, and she continued to write as the memories flowed.

We had been trying to get Dad a piece of steak for his dinner; we scoured the aisles to no avail. The man behind the counter called Mum by her name: they both glanced at me, as if they were trying to share information in coded language that I would not understand.

A bit like she used to do with Katie, she realised. Had Katie felt the same?

There had been a look of concern on the man's face. Mum and I waited while he looked out back to see if there was any more. No luck.

78

We went home to await the judgement of Dad. Would he remember? Would he be late, drunk? Who knew?

As she sat there, Sophie couldn't recall the outcome of the event, thank goodness.

She glanced across the room to the family photographs. There was one of the four of them on holiday in France in the summer. Katie looked like any other teenager, her head thrown back in a moment of captured hilarity, and Simon looked like the cat who'd got the cream, with his baby son lashed to his chest. I look so ordinary, she thought, not in a negative way but in a way that doesn't betray what the years have brought. It was a good holiday, she remembered. Katie was in her element because although they had gone alone, just the four of them, she'd made friends and spent most of the time in the sea or playing various other sports, most unlike her really.

Sophie closed her eyes and recalled the delicious southern sun bathing her body in warmth. Alfie had lain on a mat next to her in the shade and dozed. Simon had been the most content she could remember; not for many years had he relaxed and smiled and read with such voraciousness. The years had turned his once-dark hair into a more distinguished grey around the temples; he still looked young for his age, though, and women were still attracted to him.

Sophie moved across to examine the picture. The dust had given it a softer focus. Wiping it with her sleeve, she peered at her own face. I look ok really. Covered up and with a tan I look younger. She had changed her hair colour so it looked redder in the sunlight. She reached up and touched the ends that fell on her shoulder. They're dry, she noted. I need to do something about myself; my roots are showing too.

Another picture contained just the three of them. Simon looked so young, grinning in his suit, and she in a bride's dress, her body slim and firm, her hair half up half down as was the fashion. Young Katie sat astride her hip. She sat back down and peered at the faces, so young and so totally unaware of what future traumas life held.

They had finally decided to get married when Katie turned two. They really didn't want to have another child before they were married. It had been a low-key affair, just a few friends at the registry office and back to the Indian for a meal. It was all she had wanted at the time, but now, as she gazed at the image, she wished they'd had a church wedding.

Me now: I am 40. Most people say I am attractive and sometimes I think the same. I am a woman of faith, a faith that has moved with me over the years. It has never left me totally but I have felt it slipping from my grasp, only to have it returned a little battered later by someone or something. I am me, full of life and joy and pain and trouble. I am a wife and mother and a daughter and friend.

Faith came to me later in life than it does for some; it was not a childhood revelation, although I do recall some teaching from Sunday school. It was after Katie was born that I discovered faith and a love that I had not believed was possible. How did it happen?

She pushed back her chair and looked once again at the holiday photograph.

It didn't take long to retrieve the photograph album from under the bed. The pages had that dated look; the plastic folders brittle with age. Sitting back on the bed she laid her treasure of memories across her bent knees. Every now and then she would remove a picture and hold it in a better light. What am I looking for? The words, although inside her head, appeared to bounce off the walls of her bedroom. She was looking for a clue to when faith first began. I am a researcher, she smiled to herself. All writers have to do this.

Chapter seventeen

The picture showed her sitting with a group of mothers, all smiling, with babies on their laps. How different I looked then, so straight and 'Christian'. Her fingers flew across the keys as the memories flooded her mind.

> *Ruth sought me out, but I didn't realise until years later. We had been on the same ward, both having our first baby, and I did not know anyone else in the same situation as me, so it was brilliant to have a new friend with an experience in common. She eventually asked me along to a toddler group, and there I suddenly belonged to the strange new world that is motherhood. I had the correct credentials – a baby – and being part of this varied group of women was a pleasure.*

Sophie's eyes ran along the row of now less familiar faces. She could not remember most of their names, but their children she recalled. Not by name either but rather by sex, age in relation to Katie and personality types – naughty boys, annoying whining girls, and so on. It was strange how faith had evened out the rough places that would get in the way of many a friendship. This faith had welcomed her in before she had realised it, and then she had wanted it for herself. She had been hungry for it, and they were prepared to feed her hunger.

It's been a while since I felt the touch of God, Sophie thought. Where is my Bible, anyway? She cast her eyes around the room. Not in here, she realised with chagrin.

> *I remember going to church for the first time.*

She smiled at the warmth of the memory.

The church door had been swept open in welcome by a smiling lady. Her hair was held back in a tight bun, but her expression was one of overwhelming acceptance and...

She paused, not wanting to appear soppy. She took a deep breath and muttered aloud, 'Oh, what the heck.'

... and love. How strange, I thought, she doesn't even know me.

She leaned back, knowing that the passing years had revealed the lady's name and confirmed the commitment to love. The church family had swept her up in an embrace of care and support that continued to the present day. Simon had been reluctant and cautious in his journey of faith. His faith, when it came, had been based on proof – the healing of a local lady. That healing had validated the scripture that he was so sceptical about. His faith, however, had been fragile, and it had shattered with the fatal blow that had been inflicted on the family. Still, in the face of such pain, the church had continued to enfold them with love and support; meals and cards had been normal daily occurrences. And when she had finally retreated and shut everyone out, they had allowed her space, keeping in touch via Ruth.

Who am I today? Where did my passion go? I used to walk so close to God. Did pain distance me from Him, or vice versa?

Her hands paused over the keys as she pondered the roller coaster of feelings that had been her life. How had she survived? The deep sigh that her body released reminded her of those times when she had sat opposite her therapist and found herself tumbling down a rabbit hole, just like Alice. The quiet 'Breathe, Sophie, breathe,' or the touch of her hand would stop the tumble into a land where nothing existed. Were you in that land, God? she wondered.

She scanned the room to confirm that she was alone – she seemed to always worry that she had spoken her thoughts aloud. No, they're not back yet, she thought. Staring back at the screen, she felt her hands and brain start to freeze. Closing her eyes to try to jump-start her mind only released darkness and sadness, overwhelming sadness.

'Enough,' she said aloud.

***

The sound of Motown classics filled the house as she tackled the front room. The piles of clothes, like some alien landscape, were hauled up the stairs and laid in the various rooms to be sorted out at a later time. Cushions were pulled off chairs, and old biscuit crumbs, hair bands and even a pot of nail varnish were quickly dealt with as she rearranged and brought order to her mind and the room. Catching sight of herself as she swayed to the beat of a familiar tune, she smiled: her hair was caught up in a grip and a wide sweep of soot had been smeared across her cheek.

She sang aloud to the old familiar classics. Maisie looked up from her faithful place, never absent long from her mistress's side.

'Alright, Maisie?' Sophie laughed, as her companion wacked her tail against the door. 'How about a walk?' In an instant both dogs were bounding about, circling in excitement. A quick call to arrange everything with Tash, and 20 minutes later she and the dogs were in the woods.

Sophie ambled through the familiar terrain, hands plunged deep into her pockets, and scarf and hat offering protection against the biting wind. Roots were precipitous in the moist conditions, and moss covered the bare wood in its vast array of greens, so she judged her footsteps with care. The dogs ran crazily through the woodland, totally absorbed in their own canine game. She stopped to examine a branch covered in lichen that resembled lace; it stood out in sharp relief against the brown of the leaves. She pulled out her phone and snapped the image.

Her wanderings took her to a log half the size it had been when Katie had been little; another stumbling in her mind brought the familiar struggle. Steadying herself as she leaned against it, she surveyed the scene: ancient oaks and frantic dogs. She wondered, as she always did, what these magnificent giants had seen over the years – women in long dresses, Victoriana in all its glory, parasols and gentlemen, horses and carriages and babies in perambulators being pushed around by nannies. How different would life for women have been then? she wondered.

'Come on, dogs, let's go.' She called them to her with the sudden realisation that time was pressing and she was in danger of being late for meeting up with Tash.

Chapter eighteen

Pulling up outside her faithful friend's house, she experienced a surge of gratitude. Who else knew her so well? Who else had walked this awful walk with her in such intimacy?

She pondered how Tash had always encouraged her faith, even when she had questioned life itself and thought she had been abandoned by God. Why would someone who does not believe support the belief of a friend? But that was it, wasn't it? It was about what was ultimately important to the friend – that had to be what true friendship was about.

The daylight was fading now, and the lights that shone in the front room revealed Tash dancing, laughing with someone out of sight. Suddenly she disappeared from view, only to appear again with a laughing Alfie. Round and round she danced him, only to stop and point across the room to where Sophie knew a mirror hung. She watched entranced as Tash pointed and moved again and put her face against Alfie's cheek.

Sophie felt the tears prick like burning acid behind her eyes, then spill over and drop slowly onto her hands. She wiped her face with the back of her hands, one after the other, aware of an impatience settling on her. 'It's ok,' she muttered aloud. 'I'm allowed to cry. There's no time limit.'

Wiping her face again and quickly checking herself in the car mirror, she ventured out. The door was opened by Tash and 'baby boy'.

'Hey, you alright?' Tash searched her friend's face. 'Alfie, look, it's Mummy.' Alfie squirmed in Tash's arms and reached across, hugging her with delight.

'Hey, baby boy, have you missed me? I bet you had fun with Aunty Tash, didn't you?'

***

Tea and biscuits shared with the children had helped to settle Sophie as they swapped the details of their afternoons.

'What are you and Simon up to tonight? Fancy coming out for a drink?'

Sophie was aware of a quickened heartbeat. 'That would mean I'd have to get a babysitter, or ask Katie.'

'I know. Why not give it a try and see what she says. It could be cathartic for you all.'

'I don't know. I'll speak to Simon. It's been ages since we went out to the pub.'

'Just think – a nice gin and tonic, an open fire, cheese and onion crisps!' Tash enticed.

'Shall I text him?'

'Yeah, go on.'

Simon readily agreed, and in that moment she realised that the fear was hers, not his. Still, they had to wait and see what Katie would say.

Later that evening Katie and Ella were setting up the front room for a pizza and film night. Sophie had been surprised that Katie had agreed. What was it about being a mother that meant that she assumed such a heavy weight of responsibility? She pulled a shabby notebook off the recipe book shelf and wrote the thought for future reference.

The usual palaver of what to wear ensued in the bedroom, and Simon's return was greeted by the vision of his wife in black tights and bra, throwing various items of clothing around their room in outrage.

'You alright, Sophie?' he asked in that tone that annoyed her so much.

'No, I'm not. I need some new clothes. I'm so fed up with not looking good.' She slumped down on the bed and shook a handful of random clothes at the half-smiling face of her husband. 'Stop laughing at me; it's not funny. Look, these are years old. I can't go out in this stuff. And they don't fit me anyway.'

The subject of gradual weight gain hung in the air, and through her closed eyes she was aware of her husband breathing in a way that appeared to steady him before speaking. 'Why don't you go and get some new clothes at the weekend? I'll have Alfie, and you can have some fun. Take Tash. You could ask her tonight.'

Sophie looked at him. 'That's fine, but what about now? What shall I wear tonight?'

'It's only the pub, Soph. You always look fine.' She pushed his hug off her shoulders and let the tears fall in huge drops down her face.

'It will be ok.' He spoke softly, squatting in front of her in an attempt to get her to look at him. She watched as her tears dropped onto their hands that were now clasped together.

'Come here.' He tugged her towards him and she finally relented and let him cocoon her in an embrace.

'Honest, you look great. Don't worry about it.' His words were muffled by her hair but they still hit the mark.

She knew she was overweight; he did too but he was just too nice to say anything. Sitting upright again she scanned the landscape of discarded clothes – leggings, leggings and more leggings. How long had it been since she had actually squeezed herself into a pair of jeans?

'I've got to lose weight. Maybe now I have the energy, but then it's the birthday and I have to get through that.' Aware that it was a problem that Simon just didn't get, she stood up. 'Don't worry, I'll sort it.'

Dismissed, Simon left the room. Alone once again, Sophie sat and texted Tash – only she really got her struggle with weight; it was even hard for her. Her fingers flew over the keys and she sent her text. 'I hate my body. I don't know what to wear tonight. Nothing fits. What are you wearing?'

Chapter nineteen

Kate

Kate lay on her bed, legs stretched out in front of her and hands behind her head. Her eyes scanned the pictures stuck across the walls as her mind wandered back over the last few days. Mum had been so pleased with the laptop. She had known she was going to get one, but she had looked like a little kid when she had unwrapped it; her eyes were shiny, like she was going to cry. Kate knew that look and usually kept away from her when it happened.

She had sat with her a few days before, drinking tea; they didn't do it that much these days – too many arguments and too many questions; she was just so annoying. Still, she had got those really good cakes from the baker. Kate's suspicions had been raised as she realised that her mum had looked nervous, almost like she was afraid of saying the wrong thing.

'Kate?' That had made her smile. For some reason her mum found it hard to call her that: she loved her Katie, her little girl.

'Mm, I love these cakes, Mum,' she had replied, her mouth full of cream and apple.

She looked annoyed but asked a question without comment, which tricked her. 'Would you mind if I wrote my story?'

'What story?' Kate had replied stupidly.

'You know, the last few years and my childhood.'

The cake had helped her to stay calm as she suddenly realised what she meant. She had swallowed the rest of the cake in a dry gulping lump and managed to nod.

She had recounted the scene to Ella, who was all ears. It was unusual for her to be open, and the treat was not lost on her one true friend who usually had so many problems herself that they did not talk about Kate's. In fact, she had just been talking about the usual stuff

– her dad – so it was probably a relief to talk about something else instead. She nodded eagerly, encouraging Kate to continue

'So what happened? Is she writing it, your mum?'

'Yeah,' Kate mumbled, unsure how to explain to Ella the difficulty that it held for her. 'Look, Ella, I need to talk to you, but I want to know you won't tell anyone else – no one, promise?'

'Of course I won't.' She looked affronted at the thought. 'I trust you with all that stuff about my dad, don't I? So you can trust me.'

'Ok, sorry. So later, eh? You still up for babysitting?'

'Yeah great. No drink you said, right?'

'Yeah, this is a big deal, just pizza and a film. Mum's actually gonna trust me.'

Sitting up now on her bed, she was still surprised that her mum had asked her to babysit. I can't believe it. Does that mean that she actually thinks I'm adult enough now? Her thoughts ricocheted around her bedroom; music played as she surveyed her face in the mirror. Carefully she leaned forward to apply a fine line of black along the top of her eyes. As she finished the final stroke, the lid fell onto the floor and disappeared under the bed. She swore under her breath. Normally she wouldn't bother but this was a new pencil, and so she found herself on her hands and knees among the detritus that covered her carpet. She pushed a plate to one side and her hand alighted on a fork, the surface rough with whatever had been on the plate. Sightless, she pushed her hand further under the bed: nothing.

Lying flat on her stomach, she peered into the gloom. Her eyes adjusted to the light and she entered a new world of long-lost items. A half-read book: she sat up and flicked the dusty pages she had not been able to get into. Back down again, she pulled out various old exercise books, pencils and material for college projects. Growing accustomed to the gloom, her eyes caught sight of the box at the furthest point under the bed. Pushing herself quickly backwards and out into the room, she sat, leaning back against the bed. She hugged herself as the shock of its discovery arrived with force. She had pushed it out of sight, and now, just as her mum was starting to write, here it was surfacing. It was weirdly perfect timing, she realised.

Breathing in deeply, she plunged back under the bed like a deep-sea diver. She had to squeeze herself under the bed commando-style just to touch the edge of it. Somehow it had managed to get wedged. She sat up again against the side of the bed, breathing heavily. Not to be undone, she lifted the end of her bed to one side to release the prize. Its weight surprised her, and it was only determination that found it finally sitting on the bed like some large, dust-encrusted treasure chest.

Her bedroom was in a complete turmoil, her bed askew, and now the box sat there grinning like some long-forgotten monster that had lived under her bed all her childhood. She sat pondering her next move, aware of her breath coming in short bursts, hugged her knees up to her chest and rocked to and fro, surveying the scene.

Her mum's voice filtered up, announcing Ella's arrival and causing her to leap into action. Pulling the box off the bed, she pushed it into a less obvious position and chucked a few clothes over it.

'Hi.' Ella stood in the doorway, a strange expression on her face.

'Hey, what's the matter?' Kate heard the accusation in her voice and quickly rose to hug her friend. Shutting the door behind her, she turned to face her friend.

'What have you been doing? There's black stuff on your face.' Ella reached forward to touch her cheek.

Kate brushed her hand away. 'Nothing.'

'Sorry! I thought we were going into town?' Ella's voice had an unusual tremor to it.

'Yeah we are, sorry.'

Sitting down at her mirror, Kate saw clearly what Ella had been surprised at: her hair was a complete mess and looked like it had something stuck in it, and she had managed to get make-up splodges across her cheeks, too.

'I lost the top of my eyeliner and then started looking under my bed for it and found loads of stuff.' She gestured to the piles of things.

'What's that?' Ella pointed to the box, not so well disguised, after all.

Momentarily, Kate was undone and struggled to answer, but she surprised herself with the truth. 'Oh it's a box of stuff I've had for ages. I'm gonna sort it later.'

Mum had left pizza and nibbles. Later, after a chilled evening, they sat back in Kate's room.

'Your mum looked so pretty tonight, didn't she? I don't see her dressed up very often,' Ella said.

'Yeah, amazing what a bit of make-up can do,' Kate laughed.

'We could always offer to babysit again. No money required – just pizza and a film, eh?'

They had set up the spare bed on a bit of cleared floor in Kate's room. The adults hadn't come back yet and they lay there listening to music and chatting about the usual things – friends, clothes and make-up. Every now and then Kate would hush them and listen for Alfie's breathing, just as she had promised Mum.

The squeak of the door announced Mum's arrival. Her face had that rosy-cheeked look about it and her eyes were just a bit too shiny to be totally sober. 'Hey, girls. All ok? Did he wake up at all?' Mum's voice was lighter than usual and relaxed; it was so weird.

'No, Mum, he was quiet. Did you have fun?'

'Do you know what? It was really lovely; nothing like a few gin and tonics to put a smile on your face. Sorry we're so late.'

'No worries. We'll babysit again if you want, Sophie. It was fun,' Ella piped up.

'Yeah, well, don't make too many offers – I could get used to it. See you two in the morning. Thanks, hon,' Mum laughed. Kate received the look of affection her mother gave her as she retrieved the monitor.

'Your mum is so nice, Kate; I don't know why you moan about her.'

'You don't have to live with her.'

As she started to drop off to sleep, Kate suddenly thought about the trip to Whitstable. It had been so lovely, apart from the bit in the market stalls. How are we going to do this birthday thing? Even as she lay there her heart picked up, and she had to use all her energy to prevent herself crying out loud. She knew Ella was still awake by her breathing, and she would ask what was wrong.

Her tears burned behind her eyelids. 'I can't; I can't; no, no, no.'

Ella's voice startled her. 'Are you alright, Kate?'

'What? Oh yes, just... thinking.'

'What about? You sound sad. You were going to tell me about that box tonight.'

'Oh yeah, I forgot,' Kate lied.

She felt bad lying to Ella. They had become close over the years, but she didn't talk to anyone about this stuff. No, it was best if it was stuffed back in the box.

So together they discussed plans for the next day, and sleep slowly overcame them.

Chapter twenty

16th October
Wednesday

Ella's mum called in the morning to say they were moving back home, so she had left to help her. Kate found herself in the unusual situation of being at home with Mum and Alfie without any plans, apart from catching up on coursework.

'Do you have any classes today?'

'Nah, just some coursework.'

'Do you fancy a dog walk with me and Alfie before you start?'

Kate smiled at her brother who was togged up in his winter clothes, like a teddy bear. He was almost walking now. She bent down and beckoned him. 'Come on, Alfie. Walk to Kate. You can do it. Shall we go out?' Kate knew the words would not be missed by her mother.

'Ah, great, Kate. It's a lovely day.'

Alfie gingerly let go of the chair and started a slow uncertain stagger to the outstretched arms of his beloved sister.

'Yeah, clever boy.' She scooped him up in her arms and felt tears come unbidden into the back of her eyes. Brushing them brusquely aside, she kissed the top of her little brother's head. 'Let's go out, baby boy.'

A quick look at her mum revealed that her tears had been noticed, but she said nothing, much to Kate's relief.

The wind was biting in spite of the sky being a brilliant blue as they pushed the buggy across the expanse of common. They had not been here for ages; time for a change, Mum had said. The sky was dotted with kites diving and twisting against the blue expanse; faces and strange mythical creatures that appeared to have the capacity to eat the sky.

Mum had stopped and was pulling something out of the rucksack she had been carrying. As she straightened up she handed Kate a long package.

'I told Alfie I would get a kite; I thought you might like to show him how to fly it?' The caution in her mum's voice was not lost on her daughter.

The package revealed a red and blue kite that only had string, so it would be easy to fly. The nylon fabric had a long-forgotten but familiar feel to Kate, who rubbed the material between her fingers. Squatting down in front of Alfie, she offered it to him to touch. 'Look, Alfie, shall we fly it?'

Kate pushed the kite between her knees as she knelt and released her brother. Letting him cling to her like a monkey, she juggled him in one arm while picking up the kite in the other.

Mother and daughter stood face to face; a quizzical look was irritatingly visible on her mother's face. 'I can do it!' Kate's angry voice was at odds with the surroundings, and the wind snatched it away, minimising its impact with a sudden gust.

Adjusting Alfie on her hip, she flung the kite upwards. It fell to the ground in a heap. Kate looked up to see if her mum was watching, and found herself looking at her back as she leaned over and rummaged in the rucksack.

They bent down together, brother and sister, and she explained to Alfie the need to untangle it all. 'Stay here a minute, Alfie. Let me see if I can do it.'

Alfie stood swaying as his sister gingerly took away her support. She ran away from him, calling back to tell him she would be back in a minute, then turned. 'Ready, Alfie? Here it comes.'

As she ran towards her brother and mother, the kite lifted up in the sky behind her. The wind grabbed at its frail frame and it flew. Alfie's face was split in two as he grinned, now steadied by his mum's arms, pointing and laughing as the kite danced above.

Kate came to a halt next to him. Gently tugging on the string, she kept the aerial display in motion. 'Mum, can you put Alfie on my hip? I can't do it one-handed,' she asked, feeling a bashful smile appear on her face.

Alfie's little fingers held on to Kate's as she twirled the kite back and forth across the sky, their laughter mixed together in delight. Mum had brought hot chocolate, which was so delicious. Kate loved the way she did things like that. A distant memory rose and fell in her mind.

'This is really nice, Mum,' she said as their eyes met once again in peace. They sat, watching the tumbling and twisting colours of the kites.

'Sorry,' Kate mumbled, blowing the steam across her mug as her hands hugged it to her.

'Why are you sorry?'

'I keep getting mad.'

'Don't worry about it. This is so lovely. I've missed it. Maybe I should say sorry.'

'What for?' Kate questioned.

'Everything.' Mum's voice lowered as she dropped her eyes towards Alfie contentedly supping on his drink.

'We are going to have to talk, hon, about... Jakey.'

'No!' Kate's voice came low and threatening. Alfie glanced at her and she ruffled his hair. 'It's ok, baby boy, don't worry.' She pulled him towards her and sat him on her lap. From behind his body she took a deep breath. She wanted to talk about her discovery but really didn't know if she could do it. She thought her dad had put everything in it, but she wasn't sure. And she couldn't remember why they had let her have it; she just knew that they had. She had so many questions to ask but they stuck in her throat. She released a deep sigh and launched herself. 'I found the box under my bed yesterday.'

The words hung there. Mum looked shocked and looked away. But then she totally ignored what Kate had said and changed the subject. 'Kate, I'm so sorry.' She put up her hand to stop Kate speaking. 'Please don't get mad. Let me just say this: I know I haven't helped. I've been too wrapped up in myself, but now,' she paused, 'doing all the writing has shown me that I've missed you.'

'What?' Kate could feel her irritation rise as emotion showed on her mother's face.

'I've missed your growing up, and now...' Her voice trailed off as she choked up, much to Kate's annoyance. Alfie squirmed on her lap and she passed him to his mother.

'Mum, don't. Let's go home... please.' She managed to soften her tone as she got to her feet.

They drove home in silence. Kate was so mad: she had ignored her when she mentioned the box, and she decided she wouldn't mention it again. Her face felt like steel, unable to flex even for her brother, and she practically ignored him for the entire journey. He gave up trying to say her name and fell asleep.

Once home, she retreated to her room. She lay on the bed with her headphones on for what seemed like hours. The box was still waiting patiently when she finally surfaced from that place she liked to retreat to. It was strange – she wasn't sure if it was sleep or some strange phenomenon that took her away when it was all too crazy in her head. She quickly threw aside the invading thought of her mother's previous offer of counselling. How could it help? Talking was too hard. Images flung themselves around her head and she felt the tremors that heralded the arrival of a memory start again, but this time she sat up and shook herself.

Slamming the bedroom door shut behind her, she went downstairs and into the kitchen for food. The sudden realisation that she was starving and the darkened room had forced her to look at the clock. It was late – she had lost a few hours... again. She felt like she was in a scene from some film, kind of spaced out, like the time she had smoked weed.

Mum was sitting at the table, writing. She glanced up and smiled tentatively. 'Are you hungry? You've been asleep for ages.'

'Yes, what can I eat? Do we have anything nice?' The accusation in her voice curled across the room, changing her mother's demeanour in a moment.

'There's sandwich makings and crumpets. What do you want?' was the curt reply.

Kate had pulled the fridge open too abruptly; the shake of glass bottles highlighted the need to slow down. 'Mum, I just need something,' she whined.

'Do you want me to get you something?'

'Please.'

Kate knew her mum had decided not to pander to her so much; she had heard her and Dad talking the other night. They still didn't get it that their voices travelled at night, particularly when it was all quiet.

'Where's Alfie?'

'He's asleep.'

95

In the silence that followed, his breathing could be heard through the monitor. It was never switched off, with the result that conversations between Alfie and whoever was in his room with him were relayed downstairs on a regular basis.

Kate sat eating her cheese and pickle sandwich; her mum was looking at the screen, rereading – or appearing to, at least.

'I can't talk, Mum. I feel like I'm crazy. It would be easier to die.'

She regretted the words as soon as they landed, but it was too late, and it was also the truth: she had wanted to die, and still did sometimes, even now. Her mother's eyes met hers with a gasp. Hadn't she realised it was that bad? Puzzlement moved across Kate's mind and face alike. She didn't know!

The feeling of sadness overwhelmed her as she experienced a new sensation, a realisation that her mother had abandoned her to her grief, and she really had been alone. Finally, it made painful sense – she had been alone ever since the day it had happened.

'Our family is a mess!' she screamed. 'Alfie is the only normal one among us; we'd better not screw him up, too.'

Chapter twenty-one

Simon

Simon surveyed the scene: mother and daughter confronting each other across the table. Kate was enraged. He had caught the beginning of the chat as he had opened the front door but he had waited, not wanting to butt in. He had heard her thoughts about dying and had covered his mouth with his hand to prevent the cry that was threatening to burst out from invading the space. His little girl and his beautiful wife stood broken together, unable to help each other.

They both turned in surprise at his entrance. 'What's going on?' he asked, his voice barely above a whisper.

'Nothing,' flashed his daughter, her face ablaze with everything bar nothing. 'We're just arguing as normal, aren't we, Mum?' Her challenge to her mother to contradict her hung in the air.

'Don't worry. It's ok, Simon.' His wife's placating tone tried in vain to bring some relief.

'I don't know why you both think I'm immune to all this stuff. I can see and hear; I'm not stupid.' He held up his hand to silence them both, turned on his heels and retreated to Alfie's room from where sounds of life had started to come through the monitor.

Mother and daughter were left alone. The sound of Simon entering the bedroom was clearly heard. 'Hey Alfie, was that a rude awakening?' He leaned over the cot and lifted his warm son into his arms.

'They're arguing again, aren't they?' Spying the red light of the monitor, he sat and continued his conversation with none-the-wiser Alfie.

'You know what, son? I can't stand to hear them fight. Anyone would think they hated each other, but they don't, do they? No, they're so, so sad, and they think the pain is just theirs alone, but it's not. It's mine too, and it will be yours when you're older, when you know who you missed meeting.' He pulled Alfie against him to try to muffle the tears that sprung into his eyes.

He had wished time and time again that it had been him; he had begged God to take him instead, but He wasn't listening, and the tidal wave of desolation had moved relentlessly through his family. It was a miracle they had survived at all.

He was still haunted by the face of his decimated wife, and that of his daughter; their bloodless, white faces were like Halloween masks that remained in situ for weeks. The memory of his son was kept in a separate place, rarely visited. His wife had become a strange remote creature, robotic in her movements that ensured that both he and Kate were kept at arm's length. The guilt she carried had almost crushed her as it squeezed the life out of her, and he had felt so alone; only the memory of the woman she had once been had kept him faithful.

And Kate. What had happened to his little girl? Would she ever recover? Overnight she had changed from a glorious joy-filled little girl to a shadow that would seem to disappear if you tried to touch her. The grief was so huge and the trauma so awful that there was no way he could reach her. He was supposed to protect his wife and children – and he had failed. He knew in rational moments that he could not have saved them from this, but still he carried the burden. His own grief had nowhere to land, no one to help him bear it; their pain had dwarfed his in their magnitude, until today.

As Alfie leaned against his father in his sleepy waking body, Simon felt the anguish rise in his throat and release through his open mouth in a deep roar.

Suddenly he and Alfie were no longer alone. His wife and child were around him. He was hugging them both, and they sobbed together. Sounds of sorrow long held within each individual soul poured into the room as they were overwhelmed by the intensity of the wave, which finally broke with a strength of its own. Sophie fell to her knees and sobbed as Kate wrapped her arms around her daddy and finally allowed him into her grief.

'Dada,' filled the room, as the foam of the wave swirled around in a slow move of inclusive pain.

Chapter twenty-two

Kate

Kate sat on her bed. She felt as though she had done a round with Mike Tyson, as her dad would say. She wrapped her arms around herself as she recalled the cry from her father. She had excluded him, it was true – she had excluded everyone – but that sound had shocked and frightened her. He was the rock in the family and now it had all gone crazy. She still didn't want to go and see that woman, no matter how nice she was. But for him she would – anything not to hear that howl again. She turned the card over in her hand and added the number to her phone contacts list, saying to herself, I'll text her later.

Lying back on her bed, she surveyed the room. The box still sat, grinning, awaiting her attention, and she spoke aloud. 'What?' she challenged it.

She tried to imagine the things within its shell, but realised that she had put those memories far away. Spying 'that woman's' business card still next to her, she grabbed her phone and quickly typed a message. A deep breath, she pressed the button and it launched into the atmosphere. There – that should keep them quiet.

Flinging her dressing gown over the box, she turned on her laptop in search of distraction. Dad's head appeared around the door, along with the fingers of Alfie, pulling it towards them. 'Kaka.'

Her brother struggled to gain release from his father's arms. Bending down, with permission in his eyes to let Alfie go, he asked her whether she would like to have dinner with him later, just the two of them: Mum was going to stay home.

'Oh ok, sure,' she smiled. 'Hey, come here, Alfie.'

Her father left the room and she and her brother were alone. She lifted him up on the bed and sat there in the stillness with him. 'What shall we do, baby boy?'

As he sat there bouncing up and down, she pondered him – his face, his hair, his profile. It all had a familiar feel that went beyond the present time: Jakey.

His hand on her cheek brought her into the present, and the noise that heralded the arrival of a text. 'That was quick, eh?' she muttered.

She read the response and the invitation to meet. She could do the offered time, but… the sound of her father's howl revisited her, so she agreed hastily before she could change her mind.

'What shall we do, Alfie? There's nothing in here for you.' The box 'grinned' at her again: what was in there? 'Shall we look in the box?'

Alfie bounced his affirmation, his nappy-covered bottom creaking against her duvet.

A sudden surge of enthusiasm and a throwing of caution to the wind found the lid levered open. Alfie stood holding the edge, his fingers stroking the contents within. Kate held her breath as he pulled at something, and suddenly into full view flew a grey rabbit. A gasp released itself and Alfie suddenly sat down, still clutching his treasure.

The bang of the shutting lid resulted in him crying out in shock. Kate pulled him to her and sat once more on the bed with her brother and the rabbit enfolded in her arms. She wanted to touch the cuddly toy with its pink, soft inner ears; she wanted to smell it, but her senses seemed to be on full alert and she felt as though she might pass out.

Alfie pushed the rabbit against her cheek. 'Alfie, Kate doesn't want it; you have it.' Her stern voice alarmed him and he squirmed to extricate himself from her grip, clambering away along the bed, still holding on to the rabbit.

'Alfie, that is Mr Bop,' she mumbled, more to herself than to inform him.

Memories assailed her senses. She pulled up her knees and wrapped her arms around them, sinking her head down on to them as she watched him examine the rabbit's face, gently touching its eyes and ears, all the while smiling to himself.

The door was once again pushed open and her mum stood there, a cup of tea in each hand and a bottle wedged under her chin. Reaching up, Kate retrieved the bottle and passed it to Alfie, who ignored her gesture.

'Mama.' He bounced, showing off his prize. Her mother gasped, just as Kate had done.

'We had a look in the box and he found it,' Kate mumbled.

Her eyes met her mother's and they both sat on the bed, shocked at the scene before them. A sideways look at her mother informed Kate that they were both in the same state, and she leaned against her mother in the shared pain.

'Mr Bop,' muttered her mum.

Chapter twenty-three

Simon

Simon sat across the table from his daughter and watched her scan the menu. She loved Chinese food, and appeared to have put aside the earlier incident. They had walked to the restaurant and so he ordered for himself and for Kate, much to her delight, a glass of wine. The walk had been non-eventful, a father and daughter arm in arm out for an evening stroll; there was an easiness between them that was at odds with the earlier outpouring of emotion.

The wine settled the heavy coiled snake of emotion that was always ready to overwhelm; a kind of soothing solution that assisted his attempt to talk. 'So Kitty, about earlier...' He watched her face intently as she paused, and he wondered for a moment whether she would moan about his use of her childhood nickname.

Kate paused, mid scoop of chow mein, her bright eyes the image of her mother's. 'I'm sorry, Dad, I didn't mean to hurt you.'

'I know. We've all suffered; it's not your fault.'

She suddenly looked so young again and he had to steady himself, clutching his glass tightly to prevent himself getting dragged back. Is that what Sophie meant when she talked about losing time? he wondered.

Kate hesitated. Clutching her glass in both hands, she looked at him over the brim. 'I did it, Dad; I'm going to see the counsellor.' She smiled ruefully.

'Well, that's great, Kitty. I'm sure it will really help to talk. It helped Mum, didn't it?'

'And you, Dad?' Her eyes challenged him to respond.

'Well, actually, I've been seeing someone at work.'

Her eyebrows rose in a precise move, perfectly defined, depicting her surprise with elegance beyond her years.

'Well, it's not something I talk about much. See, we're more alike than you realise! That's how I know it helps. It hurts, but somehow, in some strange way, it really does help. I'm really glad you're going to see Zara.'

Her hand was soft and small in his, and her reach across the table almost unhinged him as he struggled not to cry.

The rest of the meal provided the distraction they both needed as they focused on the flavours, the hilarious use of chopsticks juggling slippery noodles, and fortune cookies. He realised that they had managed to avoid anything contentious, and it was a relief for him to have a time of respite, even though he knew the storm was still waiting somewhere. Sophie's voice dripped into his thoughts every now and then. He knew she would ask what had been said, but they had done enough, said enough, shared enough, and the rest had to be fun.

Chapter twenty-four

17th October
Thursday

Sophie

The room darkened as the predicted storm strolled into the vicinity, the heavy purple of rain unleashed its torrent and the light of day was extinguished in a moment. A sudden bright sheet of light illuminated the room.

'It's ok, Alfie, its only lightning.' Sophie found herself hugging him to her nonetheless before the thunder rumbled. The storm was not upon them fully yet.

Alfie's fingers traced the rain as it made its way down the panes. Shaking herself like a dog that has suddenly got soaked through, she moved away quickly. Memories assailed her mind again; they were coming more frequently now, as if her laptop had opened up the floodgates, and she needed a mechanism to manage them. The nearness of Mr Bop, now the constant companion of Alfie, caused her to flinch momentarily. It was a mystery as to why Alfie was so taken with the battered rabbit – he had newer teddies, after all. It was almost as if he knew the significance, the memories that the grey creature held, and so he loved him instantly. He only felt joy, like he had been reunited with an old friend.

Food had always worked before; the urge to stuff down her feelings behind a chunk of whatever was available still pursued her mind. She toyed with thoughts of white bread toasted just the right amount to allow a lashing of butter and Marmite to move in a slow, delicious melt.

Alfie was now covered in rusk; the taste had not changed since she was little, and she could not resist dipping her finger into it as she cleaned him up to taste again that strange biscuit sweetness of long ago. Alfie screwed up his face as the cool wipe made contact with the warmth of his rosy cheeks. 'There you go, gorgeous.'

She bent to kiss his face, and he thrust his sticky fingers into her hair, bringing her to a halt. His laughter echoed around the room as lightning suddenly lit up the kitchen once again. He jumped in surprise as Sophie engulfed him in her arms.

'Here comes the thunder, Alfie: listen.' She braced herself for the rumble that came quicker and louder now. Maisie and Sid started to bark their chorus of alarm.

'My mum told me it's clouds bumping into each other,' Sophie murmured to herself. 'Shh, you two. Come on, Alfie, let's go and have our drinks in the front room.'

The room never seemed to change, despite her constant attempts to bring order. Chaos reigned, and to some extent Sophie kind of liked it that way, not that she would admit it to many people. She loved the multicoloured throws that lay where they had landed the night before. Gathering them up, she folded them with an efficiency that came from years of practice. There. She surveyed the marginally tidier space and sighed with contentment. Alfie was up to his normal trick of discovery, pulling clothes from the neat piles and flinging them over his shoulder as he laughed to himself.

'Hey you, cheeky, what are you up to now?'

Diverted by the sudden appearance of toys that rained down on his mat, he turned, giving Sophie a brief interlude, space for her to grab the piles and place them on the stairs for later.

Alfie drank from his beaker while eyeing his toys out of the corner of his eye, lifting and examining them over the top of his cup. Sophie mused as she observed him. Simon had not said much the night before; he and Kate had both seemed restored in some way, and she couldn't help but feel a bit left out. It's good that they get on so well, she thought, but I miss my little girl. All the therapy had not helped her to communicate to her through the pain, and they were both locked in their own version of the past.

Scrolling back through her writing, she stopped on the words:

Dead. My dad is dead.

Alfie chuckled to himself and she found herself holding her breath again as she wrote.

> *The landing light was dim, setting the shabby décor into a sad yellow ochre hue. I went to bed early so I wouldn't hear him coming home again. Mum had warned me that there had been some problems at work. A sense of impending doom seemed to hover just below the ceiling as I tried in vain to make myself sleep. The dull sound of the television filtered up through the floor. Mum was trying to distract herself – she had made dinner, washed up, tidied the house; everything was shipshape, and yet inevitably the future held terror in its clutches, like a tiger poised to pounce.*
>
> *I jumped as the door slammed shut.*

'Mama?' Alfie's face had that concerned look again, and suddenly she was back in the present.

Surprise released her breath like a door catch, and she gasped her words. 'Hey, darling. Was Mummy busy writing?'

It was almost a relief to be distracted, but she knew it had to be faced. Like the minutes of a meeting, the truth had to be put down on the page. Later, she thought, later.

Chapter twenty-five

Sometimes the monotony of her day, the repetitive tasks of motherhood and housekeeping, meant that she yearned for more. However, close on its heels would be the feeling of guilt that she was moving on. How could she? That would mean she was getting over it, and that held a betrayal that would deny his existence.

The washing machine spoke aloud as the knock of some forgotten metallic object banged a rhythm against the drum. Alfie was fascinated and sat engrossed on the floor as the contents turned. The afternoon storm still lit the house in purple light; the kitchen had become their safe haven. Once again the creation of food: soup, warming and full of goodness, filled the room with its own particular aroma. The sound of the pressure cooker was now so familiar to the baby boy that the hiss of released steam had no effect on his absorbed self.

Sophie once again steeled herself and went back to that night.

I held my breath after the door slammed but eventually I had to expel my carbon dioxide in order to access the oxygen that I needed to live. The muffled sounds tried to get past the sound of my breathing under the covers, eventually succeeding, and I found myself standing in the open doorway as Dad's fist made contact with Mum's face. The blood that spurted out of her cheek appeared to move in slow motion as I released my scream. As she fell to the floor, he turned white with rage.

'Get out of here,' he growled.

'Sophie, go,' my mother whimpered, but I didn't move.

The washing machine beeped and Alfie banged on the door, saving her from what came next. She looked down at her hands that were shaking in her lap, and shoved them underneath herself to steady them.

The soup was hot and burning in her stomach, causing her to flinch – a desired distraction not unlike the cold pain of a cut as blood bursts through the opening in the epidermis. It's weird how pain can be soothing, she pondered, as deliberately cooled soup was spooned into Alfie's open mouth.

The ever-present laptop shone bright again, and she was transported to the doorway once more.

> *Dad moved across the floor at speed, and his open palm across my face forced me backwards onto the floor. The door slammed shut. The lino was cold and brown; small squares among the larger ones. I drew patterns around and around the edges of them with my finger as the thuds continued through the dark wood door.*
>
> *It was the first time I had to lie for Mum.*

The memory caused her to respond aloud. As Alfie banged her elbow with his spoon, the irony of Ella and Tracy in her life was not lost on her. 'Mummy had to lie, didn't I, lovely?'

Alfie looked at her with that look that said, 'What do you mean?'

The spooning of soup into both their mouths changed the subject once again. Broken pieces of bread held in his oh-so-lovely hands pulled the soup into his mouth, and the pleasure of his presence acted like a calming balm that soothed her now burning throat.

The post-storm sky still held the distant horizon as bright blue was revealed overhead and the garden released its perfume, so familiar after a downpour. The dogs ran in close circles, sensing the pending outing.

As always, the traffic had been disabled by the rain, and Alfie had to endure her mutterings as supposedly able drivers acted like two-year-olds in charge of huge machines that were beyond their capability to control. She could feel her jaw aching as she bit down in frustration.

Eventually they arrived, and the expanding blue sky lifted her mood. She swung Alfie onto her shoulders. 'You're getting so heavy, Alfie,' she said as the metal frame of the carrier dug into her flesh and refused to sit easily on her hips. She quickly dismissed the thought, My bum is too big, as she called the dogs back.

The stream that ran through the woods was deep from the rain. The dogs' joyous leaping in and out caused the path to become more treacherous. The need to cling to tree trunks and duck under low branches to prevent Alfie losing an eye ensured that it really felt like a workout. Her panting was repeated by Alfie as they moved like a slow steam train.

'Yes, hon. Mummy really needs to lose weight, eh?'

A sudden knock of dog against her leg caused a loss of balance, and she fell sideways.

The cut on his face dripped blood, which mingled with the tears as Alfie sobbed. 'Oh no, Alfie! I'm so sorry,' Sophie cried. Pulling out an old tissue, she dabbed at his face. He looked so shocked. 'Mummy fell over, didn't she? Sorry, darling.' Sophie's thoughts ran quickly through her mind: He could have died; I'm a totally useless mother.

Maisie ran around them, the cause of the trouble and the solution as she licked at Alfie to distract him and Sophie from his injury.

The hospital still looked eerily the same. The A&E department had had a facelift but the outside caused memories to stir. Sophie held her son to her and breathed deeply, unsure whether she could actually enter. Finally, she faced the glass doors, her injured son the only thing that enabled her to cross the boundary.

Alfie was engrossed with a vague semblance of toys as they waited, with what felt like the entire world, to be seen. Simon had thought it would be best to get him checked out, just in case, and so here they were, waiting. There was something about the smell of the place that brought goose pimples to the surface of her skin – and dread; awful dread. The waiting went on and on as she used her breathing techniques again.

The nurse who eventually saw to them looked much younger than she was. I really am getting on, Sophie mused. Alfie, ever compliant, sat with his upturned face towards her as she examined the cut. 'Now, what have you been up to?' the nurse asked, looking at Sophie for clarification.

'Oh, err; I was knocked over in the woods,' Sophie explained, suddenly aware that Social Services could be waiting around the corner. She thought the nurse looked at her with an expression that said, That was stupid, and Sophie found herself blustering and stuttering as if she were indeed guilty of some crime.

'I think he's fine,' the nurse said finally. Her eyes turned to the computer screen, the back of which faced Sophie. She watched the flickering of the nurse's eyebrows and imagined the record of everything being displayed before her eyes.

Finally, the young woman turned to her again. 'Your lovely boy is fine, Mrs Pritchard. No need to worry. Just keep an eye on him.' Turning to Alfie, she told him how a little scar added character.

The room began to shrink and the urge to get out overwhelmed Sophie. She muttered her thanks and fled to the safety of the car. The darkness of the day surprised her; they had been there for hours.

Alfie swallowed his drink, gurgling with pleasure as he sat on Sophie's lap and banged the steering wheel with his little fist. The sudden ring of her mobile rang startled them both.

'Is he ok?' Simon asked anxiously.

'Oh, yes. Sorry it took so long. We've only just got out. I would have rung,' she replied, feeling guilty once again. His voice cut out and she realised that he must be on his way home. 'Let's go, baby boy.'

White greasy paper held the oversized portions of fish and chips that Simon had collected on the way home. 'Where's Kate? Will she want some?' he asked.

Sophie realised that she had no idea where her daughter was or what she was doing. 'I really don't know. I'll call her.' Panic and guilt once again flooded her; it was too much for one day.

The sound of Katie's voice snapped her out of it. 'Mum, I'm upstairs,' she laughed down the phone.

They sat, the four of them, dipping chips in and out of mayonnaise and ketchup in quiet camaraderie, no one mentioning the day. Finally Katie spoke. 'You ok, Mum?' Her hand covered Sophie's still one for a moment.

Sophie's eyes stung again as she attempted to push the tears down. 'It was so awful. I can't even go for a walk without something bad happening.' She put her hopeless head in her hands.

'Sophie, that's not true. Come on, it could happen to anyone,' Simon placated.

110

'But look at his face!' she cried, tears now freely flowing. Alfie had a big shiner. The strips of plaster above his eye and the spreading dark bruise made him look like a trainee pirate.

'You're ok, aren't you, Alfie?' Simon smiled at his son as he stuffed an oversized fistful of chips into his face.

'Mum, you couldn't help it; it was Maisie's fault. It could have happened to anyone.' Katie's voice of reason stopped her mid-sob as she turned to look at her. Here was her lost daughter.

Chapter twenty-six

18th October
Friday

The day shone bright with potential as they packed the car with dogs and rugs and children. Tash had suggested a trip to the seaside. Katie had declined the offer to come with them, and appeared to be almost hurrying them out with her offers of help.

'What are you going to do?' Sophie asked suspiciously.

'Nothing, Mum. I have loads of work to do. Ella might come over later. What time will you be back?'

Sophie glanced at Tash – she was driving, after all.

'I don't know, she said. 'When the kids get bored. It might be freezing too, so it depends.'

As they left, Sophie voiced her concern. 'Katie was a bit too pleased to see me leave, wasn't she?'

'I'd be the same – a chance to lay about all day and watch TV, no little brother or annoying mum about to give me jobs. Don't worry, Soph,' Tash soothed.

The waves at Broomhill Sands sounded distantly across the wide expanse, and kites in glorious colours sped across the open sky. Daring young men and women leapt out of the water in aerial displays as they hung beneath them, or drove pell-mell across the surface of the sand on buggies that would perform a slow curve before returning the way they had come.

The sand held a vague sense of warmth as they spread the picnic rug that had only been thrown in at the last minute, just in case.

'It's so beautiful here,' Sophie muttered, as a cape of calm settled around her.

Alfie sat with Naomi. They were both covered in padded all-in-one winter coats as Naomi attempted to show Alfie how to fill a bucket with sand.

The sand ran through Sophie's fingers, just like time, she thought. 'Can you believe I actually fell over?' she said as she surveyed the damage on his little face. The bruise had completed its arrival and sat like a conqueror across Alfie's cheek in brazen glory, a perfect reminder of her stupidity.

'Sophie, it could have happened to anyone. It's not your fault.' Tash handed her a sandwich along with her comfort.

'Sorry. I'm sure I must be getting on everyone nerves. I just feel so awful about it. Look at him.'

'I know, he does look rather bashed up, but *we* know what happened. It really doesn't matter what anyone else thinks, does it?'

Sophie bit into the baguette and became aware of Alfie's eyes on her. Laughing, she realised how alike they were: he didn't miss a thing where food was concerned. 'Are you hungry, baby boy?' she asked.

It really was a lovely day. The children provided a distraction as they played. What is it about seeing something through the eyes of a child that lifts our spirits? Sophie wondered.

Pebbles in their variety were so fascinating, especially to taste, as it turned out. Frequent cries of 'Aunty Sophie, he's got another one,' resulted in her finger prising a pebble from his determined mouth on more than one occasion.

Even the dogs behaved. Thankfully there were no other people around or it could have been a different story, with the dogs' penchant for picnic rugs and the food that covered them.

As the tide moved further out, the revealed expanse of sand shone with the late autumn sun, and she decided to risk the baby carrier again. What was that saying about getting back on the horse? she pondered. Alfie's laughter released itself as he watched Naomi skipping alongside them, revealing no deep trauma from the fall, and she recognised Tash's plan.

'Thanks, Tash,' she smiled.

'You're ok, then?'

'Yes.'

'Sophie, you're a great mum. Don't believe the negative thoughts that run around your head. Didn't you say it is the voice of the enemy?' she enquired.

Sophie was surprised to hear her say that, but it was true – she did believe that the enemy, Satan, used the negative things in people's lives to manipulate their thinking. It was just strange to hear Tash say that.

'You're right; it's just so hard sometimes with everything that's happened,' she replied.

'Do you think writing your story is helping you?' Tash voiced her concern as her eyebrows raised, her blue eyes glinting expectantly.

'Well, it's hard, but I think I'm supposed to write it, almost as if I need to finally face some things,' she answered, forming her answer on the hoof. She was unsure how much to speak of, even to Tash. Her writing had revealed how much she had put away – 'for safety', as her therapist had said. Now it was flooding her mind thick and fast.

Tash smiled, and in her matter-of-fact way just said, 'Ok, just take care.'

The sand lightened with each footstep, as if the weight of their feet caused the water beneath to flee. Distant oil tankers hugged the horizon, and the submerged wreck was revealed again, a long-forgotten image of past days on this beach. 'It's the Mexican,' Sophie said aloud.

'What?'

'See, look – there's the head in profile wearing a hat like a sombrero. And his feet – can you see? He looks like he's lying down.'

'Oh yes, I can. Can you see it, Naomi?' Tash picked up her daughter and pointed at the silhouette of the wreck. 'Can you see the funny man wearing a hat?'

'No, Mummy,' she replied.

'When we used to come here years ago, Simon would swim out there. It seems like a different life now,' Sophie whispered.

She realised that as a family they had gone into a kind of cold storage since it happened. Where had joy gone? Jake had taken it with him, and all that remained was a kind of managing to survive.

What about Katie? How did she manage? Her childhood had been stolen. Once again the villain, guilt, took her captive as she thought on.

Tash had, of course, been right: Katie had spent the day lying around eating pizza, as the discarded delivery box proclaimed from the recycling bin. Ella and she were engrossed in a film when they made their entrance. Sophie needed to write, she realised, as she released Alfie into the room.

'Can he play here, while I write for a while?' she asked.

'Doesn't he need a sleep?' Katie asked, her voice tinged with irritation.

'No, he slept in the car. Just for half an hour, please?' she pleaded.

'It's ok, Sophie, he'll be alright. The film's nearly finished,' Ella voiced. 'Come here, baby boy. Let's find your toys.'

Her tea steamed in the mug as she pulled up the familiar page.

> *It was the first time I had to lie for Mum.*
>
> *The nurse looked at me as if she could read my mind. Mum had told me time and time again what I had to say.*
>
> *'Yes, she fell down the stairs.'*
>
> *But the nurse said, 'Josie, love, are you sure about this? It looks like you've been punched in the face. There's a lot of damage. You'll need an X-ray.' She had obviously seen these sorts of injuries before.*
>
> *I remember Mum trying to protest, but her face hurt so badly there was no choice. Her right eye was gradually disappearing into a bloody mess. She tried to smile at me.*

She sat back and remembered the wait; she could still smell the hospital and see the coloured paint on the walls. She was glad they had repainted before she took Alfie there, even if the smell was the same. Eventually they had told her mum she would need surgery and that she had nearly lost her eye. They said it was brutal: her cheek bone was shattered. The similarity to Tracy's injuries brought her up short, and the realisation that what starts as hidden assault often materialises in blatant visual harm.

She paused with her fingers above the keyboard. Should she write all the details? she wondered. It was a bit of a blur, to say the least; it was as if only key words and phrases existed. Some details were as clear as if it had happened yesterday, and others were veiled in the mists of time.

> *I had to stay with friends, but I can't remember who now. I just remember visiting Mum in hospital. Her face was all black, and she had a huge bandage and plaster across her face. She tried to smile then, too. They wouldn't let me sit on the bed so I sat and reached through the bars of the bed to hold her hand.*

Leaning back in her seat in her adult awareness, she realised that Social Services must have found her somewhere to stay. She could see in her mind's eye a big house with fir trees, but she had no idea where it was. She supposed it would come back if she sought it hard enough, but she needed all her energy to write about the violence and the fear. Her mother's shame had covered her, too.

She realised as she wrote that that was the time that marked the beginning of the end for her parents' marriage. It was probably true, as her therapist had mentioned, that perpetrators finally overstep the mark when they start on the children. And she had been that child.

> *Mum and I moved into a refuge. There were women and children from all over the place. There was one other girl my age but she had little brothers to look after all the time so we didn't talk much.*
>
> *I think we were like war-torn refugees, in shock at what our dads could do to us.*
>
> *I remember playing Scrabble with a rather bashed-up board. Most of the toys were broken or damaged in some way or another. A lot of the children had a crazy edge to them, like they had been released from a prison and now couldn't manage the lack of boundaries. Others, like me, were quiet and spoke little, nursing our pain like a newborn baby, not wanting to share it with anyone. The people who worked there were really kind and tried to get me to talk, but it was too hard, and so I stayed silent.*

Her tea had gone cold, and as she reheated it she wondered if it was alright to write with an adult's knowledge that had only been acquired in later years.

116

The door swung open as Ella brought Alfie in for a desperately needed nappy change. 'How's your mum, hon?' Sophie asked her.

'Actually, she's alright thanks, Sophie. Dad has not been near us.' Her eyes smiled at Sophie without their usual hoodedness, and looked bright and alive.

'I'm so pleased.'

Chapter twenty-seven

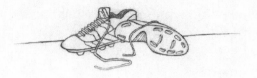

Over the evening meal she continued her musings into the past as she listened to Ella's hopes and dreams for the future, all so dependent on the behaviour of both of her parents. The ebb and flow of comments as sympathetic nods and encouragements were shared pointed out in sharp contrast the differences in all their lives. Her therapist had been the only one she had truly shared the horror of her life with; even Simon did not know the full extent of her pain. She looked at Simon as he commented on university choices, and her heart stirred with love. He caught her looking and smiled, his eyes alight with enthusiasm for life.

'It will be so good. Edinburgh sounds amazing – that or Hull, eh? I reckon Edinburgh would be a nicer place, though. I know it's a long way, but it would give you space. What do you think, Soph?'

Their faces turned to her in expectation. 'Yes, yes, sounds great, Ella, you should go for it. Your mum still has a year to get used to it.' Her words dropped like stones in her mind as she realised time was falling through her fingers and that she, too, only had a year.

As they cleared the dishes later, he came and wrapped his arms around her waist while she continued to scrape the stubborn potato from the pan.

'We'll sort it, don't worry,' he muttered, his voice low.

She shrugged him off and turned in busy avoidance, continuing to clean.

'What is it? Are you upset about the talk of universities?'

'I can't go there. She'll be gone and I've missed the last seven years of her life. We can't even talk about Alfie's birthday, let alone university.'

Katie's sudden entrance into the room stopped them, and she eyed them suspiciously. As usual, Simon stepped into the gap and swept her up in some idea or other – Sophie wasn't really listening. Alone again, she pondered the upcoming birthday and realised to her chagrin that she had no memory of Katie's birthdays since it had happened. They had passed with Simon running the show – she had been just a bystander. Her fortieth had broken a pattern that she had not known was there.

I am a selfish woman.

The words spoke loudly into the room as she stared at the screen, the words getting bigger and bigger as she increased the font size. What had she been thinking of? How had she managed to lose so many years?

She jumped as the breath and words of her daughter touched her neck. 'Why are you doing that, Mum?' Her eyes looked large and black in her beautiful face as she challenged her.

'I don't know, hon. Sorry.' Sophie's tone was hushed.

Katie righted herself. Sophie saw a determination not to be drawn in set itself across her mouth as she asked her mum to come and play Uno.

Later, as Simon slept, the steady breathing of satisfied slumber quietly filled the room. She lay awake, the night light setting a pale yellow gloom as she reflected on the day. How could she have lived – no, not lived – existed like she had? How had Katie managed without her, or rather, managed with the broken, shutdown version of her? How could she have abandoned her? She herself had been left totally alone by her own mother's selfishness and self-obsessed grief, and she had done the same to her own daughter. Her heart banged loudly under her ribs as she continued in her thoughts. Was she being over the top, as was her way so often, or was it a true assessment of how the ground lay?

She curled against Simon's warm back as she reached further into her past. Her mum had appeared robotic so often. She knew now that she had been afraid, but as a child she had experienced her as aloof, like she didn't really care about her. She had thought of her as selfish and self-obsessed, but really she had just been surviving. In recent years she had learnt about the cycle of domestic abuse and how long women stayed on it, and how it often took an attack on a child for them to break out of it. It was the trick of the perpetrator to ensure that the woman thought she would not be believed, that she would lose her children and be thought to be insane. The isolation that he ensured completed the picture and prevented any outside perspective from changing her opinion. Still, even with this knowledge, Sophie had been the child and so a victim too, and her view of her mother remained stubbornly the same.

Simon murmured and pulled her closer to him. She kissed his shoulder and lay for a while with her legs entwined in his before her overactive mind meant that she had to move. Stroking his hair, she whispered her need for a drink and slid gently out from under the duvet.

Hot milk filled to the brim threatened to spill as she edged cautiously into the front room. The darkened mess embraced her as she pulled discarded throws over herself.

I am a selfish woman.

The words still filled the screen as the door was pushed open. Katie stood there, her silhouette framed in the entrance. 'I can't sleep. Can I come in?'

Snapping the laptop shut, she lifted the throw and Katie moved into her embrace. To have her settle into the crook of her arm was so delicious, and they shared the milk, like days long ago.

Katie talked, asking about the writing. Sophie had known it would come and just didn't know what to say. Her question did something to her and she couldn't stop crying, but Katie didn't move; she didn't run away, and that almost made it worse, like she was giving her permission. Then she brought out *Dogger* and laid the long-hidden, cherished children's picture book on Sophie's lap, and it almost unhinged her.

It still smelt the same. The edges were rounded from Jake's practice of sucking the pages. Katie picked it up and slowly opened it, carefully leafing through it as familiar images flicked into view and retreated. Katie's young hands, perfectly manicured, held the treasure with an awed respect as she continued to open it up for them both.

'Alfie loves it.' Her blank statement hung there.

'Oh, have you shown it to him?'

'I *do* spend some time with him, you know.'

'Yes, yes, I know you do, hon.' Sophie tried to placate. She imagined that she could feel Katie's pulse through their nightclothes – or was it just her imagination? – and her breath, fast and steady.

'He loved it.'

'I am glad he does,' Sophie replied.

'No, *he* loved it!' Katie's voice rose in a loud, irritated response.

'Oh… yes.' Suddenly Sophie realised what she meant, and was stunned into silence.

As the book fell silent and still on her lap, they became still together too. She didn't want to break the spell or lose the moment, but she also didn't want to waste an opportunity to talk about the upcoming birthday. Katie beat her to it with a change of subject. 'I'm going to see that woman tomorrow.'

Sophie sat up and looked at her in the gloom. 'I'm so pleased, Kate. It will help in the end, I promise.'

'Well, maybe. She had better be ok. I can't talk – you know that.' Katie's voice returned to the low growling tone that had become all too familiar in recent months. But she returned to Sophie's shoulder, to her relief, as she confirmed that Zara was recommended and was supposed to be really good.

Chapter twenty-eight

Kate

Kate listened as her mum moved down the stairs and into the kitchen. It had been so weird earlier when she had seen those words on the screen. Kate had thought she was writing the story of her life. She didn't get it – one moment she was so able to help Ella, and in the next moment she went all strange.

She turned on the bedside light and picked up the book she had been trying to look at, another treasure the box had released: *Dogger*. The pages still had the lines where they had been bent and restraightened; the image of the boy and his toy on the cover still held the promise of adventure. She realised that the main character in the story was called Alfie and wondered at the coincidence. Alfie had stroked the picture earlier as they had looked together. He was so lovely sometimes, sitting on her crossed legs and leaning back on her, his head under her chin, but he triggered memories, and that was hard.

She heard her words speak into the room. 'You're nearly one, baby boy. What are we gonna do?'

She knew her mum wanted to talk about it, but she still had that pain that her mum didn't know about, like someone was sitting on her chest, crushing her. The appointment was tomorrow. How am I supposed to talk to a stranger? I can't talk about it at all. Her thoughts ran in free will round the room.

'I miss you, Jake,' she whispered to the walls. *Vogue* models stared back at her, unable to respond as she pulled her childhood pillow into her mouth.

Later she found her mum sitting downstairs in the dark. Her face looked pale blue as she stared at the screen. As soon as she saw her she shut it quickly and lifted the throw. It was strange and nice to be with her in the dark, and the milk was hot as she shared it with her. Then she spoke: 'What are you doing, Mum?'

'I can't sleep so I thought I would write, that's all. Nothing to worry about.' Her mother's voice had that soothing sound. She cried when Kate had asked why she had written what she had seen on the screen. They just sat together as she cried, and Kate didn't leave the room – she suddenly felt able to cope... She realised that they hadn't sat together like this for ages; it was familiar but different, somehow.

'Sorry,' her mum whispered.

Finally Kate responded, 'Why are you awake, Mum? Did you have a dream?'

'No, I just couldn't sleep. I was thinking about today.'

'Did you enjoy it?'

'Yes, I had a lovely day with Tash. She had a plan to get me to walk with Alfie in the carrier, and it worked, and the beach was so beautiful. We saw the Mexican. Do you remember him?'

'*We* haven't been to that beach for ages, have we?' She could hear her accusing voice but couldn't stop the words. She felt her mother stiffen and move away a bit, but she held on; she didn't want her to go. Placing *Dogger* on her lap, she looked up into her face. 'Alfie loves it.'

'Oh?'

Her mother's surprised response nearly made her push her away: how come she had no idea that she spent time with Alfie?

Suddenly Sophie kissed the top of her head and mumbled that she loved her. Now that was really weird; she suddenly felt young, and she liked it, and didn't at the same time. Slowly, Kate turned the pages as they sat there looking at the pictures. Steadying herself she took the plunge: 'He loved it,' she spoke aloud.

Her mother had not known what she meant and she felt misunderstood again. Her rage started to rise as she repeated, 'No, *he* loved it!'

She watched her mother's face as the penny dropped.

Kate felt time slow down as she heard Jake's name in her head. Turning her thoughts away from him quickly, she told her mother that she was going to see the counsellor. 'That put a smile on your face, Mum,' she thought.

Chapter twenty-nine

19th October
Saturday

Sophie

The café was buzzing with conversations around the various tables. They had managed to get the last available space. The atmosphere was charged with words that moved like electric currents criss-crossing each other, sparking as they intersected. Alfie's buggy was squeezed between two tables as understanding mothers smiled and moved up to accommodate his sleeping form.

Rebecca sat with her cappuccino clasped in her hands as she leaned forward in concentration. She had been in Sophie's life for more than ten years and had known the whole family. Her support had been close, but not so close that they would go out socially together very often. She was the sort of friend who was a burden-bearer; a Christian who was familiar with her own pain and was not afraid of others'. As a pastor's wife she supported many people, but Sophie had always felt special; maybe everyone she helped felt the same? As she looked into her eyes, Sophie wondered if that would or could change as she moved through this last stage. She knew she would never forget the unconditional support Rebecca had shown her.

'So, today she's going to see her,' she said, recalling the conversation of the previous night. 'That's so good, Sophie. It will help, I'm sure. It helped you and Simon, didn't it?'

Sophie nodded, concern written across her face. 'Alfie will be one next week.'

The blank statement met compassion in the eyes of her friend. 'I know.'

'I don't know what to do. I realised yesterday that I don't have a memory of any birthdays since then. It's like time stood still until I turned 40.'

'Maybe it did for you, Sophie. It's been a terrible time.' Rebecca's hands reached across to hers.

'But that's not ok. Katie has had seven birthdays since then. I feel so terrible, like I've woken from some nightmare and now I suddenly realise what's been going on. I've left everything to Simon.'

Rebecca's hands steadied hers as she stared truth in the face. 'Have I been really crazy for the past seven years?' Sophie heard herself whisper.

'You've been grieving.' Rebecca paused and appeared to be making a decision before she said what came next. 'I think Alfie is the healing balm that will break through the pain for you all.' Her gentle voice seemed to hover and land just in front of Sophie's eyes.

'Yes, he really is a joy for all of us, even for Katie. But then I feel guilty for the joy, as if...' Sophie paused and then continued, '... as if Jake didn't matter. Even though I know that's not true. I miss him so much. And I'm terrified of something happening to Alfie.' Her words moved like a wave that she could not contain. 'When I had to go to the hospital after I fell over with him, I kept thinking he could die, even though I knew it wasn't true. The two thoughts kind of held space in my mind together equally; I thought I could go insane. It was awful.'

Leaning back, Sophie caught her breath as her friend continued to hold and stroke her hands. 'It will be ok. The birthday will be ok too. Why not let Simon make some decisions? It may help him too. What does he think? And Katie, what about her?'

'It's a no-go area; she's so unpredictable. She was so lovely for my birthday and she actually mentioned his birthday when we went to Whitstable, but then she had a mini meltdown. I'm hoping that seeing someone will help her.'

'Counselling helped you, Sophie, but it wasn't quick,' Rebecca replied.

Alfie grinned at her as she retrieved the dogs from the kitchen. The conversation with Rebecca, although good, had not sorted out her dilemma.

'Come on, kiddo, let's take the dogs out,' she said as she fastened him into his car seat.

She nipped down some back roads, trying to avoid the traffic. At the intersection she saw a familiar figure walking head down against the wind with a determined stride. She crossed the lane of traffic, parked and waited for her to come alongside. Katie looked up, surprised to see her.

'Kate, where are you going?' Sophie asked.

Her mascara-streaked face looked back at her. 'Home,' she muttered.

'Come on, hon. I'll take you.'

It seemed for a moment that she was going to decline her offer, but instead she came round, deposited herself in the passenger seat and turned the fan heater on full blast. 'Please, Mum, don't say anything,' she said, staring straight ahead.

Once again the cold parkland let her release her feelings into the air. She breathed and exhaled deeply as she pushed the buggy up the hill towards the view. Gulls wheeled and cried overhead as the wind gusted into her face, and the thought that it must be stormy at the coast flitted in and out of her mind. Alfie, firmly ensconced under the plastic cover, was safe from the elements.

Katie, I'm so sorry. Her thoughts rang out for only her to hear. My little girl is in pieces as she starts her journey of memory. How could I have let this happen? His face, cherubic and alive, danced in memory in front of her eyes as she continued to blindly push on up the hill.

Maisie and Sid suddenly reappeared and barked her back into the present. A horse rider shouted to her to keep her dogs under control as she scrambled to grab their collars. As Sophie held them tightly, the woman swung her horse round and gave a curt nod of her head before galloping off, her horse kicking up huge clods of earth in its wake.

Sophie hung her head and cried loud tears into the wind.

Kate

Zara was really nice – not at all what Kate had expected. She looked quite young, and her room, although small, was calm, with lovely pictures on the wall. There was a sand tray and figures and games, plus paper and art materials which, she later discovered, she was allowed to use whenever she wanted to. Zara did not let her struggle like she had imagined, so that was alright; she had been terrified of her sitting there looking at her, waiting for her to speak.

'Hi, Kate. It's really nice to meet you. I'm so glad you got in touch. How are you feeling now you get to meet me face to face? It's always a bit scary, I think.'

Kate mumbled her reply. Zara didn't ask her to speak up but leaned towards her so she could hear. Kate had no idea why she noticed that; she wouldn't usually – it just felt kind of grown up, like she could do what she wanted.

Zara told her what she knew of the situation, and that shocked Kate; usually people fannied about not wanting to speak about it. It was weird, and good too; she didn't need to explain to her. Zara asked her what she should call her and told her she had a habit of abbreviating names, but that she would call her whatever she wanted. That had made Kate smile.

They did all that form-filling stuff and then started a timeline. Zara told her that it was useful to see and understand her life, for both of them. It was strange seeing her life laid out like that, and to remember some good things that she had forgotten about. Zara said she couldn't get it wrong – it was her life and she could show it how she liked, so Kate did. They got out paper and pens and she drew their house and the swing in the garden and the park, her college and some friends, and before she knew it her time was up.

'How can talking to a stranger make any difference?' Kate had asked, and Zara had told her that it was in the sharing of the story that people were no longer alone, and in the sharing of the pain that people didn't carry it alone any more.

'I know it's hard to trust someone you have only just met, but I hope you will feel safe here eventually, Kate. It takes time. Will you come again? I can see you next week.'

Before she had known it, she had agreed. She liked Zara, and for the first time in ages she thought maybe it would be ok.

When Kate had got outside in the freezing cold she couldn't stop crying. Suddenly her mum was there, as if by magic. She gave her a lift home and took Alfie and the dogs out, so that was good, and she didn't question her like she usually did, so that was good too.

She ran a really deep bath and put some of her mum's special bath stuff in it. She kept slipping down but managed to wedge a flannel on the side under her foot to keep herself still. Lying there, she thought about her mum at the park with Alfie, how she had bought a kite – they must have had one before...

She had another strange memory of jam tarts and pastry, which she rolled out and then stuck back together. All the odd bits of pastry rerolled and pushed into those old tins that she always used. The jam would be so hot it would stick and burn her fingers if she tried to eat them too soon. Was that before? And school – she had definitely started there years before. She remembered going to ballet lessons too. Why had she stopped going?

Her thoughts seemed to have become fluid, like the therapy session had unlocked something. She stayed there, the water lying level with her chin, until it started to get cold and she heard the front door slam in the wind as her mum and Alfie returned.

Sitting on her bed looking at the box she wondered if her mum would open it with her. She had asked Zara if she thought her mum would have done a timeline too, and she had said maybe. The thought of her doing a timeline too upset her for some strange reason: she would have had to do before – before her, and before Dad; when she was a little girl, and she knew she had had a hard time before Gran was married to Granddad. For the first time she felt sorry for her, and also like her in some way, too.

The suggestion of cooking dinner had just come out of her mouth before she had time to think about it. Her Mum had looked surprised, but she had no idea how surprised Kate was too. But it was good – she actually enjoyed it – and then when Mum had put Alfie to bed they had sat together and Kate had mentioned the box. But now what? They sat there in silence and looked across the room at it.

Breaking the silence, Mum spoke: 'Shall we do it together?' And with that she slid off the sofa on to her knees.

Sophie

Simon had gone into the office even though it was Saturday. She wished he had said no, but the job did bring with it some flexibility, so she tried not to complain, but now he was late again – more train trouble – so Alfie and Sophie were left alone. Katie had not come out of her room since she had come home and so she was left to stew in her own juices, as her mother used to say. She was wishing she had a playpen as she juggled Alfie's increased mobility and her urge to write, when suddenly Katie appeared.

'Where's Dad, Mum?'

'He's stuck in London. The trains are all messed up. You ok?'

'Do you fancy pasta for dinner?' Katie suddenly asked.

Shock must have been written all over Sophie's face as she watched Katie change her body position in response, placing a deliberate hand on one hip and sticking it out to one side in a questioning stance.

'Err, yes please. That would be great. You can make it spicy for Dad, if you want. There are some sauces in the cupboard.' Sophie tried to keep her voice level and her smile in check, and she managed it… just.

The music sounded through the wall of the kitchen as she vacated the room.

'Well, Alfie, what do you reckon?' she asked her son. The television lit up with strange creatures as Alfie sat engrossed, and so she opened her laptop once again.

As she pressed the delete key, the words *I am a selfish woman* were eaten by some invisible force, and the page waited, empty, for her words.

Scrolling back through the writing she settled on the part about God. What would Katie say about God? she wondered. Nothing good, she thought. And me, how did I manage to hold on to Him, or did He hold on to me?

When I was truly alone, desperate for him, when my arms ached, empty with heaviness, the absence too overwhelming to draw breath, were You there somewhere, Lord?

At night, when our sobs merged and we could not reach each other, were You there?

As we laid his broken —

Alfie appeared above the screen with a questioning look across his little face.

'Did Mummy say something, Alfie?' He reached across and touched her face, and only then did she realise she had been crying. Wiping her face, she lifted him onto her lap, her computer once again left in favour of her beautiful boy.

Sitting across the table, Sophie watched as Katie scooped pasta into bowls. Alfie banged his spoon impatiently as she handed his bowl to Sophie to blow on.

'This is really nice, Kate.'

Katie pulled Alfie's chair towards her and Sophie watched as she fed him his food. There appeared to be a quiet settling to her, even though her face still betrayed the signs of the recently shed tears.

'Shall we light a fire for when Dad gets home? It's freezing, isn't it?' Katie suggested.

Sophie pondered this change in her child, unsure what her therapy session had revealed to her. She did not want to assume anything; it was only the first session, after all.

'Good idea, hon. I'll do it after dinner. This is really good, by the way.'

Her eyes met her mother's briefly.

Over the last year or two they had seemed to avoid each other's company at all costs, and so this situation of mother and daughter alone in front of the fire was new to them both. The flames licked enthusiastically at the dry logs, hissing and popping in gusto as they sat in silence.

'Mum?' Katie asked

'Mm?' Sophie looked at her face.

'I want to look in the box with you.'

She looked away quickly as Sophie realised what she meant. 'Oh. Ok, if you like,' she stammered. Questions about how the therapy session had gone quickly disappeared in her mind as she recognised the fragility of the ground they were standing on.

'Shall I bring it down here?' Katie asked.

'Now?'

Sophie's surprise was far too evident as her child sank into her onesie and pulled the hood over her head.

'Kate, of course you can,' she countered. 'Sorry, I was just surprised, that's all.'

Simon had called. Something had happened on the line so he was going to stay over at Giles' place.

And now the box sat waiting, covered in dust, as they stared at it together. Mother and daughter mirrored each other as they sat on the floor, leaning against the sofa.

'I fancy a glass of wine. What do you think? Do you want a small one?' Sophie suggested.

Kate looked surprised at her suggestion but jumped at the chance. 'Sure, why not.'

So now they both held their respective drinks, and still looked.

'We need Alfie here,' Katie suddenly said. 'He's well up for getting in there.'

Her half-hearted laughter sounded rather hollow, and they smiled weakly at each other.

'I have no idea why it ended up in your room, you know,' Sophie said.

'I wanted it, especially after we started to redecorate the room. I hated that.' Katie's voice quietly offered the information.

The silence was loud and echoed in Sophie's ears as she pondered the next move.

Chapter thirty

They lifted the lid and sat back on their heels together, united for the first time in ages.

'It's so hard, isn't it?' Sophie said. Katie nodded next to her.

'I don't know how Dad did it. Getting all this together. I know I couldn't have done it, that's for sure.' Katie slid sideways and leaned against her mother. 'Dad's great, isn't he?' she offered, as Sophie nodded in agreement.

Sophie knelt up and lifted out the yellow blanket from the corner it was tucked into; the silky edge invited her fingers to stroke it. Sitting back once again, she laid it across her lap and Katie pulled it over her knees too. The holes widened as it stretched.

'Blankey,' they said in unison.

The word spoken aloud filled her mind with memories. Did it do the same for Katie? Are her memories like mine? Sophie wondered.

Katie lifted the silk edge and stroked her cheek; she remembered.

A bear landed on her lap as she plucked up the courage to investigate and pushed her hand in the box. 'What's his name, Mum?' she whispered.

'Wasn't he called Bear?'

'Oh yes, you're right: Bear.'

Katie held him at eye level and stared at him with renewed interest. 'I remember you now, Bear.'

'Bear and Mr Bop,' Sophie ventured.

'Shall we watch a film? I don't think I can do any more right now,' Sophie suddenly stated, aware of the risk of Katie running away.

'Ok.' She surprised her.

Alfie's murmurs sounded through the monitor. What's he dreaming about? she wondered.

'He doesn't want to be left out,' Sophie heard Katie say. 'He'll be one soon.' Her back as she left the room in search of a film once again closed the conversation, but it was a start.

Chapter thirty-one

20th October
Sunday

Simon

He had been so pleased when he had received the text from Katie last night, telling him that she had been to see Zara. But he couldn't get home to see her. Sophie had called later, too, speaking in hushed tones from their bedroom. She had recounted the events of the evening, sharing her joy at Katie's communication and the time they had spent together.

Now home, he sat in the front room, mug of coffee in his hand and Alfie leaning against him, banging his car on his knee. The box was still in the corner of the room.

Katie appeared in the doorway, all showered and shiny, her hair still wet. 'Dad, you're back,' she smiled. 'I missed you. Not going to church today?'

'We're staying home. I need a day to chill after working yesterday,' Simon replied.

She linked her arm in his as she sat down next to him. 'Did you work yesterday?' Simon asked.

'I had a day off. Sometimes I can swap and do a shift in the week, so I can see friends. The joy of college!' she laughed.

'Are you enjoying working there?' Simon asked. 'I hope you're saving for those driving lessons.'

Her job as a waitress had surprised them. They kept forgetting that she was nearly 18.

'Hey, baby boy, what are you doing?' She reached out and held his hand as he moved round his father's legs towards his sister. 'Come on, you,' she said as she lifted him onto her lap.

'So you went to see Zara. How was it?'

'It was fine, Dad, but you know I'm not going to talk about it.'

'Ok, but I'm glad you've been. She's meant to be good. I see the box is still here.'

'Mm. Mum and I started to look in it. Come on, she told you, didn't she?' Katie nudged him.

He was so pleased to see his daughter smiling at him that he was almost undone and struggled to keep a grip. 'Oh Dad, I love you.' That did the trick, and his tears started as he kissed the top of her head.

'I love you too, Kitty,' he mumbled.

Sophie appeared around the kitchen door, another meal prepared.

'Want it on your laps? Well, actually, we'd better not, eh, Alfie? Come on, you lot, fish pie is ready.'

He hadn't seen her look so well in a long time. She had a smile on her face that reflected it. Alfie was also full of beans, chattering on in his own fashion.

'Come on, Alfie, say my name: Kaayyteee.' Katie drew out her name with deliberation.

'Kaka,' Alfie echoed.

'Isn't that a word for poo, Dad?' Katie laughed.

'Yep,' he grinned.

Hot fish pie released its aroma in the room. 'Sophie, I love this. You know it's my favourite,' Simon voiced.

Mashed potato sat over the top of white fish and prawns, and bright green vegetables sat alongside. He watched while a knob of butter started its slow melt.

'I know – that's why I made it for my hunter-gatherer.' Her smile lit up her face afresh.

'Mum, it's my favourite too, you know,' Kate chipped in.

Simon laughed as he recalled how his little girl would get between them as they hugged when she was young. 'Do you remember what she was like when she was little?' He spoke aloud.

'Oh yes, you were such a minx, always wanting to be included in our cuddles,' Sophie laughed.

'I was a perfect child and you know it,' she replied with a smile.

Alfie banged his spoon to bring order.

'Leaving you out, were we? See, he's just like you, Kate,' Simon responded. As silence moved in, he realised that his daughter was recalling something from before.

'How was college on Friday?' he offered as way of distraction. 'Have you decided what to do?' The mention of universities for Ella had resulted in mutterings about a year out.

'I met up with Miss Watson. She's sure I'll do well and she thinks I should apply to do art. I could do it in London, then I could still live at home.'

'Wow, that sounds like a great idea.' Sophie's joyful response was laid bare for all to see.

'Don't think I'm ready to leave yet.' Katie stated as she pushed her chair back from the table. 'Can I have it later, Mum? I'm not hungry.'

Sophie agreed, and as she vacated the space, Katie reassured them that she would be back.

Alfie sat in his ring in the bath as Simon watched him smack the water with his toy duck. He reminded him so much of Jake, more and more as the days went by. His laughter echoed, and even more memories stirred.

'What are we going to do about the girls, eh, my boy?' My son, my second son. He missed his first boy with a deep ache that sometimes would double him over if he let it. But he couldn't – not often anyway; he had to be strong for his girls, for his broken, troubled girls.

The door was pushed open. Katie stood there, her hair pulled back from her face, her skin shiny and clear, her beautiful face make-up free, and she smiled.

'Kate!' He could hear the delight in his voice; he was so pleased she had reappeared before the day was over. 'You look lovely.'

'What are you talking about, Dad? I've just cleaned my face.' Her disparaging tone rang around the room.

'Yes, I know, and you look lovely, doesn't she, Alfie?' Simon replied.

'Kaka,' laughed her brother.

'I think he's trying to say Kitty.'

'He'd better not; only you can call me that, Dad!' Kate countered with a laugh.

She moved in to splash Alfie, much to his delight, and sat with her knees bent up opposite him on the bath mat.

'It's his birthday next week,' she whispered. He heard her stumbling words. 'What shall we do?'

Her eyes brimmed full as she looked away, staring intently at the bubbles that shone on the water.

'Well, we did something for Mum, didn't we? How about just a little tea for the four of us, or would you prefer some others to come too?' He tried to speak in level tones, all too aware of how hard this conversation was.

She leaned back on the wall and closed her eyes. Alfie tried to release the suctions of the ring in a vain attempt to get to her, his little fingers turning white with effort as they gripped the side of the bath in earnest. 'Kaka,' he almost whispered.

He watched as she turned her head towards his voice and slowly opened her eyes. 'Hey, baby boy, what you doing? Are you trying to get out? Is he finished, Dad? I could dry him.'

'Sure, go for it.'

He stood up and watched as she lifted him onto her now towel-covered lap and pulled him close. He was constantly amazed at how his daughter changed like a chameleon from moment to moment, a woman–child, unpredictable like the weather. She was so like Sophie in her movements, too.

'You look just like your mum, Kitty,' he uttered as he left the room.

He found Sophie once again on her laptop, her brow furrowed with concentration. She glanced up as he walked in.

'Where's Alfie?' she challenged.

'Kate's drying him. She looks more like you every day, and he looks more like his brother.'

Sophie held her breath as she took in what he had said, and as she expelled her breath she said, 'I know. I don't know if it makes it better or worse. Do you think she sees the same? She was only ten.'

'She spoke about his birthday.'

'No? Really? I can't believe it! What did she say?'

'Well, just that it was coming up. I don't think she knows what to think either. We need to take the lead. How about we go somewhere away from here for the day? We don't have to make it a big thing. After all, it's the first of many.'

Too late the words came out of his mouth without censure. The shock registered across her face as if he had slapped her.

'No, no, Sophie, I didn't mean to say that.' He made to pull her to him in a forced embrace but, not unlike her daughter, she pushed him away and left him alone, with only her laptop for company. He glanced at the screen without the intention of reading, when some words caught his attention.

I am glad my dad is dead. He hurt me and he hurt my mum. He made me keep horrid secrets and now I am glad he has gone.

The spoken words of a child were written in italics across the screen. He moved the cursor up the page to see the rest of the writing.

Sometimes I was afraid to go to school because he might hurt Mum when I wasn't there, and sometimes I was afraid at home in case he hurt me too.

*I remember writing 'I hate you' in a book and getting into big trouble in school because the teacher thought I was being mean to another child, but I wasn't – I hated **him**.*

'Where's Mum? Alfie needs a bottle before bed.' Katie's sudden appearance made him shut the laptop hurriedly.

'Oh, I don't know. She might be upstairs. Come here, Alfie. Daddy wants a cuddle.' He stretched out his arms for his son, now all clean in his pjs.

'Mum!' Katie's voice rang out.

As her footsteps sounded up the stairs he took in the face of his son. His rosy cheeks shone with post-bath sheen as he pulled his face towards him, tugging on his father's ears.

'Hello there, what are you doing?'

'Dada.'

His heart choked up his throat in an overflow of love for this lovely boy. 'Thank you, God,' he said aloud.

Chapter thirty-two

21st October
Monday

Sophie

She was sure he had read it. She didn't remember shutting it down at that point. It didn't really matter – he knew it had happened, but he shouldn't have looked. She still couldn't believe he had said that about the first of many birthdays.

The house lay silent. Alfie was having a nap: she had actually put him in his cot thinking he needed more boundaries, and so did she, and so now peace reigned and she wanted to write again. This time, though, she had with her something she had not looked at for a very long time, not since she had taken it to therapy that day. Carefully, she pulled out from behind a picture of Katie – a school picture that she kept in her purse – a small photograph. It had been taken in one of those passport picture booths. His dark fringe hung low over his face; it had needed a cut, she remembered saying. His eyes shone with life as he grinned at the screen. They had waited at the magic window for the pictures to appear. Some were of the both of them, and this one was when she had lifted him up alone.

Her fingers traced the outline of his face. 'My Jakey, my son, my boy.' And clutching the picture to her, she rocked to and fro in agony. 'Darling you,' she heard herself say, 'Mummy is going to write about her life and about you, lovely you. I miss you so much.'

She placed his picture on the corner of the screen and steeled herself to write as he watched her intently, his smile frozen in time.

She scrolled through the writing, adding words and correcting sections here and there as her meeting with Simon and pregnancy with Katie and her subsequent birth were fleshed out.

Growing up. Now this was tricky. She found herself talking to Jake as she tried to find the words to describe the outrage she felt at the abuse they had suffered at the hands of her father.

> *One day I came home to discover my parents in the middle of a sexual act, and not one that my mother wanted. He had her bent over the kitchen work surface. Her face was pressed to one side so she could see me as I stood there in the doorway. He had his back to me; his trousers were around his ankles and his shirt hung over his backside, he was grunting like some sort of animal and swearing at her as he pushed on her.*
>
> *What I remember most was her pleading eyes – they begged me to go, and so I did, and I did not speak about it to her.*

She wondered at her mother. How she had managed to stay with a man who beat her and raped her at will? His hand on her child's face, however, was the one thing she was not prepared to tolerate.

> *Mum said she would not go back after he smashed her cheekbone. She promised, but she did anyway, and we were asked to leave the refuge when they realised she was in contact with him and the secret location was in danger of being revealed.*

She knew now that her mother had been caught up in the almost addictive cycle of abuse, that it had been impossible for her to break free. She had been a prisoner in her own mind, confusing love with control and power, flattery with truth.

> *He was really strange when we got home, all lovely and funny. He bought flowers and told Mum she was beautiful, which was weird considering she still had the faint remnants of the bruising from the beating. I was almost happy, until one day I heard her screaming again as I came in from school.*

I heard the thumps on the floor above and caught a glimpse of him as he dragged her by the hair across the landing. His voice foul and loud added to her screams.

'Dad, stop!' I screamed.

His eyes as they met mine were like a wild animal. Fear released urine, warm and fluid down my legs, and as the puddle grew he flew with force towards me. As my head hit the front door, I blacked out, and darkness overwhelmed me.

I was cold when I awoke. The house was silent and dark. The back of my head was sticky with blood. I listened over my loud banging heart for signs of him, but all was quiet.

I remembered crawling up the stairs to find my mother; she was no longer on the landing. I found her unconscious down the side of their bed. She had no clothes on, she was bleeding on her face again and her white body was covered in long purple bruises. He had beaten her with his belt.

Later in the hospital I stopped lying. The policewoman was not angry with me, after all.

Alfie's voice through the monitor snapped her back into the present day, and Jake continued to smile.

Chapter thirty-three

Kate

Ella was fed up when she came back. Her mum was talking about moving away, something about not feeling safe if they stayed near her dad, with or without a restraining order. Kate didn't know what to say, she was so upset. She would have asked her to stay, but now was not a good time, just as things were starting to get sorted.

Mum sat across the room. She had been writing; her laptop was still on her knees. Kate knew this wasn't the best time to talk, but when she wanted her mum she didn't care. As she recounted the situation, her mum nodded in all the right places, but something about it made her think she was not paying proper attention, and she told her so.

'I've been writing today,' she tried to explain. 'It's been hard.'

'Yeah, well, I was telling you something. Why aren't you listening?' Kate responded, whining with frustration.

Mum sighed and looked at her, and then she said, 'That's just it. I was writing about domestic abuse.'

'Why did you do *that*?' Kate's words were tinged with a hint of sarcasm.

'Kate, please stop talking to me like that. I'm trying to explain. I've never spoken about this before. I just understand why Tracy wants to move away, ok? ' Her voice started to rise and she leaned back and ran her fingers through her hair, tugging at its length. She suddenly looked tired.

Kate felt bad, then. She knew she had been writing, but she didn't want to upset her. She moved to sit next to her as her mother lowered the screen. 'Sorry, Mum,' she whispered.

Mum reached out and took her hand as she spoke. 'I understand what Tracy is going through because I lived with violence when I was younger, too.'

Kate was so shocked; she felt her mouth drop open. 'What do you mean? Who hurt you?'

The silence seemed to swell before her mum spoke. 'My father.'

Then, and only then, did she realise what her mum was saying. She knew – she had known all along – what Ella was going through. That's why she had got in touch with Tracy.

'Oh, Mum, I'm so sorry.' Kate reached across and held her mother's other hand.

'It's not your fault I never told you. There was no need. I was ashamed of him. I didn't want you to know about him,' she responded.

'Does Dad know?'

'Yes, hon, but only the facts; not what it felt like. I've really kept the secret all my life, but Joanna – do you remember her? She was my therapist – she suggested I write after I had been seeing her for a few years. She said it was not my secret to keep.'

Mum looked different somehow. Kate had always thought she was brave for some reason, and now she understood why. 'Can I read it? When it's finished?'

'Yes, if you want to.'

'You think it's a good idea that Ella moves, then?' Kate asked, a new level of respect obvious in her tone.

'I think it's good that her mum is keeping her safe.'

'Why? Didn't Gran do that for you? Did he hurt her too?'

'He hurt us both, but you need to talk to Gran about her story. All I know is that she didn't keep me safe. I can give you all the reasons why. I've learnt about it as an adult, but when I was little I hated that she was afraid of him, and I thought she was a coward. I was really angry with her.'

'Did you stop being angry with her? You don't see her much.' Kate voiced her gentle challenge, aware that she would love them to spend more time together.

'I struggled with it for a long time, and then she married Granddad and it all changed again.'

'So what happened to your dad?' Kate asked with gentleness.

'He's dead, darling. He died a long time ago now.'

Shocked, Kate was suddenly aware that she knew so little about her mother's life from when she was young. She had kept it all a secret, even that her father was dead.

143

Her mum's face looked different suddenly, and she just had to hug her when she thought she was going to cry. Side by side they sat, her mum crying and Kate not saying anything, just holding her hands. Then her mum got up and made a cup of tea; she wouldn't let Kate do it, even though she offered to.

Kate now knew that her mum was not just writing about Jakey; he was the reason she had seen Joanna, but it was her past that had made her the person she was today. Thinking about what her timeline must look like made her feel really sad. On the shelf of her room was a youth Bible. Her mum had given it to her. She had no idea why her mum believed in God after what had happened, and now she'd added to it and told her that her dad had hurt her too.

'Where were you, God?' Kate muttered under her breath.

Chapter thirty-four

Sophie

The soup glugged like an awakening volcano and splattered its vegetable residue up the walls and over the cooker top. She grabbed a cloth and rescued the walls from the slow-moving potato and carrots. 'Come on, Sophie, get a grip.' She spoke aloud to the room.

She had surprised herself, speaking to Katie like that. Although she had looked shocked, there was also pride in her eyes when she realised what she had come through, but now she faced her dad. Writing about what happened to him. Could she do that? What would Mum say?

Slamming down the spoon with greater force than necessary, she opened the laptop once again.

> *After the beating I was told he would never come back again, but he did.*
>
> *He looked awake, but really he was not. I was afraid to go into the room. Where was Mum? She promised she would be home when I got back from school. I was always afraid, even though he wasn't there any more.*
>
> *That was my bed, my room. What was he doing there?*
>
> *The police said he would go down this time for sure. I had to do that interview with the video saying what had happened. It was so terrible. I was afraid even though they said they had him; I wanted it all to be ok, but it wasn't.*
>
> *Mum left me on my own even then; she could have stayed but she said she couldn't face listening to me, so that social worker was there. She was alright, but Mum still should have been there. She told me she had done a video of her own, too.*

Her heart pounded loudly as her thoughts ran in manic fashion across the page and in her mind. Injunctions are all very well; they are meant to keep you safe, but it didn't stop *him*, did it? She felt so angry, even though it was years later. It was a good idea to start again somewhere else, as she had said to Tracy earlier today, but it was really important that he didn't know where they were.

She turned off the soup and got out the rolls to heat through. Make the most of the time, she thought; Simon was out with the dogs and Alfie. It was great that he had flexi-working. So now make the most, she thought, and get writing.

After the belt incident I had eight stitches in my head and an X-ray. Mum had to stay in hospital so she couldn't be with me. I stayed in a foster home; Jo and Michael were nice. They had a King Charles spaniel who was cuddly and allowed on my bed. It was strange being there, but they took me to the hospital every day to see Mum. She looked so terrible – she couldn't open her eyes and her body hurt all over. The police were there sometimes, asking her questions, but she didn't talk. It was only later that I realised she had not told them anything and it was because of me that he was going to prison.

Sitting back, she wondered what had happened that had resulted in him being released. It had been one almighty mess-up, that was for sure.

I stood outside my bedroom door like a statue. I could feel my wee coming. I tried to stop breathing but when I did it would come in a loud gasp. Slowly, slowly, I moved to the side of the door. It was then that I saw the bottles and pills. He had spilt something all over my books, and then the smell hit me. Puke. He had puked over my bed.

I was sure he was tricking me, staring at the walls like that, and I started to cry quietly. 'Please, Dad, don't. Please, Dad, don't.'

And he didn't. He didn't answer me. He didn't growl or swear and jump up and take a swipe at me. He didn't move at all.

The kitchen door banged open to reveal her boys and dogs, all soaked. 'What happened?' Sophie gasped, making a move for Alfie.

'Where have you been for the last hour?' Simon asked with surprise.

'Well, here, cooking and writing.' She started to laugh at the sight of them. Where they stood, dogs and man, large brown puddles grew. Flinging some towels to Simon, she yanked off Alfie's suit. 'Why didn't you take the buggy?'

'We thought we'd have a man walk, didn't we, buddy? A shoulder ride, but the storm arrived before we noticed. We went to the park and it was there suddenly, over the hill. Weird, really, it snuck up on us, but we're men, aren't we, Alfie? We can take it, yeah? Where's my high five?' Simon thrust his open palm towards his son, who just grinned in Sophie's arms.

'You'll need to teach him that. I'll put him in the bath. Can you move those rolls out of reach of the dogs?'

Later, baby bathed and dried, soup eaten and fire made, Sophie felt distracted and retreated to write in the kitchen while Simon sorted Alfie. She needed this part over and done with; she needed freedom, and she needed to remember that she was not to blame.

Joanna had sat with her for many hours as she recalled her father's threats. His menacing face would draw so near to her that the spit loitering on his lips would touch hers in the most repulsive way. She would gag as she recalled the many scenes. Often Joanna would have to tell her what she had spoken about, what she had drawn, as she disappeared, dissociating in the sessions, as memories overwhelmed her. She was shocked at the power of the mind to keep her 'safe'.

He still lay there. The smell of him came at me in waves as I slowly realised he was not going to wake up. Still I backed away and then ran out of the house to our neighbour. She had often called the police over the years, only to have my mum deny anything had happened.

The sirens came, blazing into the street, first to see me and then into the house. I did not go, and still my mum did not come home. I still didn't know where she was, but I thought she was probably with my stepdad. I had tea, really sweet. I never had sugar but this was needed, I was told. I was in shock and the tea tasted good, so hot it burnt my throat with the necessary pain to extinguish the image from my mind.

I watched from the window as a black van turned up and two men brought a trolley-like thing into my house. Later I saw them take something – my dad, I realised – out in a long bag. He was gone.

Mum arrived as they were shutting the doors. I watched as she screamed and shouted, demanding that they open the doors. The men pointed to where I sat staring out of the window, and she came running up the path, shouting my name.

I did not want her hugs or her tears. She had not been there. He had hurt me again and she had not kept me safe. He had managed a final blow, and won.

Later, much later, I listened to her pathetic excuses as to where she had been. I knew what a lie looked like and saw it play out across her face. I could not forgive her.

The clink of a carefully placed glass of wine brought Sophie out of the scene. Simon's arm placed tenderly around her shoulder and his kiss, light and undemanding, saved her.

'Are you ok? Do you want a break or do you need to do this now?'

'I have to do this.'

She pulled out the chair next to her in silent invitation to the man who had changed everything. His hair hung down just like Jake's, low across his eyes, but his were blue. She loved this man, and her heart filled with gratitude that she had someone who was safe and trustworthy. 'I'm writing about something I've not spoken to you about.'

His eyes had a quizzical expression.

'You know my dad died, don't you?' He nodded. 'But you don't know that I found his body.'

He sat stock still as it registered, then slowly reached over. Pushing the laptop to one side he pulled her towards him until she sat on his lap, arms around his neck. Her sobs felt young; teenage grief and rage mixed with adult awareness.

'My mum left me on my own. It's her fault. I can't forgive her. She was with Brian, I'm sure.' She mumbled the words into his neck and heaved huge, deep sobs.

148

Kate

Kate was just about to press the play button when she heard her. It was her mum, she was sure, but she had not heard her cry like that before. Standing against the kitchen door, she listened to them. She had to stuff her hand across her mouth to stop any noise. How could Grandma do that to her? My mum, my lovely mum. She couldn't believe it.

Later, as the light was fading, they all sat together on the sofa. Kate moved into Dad's other arm and the three of them sat as dark came and the fire glowed. 'Mum, I love you.' Kate heard the words she did not say enough, as her mother breathed them in.

'I love you too, hon,' she replied, as her hand found Kate's.

'Shall we go back to the beach for Alfie's birthday?' Kate whispered. The squeeze of her hand affirmed her choice, as Dad's gentle breathing informed them that he was asleep. They lay there together, safe and quiet, until the fire became white and calm. Only Alfie dreaming his dreams made any noise.

Chapter thirty-five

22nd October
Tuesday

The next morning Kate found Alfie in bed between her mum and dad. They all slept the same way, with their arms above their heads like frozen ballet dancers. They looked pleased and rather surprised with the breakfast she presented them with. Alfie sat on her lap, glugging back his bottle like a drain.

'I have no classes today. Do you fancy going out somewhere?' Kate asked. 'What do you think? It's actually sunny; we could go up to the forest and have coffee out. You'd love it, wouldn't you, Alfie?'

Dad reached across to pull the curtain, revealing the unbroken blue of the sky. 'Do you fancy it?' He looked at Mum, who smiled wearily. 'I'm still due some time off.'

'Sure. I probably need some air after all that writing, eh?'

Kate realised that Mum knew she had heard her. 'Great! Come on, baby boy, I'll get you sorted. Ugh, you stink.' Kate scooped up her brother and carried him at arm's length into the bathroom. 'You are really disgusting, Alfie. It'll be so much better when you use a potty,' she told him.

It was not easy dealing with his wriggling chubby legs as she tried to clean him up. Her eyes watered and she had trouble breathing, but she wanted Mum to know how much she cared, and this seemed to be a good way to do it. Later, as they sat in the car, Mum told her how grateful she was for her help, so at least she'd noticed.

The sky was so blue, but you could see your breath. She loved that – warm on the inside, loads of layers, but freezing air. Mum always said that was what the English were like – they loved the change of seasons, and Kate definitely did. Mum looked much more chilled today; her laugh seemed more real somehow, and she was doing that throwing her head back thing like she meant it.

The forest triggered all sorts of memories – not full on, but around the edge of her mind. She hadn't been able to stop thinking about Jakey ever since she had met Zara. They hadn't really spoken about him even then; well, Zara had, but Kate hadn't. Kate had told her that she wanted to see his face, to look at some pictures, but she was afraid: 'I don't know what will happen,' she had said. Zara said she could bring anything she wanted to the sessions so she supposed she could bring photos, but what if she couldn't stop crying? Her thoughts pursued her as she walked.

'Look at Maisie!' Dad cried, pulling her out of her wonderings. The dog was covered in some sort of brown boggy stuff and was hurtling in their direction.

'Watch out, Mum!' Kate called, running up to her as she was bending down to examine something with Alfie. Maisie bowled into Alfie, sending him swinging round. Luckily Mum had his hand.

'Alfie, you nearly had a flying lesson!' Kate cried as she grabbed his other one. Swinging him high into the winter sky together, they laughed.

Sophie

All together they walked, the air charged with restorative power that had been absent for too long. Katie, now running with the filthy dogs, had once again relinquished Alfie into her care. Her long hair flew out behind her as she increased her pace.

Hands on hips, Simon stood and laughed loud and deep. Now the pressure for her to keep silent had been released, it seemed to have freed him too. In the distance she stood, his once baby girl calling for him, and he loped off after her.

Simon

The forest was golden against the blue sky. He really noticed now that he had a camera. Alfie in his red wellies was laughing and screaming with joy as he swung between Sophie and Kate.

He had been taken aback when Katie had arrived with breakfast. Alfie had woken in the night and, unusually, Sophie had brought him exhaustedly into their bed. As they sat all together, Katie had suggested the walk.

He was sure she had heard what Sophie had said the night before, and now they were experiencing the Kate that everyone spoke about when they met her: charming, friendly and helpful.

He was gobsmacked when she changed Alfie's nappy; she didn't realise until she lifted him up that he had produced his usual awful morning mess. Sophie and he had smothered their laughs into the pillows together – a bit mean really, but it was so funny. And now here they were all together again.

Chapter thirty-six

23rd October
Wednesday

Sophie

A few hours at a childminder for Alfie gave Sophie the space she needed to do her food shop online and to get on with her story. Katie had gone off to college with her decision made: she would have a year out and then would try to get into a London university. The decision seemed to have rejuvenated her and she seemed suddenly happier.

Sophie pondered the recent turn of events and wondered aloud to God about His part in all of this. What had happened was not His fault, but she thanked Him for the perfect timing of now – the finding of the box and the fact that Alfie's birthday was in only a few days.

Mum and Brian.

The words sat on the page as she recognised her teenage anger again – or was it adult anger? These days she was able to tolerate spending some time with them, and the children loved them. To Katie, Brian was Granddad, but *she* still held resentment like a prized cup against him: he was not her father!

Sophie's diatribe was strewn across the page as the pain and anger at her abandonment flooded her brain.

I would never do that to a child of mine she finished with a flourish.

Her sandwich still sat in miraculous untouched silence, her tea brown and cold, as she paused for breath and surveyed the pages. Suddenly the realisation that she had done just that hit her with force as she doubled over.

'Katie, I am so sorry.' Her voice filled the room in whispered acknowledgement. She had done just that, like Joanna had said – she had continued her family script of silence into her marriage. 'You must keep secrets and not respond to pain.' She had mimicked her mother's behaviour, pretending that all was fine – or at least keeping the pain that she felt on a daily basis within, behind her self-imposed wall. No one, not even Simon, had penetrated her defences.

She retrieved her folder from its hiding place and released the voices of years of therapy. She had chosen to keep it all, just in case, and now she was glad she had, in some strange way.

The pages fell onto the cleared table, pages of different colours and sizes, pages with drawings, and some folded over and taped together to enlarge the page. Gingerly she lifted a light blue page and took it towards the window; it was too lightly drawn to see easily the pencil marks of a child. A small figure sat on one side of the page while diagonally across a monster stood tall over another person; stick people of clear meaning, fear in pencil.

The sickness grew within her. How old had she been when it started? she wondered, as she handled the traumatic images. Another page, another image, this time in black marker, hatred spewing out of an open mouth. Hers or her father's? she pondered, clutching her stomach.

The minute minder on the cooker released its beep: it was time to get Alfie. The papers were once again packed in their folder and stuffed behind the chair as she swallowed her pain and re-entered the present day.

The dogs and Alfie were in the back of the car. She wiped the screen to rid it of the sudden condensation that had risen in response to the hot panting breath of her exercised dogs. Alfie drank from his cup as she drove slowly, waiting for the condensation to clear.

Suddenly her phone rang, and she peered at the name of the caller: Tracy. Cars passed her in obvious irritation as she parked hurriedly and listened to the quiet terrified voice of her friend. He had appeared at the house; no order was going to keep his kids away from him. She had used her newly installed panic button, but now she would have to move for sure.

Sophie was more affected by the phone call than she liked to acknowledge. She had texted both Simon and Katie to ask where they were, and their responses – work and college – led to the obvious enquiry as to her welfare.

She couldn't shake off her fear and waited with her oblivious but bored son for Katie to come out of college. She had reluctantly agreed to be collected, unclear as to why. Once again the windows were steaming up as she waited for college to end.

A clap of thunder and the predicted hailstorm arrived with a flourish, pounding on the roof of the car. Alfie jumped in alarm and Sophie cranked up the sound of Postman Pat. 'It's ok, darling, it's only hail,' she soothed.

The pavement danced with white peas of hail, all out of rhythm with each other, and students like Lowry silhouettes started to rush by, bending over against the onslaught.

Katie's sudden arrival, banging on the passenger window, made them both jump. 'Oh, there you are,' Sophie breathed in relief.

'Good thing you texted, Mum. I would have got soaked. What's up, baby boy?' She turned to the thumps of Alfie's feet against her seat. 'What's the matter, Mum? You don't look good.'

Turning the rear mirror towards her, Sophie saw her sunken eyes. 'Was Ella in college?'

'She was this morning but she wasn't at lunch and someone said she'd gone home. Why, what's happened?'

'Tracy said her dad had turned up and they had to call the police.' Katie's hand was clamped over her mouth in horror. 'Is she ok?'

'She must be or Tracy would have rung.'

Their hands linked over the gear stick as the hail continued its show.

'Sorry I texted. I was suddenly so afraid. My writing is stirring up stuff for me.'

Katie tried to call before they moved off. Ella was not answering.

The supermarket was crammed with mothers who, like Sophie, appeared to have wished they had shopped earlier in the day before the storm broke. Fortunately she only needed a few things until her large shop arrived tomorrow. Rushing down the aisles, list in hand, she dispatched Katie on various missions while Alfie sat strapped in the trolley munching on French bread. Only the totally empty cupboards had forced the trip, otherwise with all the Tracy business she would have gone straight home. Queuing finally to pay, she tried Tracy's number to no avail – there was no signal, so she sent Katie out to the car to try from there.

Chapter thirty-seven

Simon

Meanwhile, Simon sat on the earlier train, attempting to beat the weather. The trains had a habit of giving way to extreme precipitation, and now the power had been lost and they were all sitting there in frozen silence as darkness descended. Only the light of mobiles and laptops revealed the irritated faces of his fellow commuters. Conversations to spouses and girlfriends, parents and friends, punctuated the air as they sat captive in the countryside. The storm lit up distant houses that had also been plunged into darkness, and hills and fields.

'Sophie, you alright?' Simon responded to the sudden buzzing in his pocket. He had a signal again. Her voice sounded flat and troubled. 'What's the matter?'

'It's Ella's dad. He went round to their house and lost it and now no one knows where Ella is. I'm scared. When will you be home?' She recalled the events without appearing to catch her breath.

Simon felt his heart start to pound. He had no idea how long it would take to get home; all his good intentions had been to no avail. 'Is Katie with you?'

'Yes, she's here.'

'Please lock all the windows and doors and don't answer the door to anyone. Ok?'

'I have locked them already. I hate this. I'm afraid. I need you home.' He heard her breathe deeply and gain a modicum of control. 'We're alright. I just hope we don't have a power cut again – we had one earlier.'

'Light a fire and get the torches and the candles just in case, ok?'

'Ok.'

The line went dead. He redialled but could not get through.

Sophie

Katie had tried again and again to reach Ella, to no avail.

'Kate, Dad said to light a fire and get all the torches and candles out in case there's another power cut. He's stuck on a train in the middle of nowhere and can't get back straight away.'

'I'm scared, Mum. What if Ella's dad comes here again?' Katie looked flushed with fear.

'Oh, I'm sure he won't,' Sophie replied. Her eyes felt a little too bright, and she realised that Katie had noticed. 'Grab the candles, hon. There are some in the cupboard under the kitchen sink.'

Alfie had been fed and now was in bed safe and sound as his breathing revealed, filling the silence of the room through the monitor.

The pizza, in spite of the anxiety, was delicious. Maybe Katie was more like her than she thought. They sat together. Katie had relaxed and found a chick flick to watch with her. It wasn't really Sophie's thing, but it was good to be with her anyway. Every now and then she allowed her to mute it to listen to the monitor. Sophie leaned back and held up her phone, redialling Tracy's number. No answer. Katie did the same for Ella, with the same result.

'Where can they be, Mum?' she asked.

'Well, hopefully together somewhere safe, hon,' Sophie replied.

Simon had called. The train had started to move now so he should be back soon.

'Can you mute it, hon? I thought I heard Alfie.'

The dogs ran into the room, barking, their tales knocking into the plates. 'Stop it! Come here and sit down!'

Katie grabbed their collars and wrapped her arms around their necks. Sophie's heart jumped into her mouth as the sound of banging reverberated through the house.

Chapter thirty-eight

Simon

She was screaming. Katie's voice reverberated off the train walls as he tried to decipher her words. What did she mean, he was at the house? Who was she talking about? Suddenly the truth slammed into his chest. 'Where are you? Where's your mum and Alfie?'

Passengers shot furtive glances at the now frantic Simon. 'Stay inside. Don't open the door. I'm coming.'

'Are you alright, Simon?' Looking up, he saw someone he recognised, sort of. 'Mike from church, remember? You ok?'

The offered lift was gratefully accepted as he dialled and redialled the house phone and Sophie's mobile, to no avail.

Sophie

They could hear his voice echoing through the house. The letter box lifted and dropped as he drew breath. 'Tracy, are you in there? Ella, come out here to your dad.' His voice alternated between pleading and rage. Alfie's cries started up through the monitor, awakened from his slumber.

They stood by the doorway as he continued his tirade, kicking violently at the front door as his frustration grew. 'Get out here, you stupid cow!'

The words spurred Sophie into action. She held the dogs by their collars and entered the hallway as the letter box lifted up again. 'Where's my wife and daughter?' his faceless mouthed threatened.

'They're not here. Please go away.' Sophie's voice quaked as she tried to brave it out. Katie stood to one side, out of the line of sight, her eyes pleading with her, fear written across her face.

'I know they're there. Tell 'em to come out or I'll come in.'

'I promise they're not here. I really don't know where they are.'

Kate suddenly launched herself down the hall and slammed the letter box shut. 'Go away! You hurt Tracy. Go away!' she screamed.

The dogs, released by Sophie, now ran towards the door, followed by their mistress. Sophie slammed her body against the door, shutting the once again open letter box, and wrapped Katie in her arms as they stood leaning hard against the door. They stood together in a solid embrace and waited, until all was quiet.

Kate

Later, at the sound of sirens, Kate ran out the door. She raced around the corner to see Ella's dad on the ground, shouting and swearing, as a policeman knelt on his back. Dad, with his back to her, said something about a knife, then suddenly vomited on the grass in front of him.

He turned round as she said his name. His face was so white, even in the dark. He looked like a ghost. He mumbled her name, holding out his arms for her.

Sophie

They stood together, a huddle of shocked humanity, watching as he was led away, and they all cried in unashamed relief. Sophie's heart banged and raced so hard that it almost hurt, despite the exhaustion that filled her bones so totally that she thought she might collapse. It was then that she saw them bagging up the knife. She had been totally unaware of it. Only then did she realise that their lives – all of them – had really been in danger, and suddenly all was quiet.

Chapter thirty-nine

24th October
Thursday

Simon

Alfie sat in his chair, munching obliviously on his toast. Just the way it should be, Simon thought, as he took the tea bag out of the mug. He felt exhausted, like an old man. His arms were heavy, as though he had returned from a massive workout. The image of the knife still careered unbidden across his mind. He absent-mindedly stroked Maisie's head; even the dogs seemed to know he was delicate and were undemanding.

I could have lost them all. The words kept going round and round his mind. He had almost arrived too late. As it was he hadn't prevented their terror. The déjà vu of the situation was not lost on him.

He had actually wanted to kill him, and possibly it was only the young policeman's hand on his shoulder that had enabled him to control the rage that had surfaced. He had a sudden realisation that any man can be pushed to kill for those he loves.

Sophie's collapse had taken him by surprise, as in an almost slow motion sequence she had slipped between them onto the grass. The ambulance man appeared as if by magic, and the realisation that they had come as well as the police seemed to loosen something in him. He didn't know what: rage, fear? Anyway, he lost it and cried in front of Katie.

'What an idiot,' he muttered to himself.

'What, Dad?' There she stood, panda eyes glassy, looking at him with renewed concern.

'Kitty, honey, you ok?'

'Yeah. You?'

Quick as a flash she was there again, his child–woman, his daughter, and his fellow survivor, soothing him. 'I should be hugging *you*, Kitty,' he muttered into her hair.

'Dad, I love you.' That was all. Just four words, and like a plug pulled from a very full bath, his tears overflowed in a rushing torrent, and she stood still to hold him.

Kate

The smell of toast had woken her from a dreamless sleep and she stood watching as he absent-mindedly dipped the tea bag in and out of the cup. Alfie grinned at her as she stood out of view from her father.

His words had surprised her, as had his crying; and now, watching Alfie over his shoulder, she saw baby boy's eyes fill up.

'Dad, it's ok.' My turn to hold his shoulders now, was the random thought in her head as she moved past him to take Alfie into her arms.

The three of them heard Sophie as her dream-held voice invaded the kitchen, screaming out again and again, 'Jakey! Jakey!'

Sophie

The sun fell warm on her face as she turned to see him, Jakey racing across the park ringing and ringing and ringing his bell. He was shouting at her to watch but she couldn't hear him. She tried to call out but the words were stuck somewhere and she couldn't move. In panic she breathed deeply and forced out his name. He did not turn.

Sophie peered through her sleep-fogged eyes. Simon was panting as he called her name from the doorway. Concern was written across his eyes and in his voice as he and Katie, holding baby boy, moved to stand at the foot of the bed. She realised in an instant that Alfie was gulping in air through his crying again. 'Alfie, Mummy is ok, darling,' she croaked. Her throat ached and felt as dry as sandpaper.

Katie moved towards her and handed Alfie over to her as she stepped back. Remembrance of her dream flooded her mind. 'Did I shout out?' she whispered.

'Yes, for Jakey.' Simon spoke.

She hadn't heard him say his name for so long that she gasped. 'Sorry, sorry.' She felt her shame rise like a cape to smother her.

Looking at Katie over his shoulder she saw her daughter, her 10-year-old daughter, arrive and depart in a flash as her 17-year-old adult self gained control once more. 'I'm so sorry, Kate. I had a nightmare.'

'I know, Mum. It's ok.'

She sat at the end of the bed, just out of reach, but she stayed, much to Sophie's relief.

Chapter forty

Simon

The doorbell rang and snapped him out of a place he would prefer never to go to again. The supermarket shop had arrived, along with the police, and a bizarre scene unrolled as the bags were manhandled by all into the kitchen.

The two police officers accepted the offer of tea and now they sat, the six of them, around the table, Alfie's presence bringing a level of calmness no one felt. They brought them up to date about everything that had happened: Ella's dad would not get bail after the knife incident and in fact was likely to go to prison for a considerable while. Tracy and Ella and the rest of the family were safe and most likely would be able to move home now.

They offered help from the victim support team, but each of them shook their head as they dismissed the suggestion. They asked about Sophie's well-being after the night before, and it was then that Simon realised she had no recollection of her collapse. Her expression of abject shock ensured she was offered space to get herself together before she gave a statement.

Turning to Katie, they asked if she was up to the task. She nodded her compliance, and also her agreement that she did not need her parents to be present.

Kate

It was strange to talk to the policewoman. The policeman had left them to get on with it alone, and the officer listened to Kate's every word with her head tilted towards her. It was hard to get the words out – even to her it sounded confused so she guessed she must be having trouble, but the policewoman seemed unfazed by her stumbling and crying.

Dad then came in to make his statement and she took Alfie in search of Mum. She was lying outstretched in a deep bubble bath, her body covered apart from her breasts. She seemed to have moved from a place of embarrassment to them just being women together, not that Kate would do the same. She sat on the edge of the bath, suddenly aware of a large red area under the mug that was sitting on her mother's skin.

'Mum, you're burning!' she shouted, and hastily put a cold wet flannel on her skin, causing her to jump in shock.

'Oh, I didn't realise,' she murmured.

'What are you doing?' Kate's voice rose in volume.

Alfie's 'Kaka' caused her to lift him onto her lap.

'Alfie, Mummy is being very silly – she burnt herself,' she told him. With that, her mum slid beneath the water, mumbling her sorry again.

'Come on, kiddo, let's find some toys. Look, there are some bricks. Go get them.'

Set down again, Alfie crawled across the floor while she pushed her hand into the water to touch her mum's skin. Sophie came up for air, turning on to her side to watch Alfie. Her eyes still on him, she said, 'Kate, I'm so sorry for all the years, all the silence, the shutdown me you've had to live with. Last night was like the final straw. I really thought I would lose everything – you, Dad and Alfie. My writing has been making me a bit crazy. I had no idea it would do that. I'm sorry. We need to talk. Not today, but before Alfie's birthday, eh?'

Kate turned to look at her, feeling her shrug before it arrived. 'Ok.' It was all she could say at that moment. She was overwhelmed with memories and really didn't want to tell her about them.

Sophie

Simon had filled the bath to the brim. The scented bubbles shone their invitation as she slipped beneath them. Running her fingers through her loosened hair, she lay in watery silence and waited until her need for oxygen overwhelmed her. Surfacing, breathing deeply, she hugged her tea in her cupped hands as she leaned back, holding it against her breasts.

She couldn't believe she had collapsed. Then, on top of that, she had awoken to find them all around her. She had screamed Jakey's name out loud, for goodness' sake. Why? Katie had looked so terrified and young, so very young. Memories flooded her mind as she pushed the hot cup against her skin.

The knock was quiet against the door and the voice timid as she asked permission to come in. Katie stood there with Alfie perched on her hip.

'Are you ok, Mum?' Her eyes were red rimmed as she scanned her face.

'Yes, lovely, I'm ok. Are you? I'm so sorry; I can't believe I called out like that. It must have been because the drugs made me sleep so deeply.'

Katie sat down on the edge of the bath, setting Alfie on his feet so he could reach over and play with the bubbles. 'Mum, you're burning yourself!' she shouted.

She grabbed the cup out of her hands and ran a flannel under the cold tap before placing it across her now red skin. It made her jump. She was surprised at her daughter's innate ability to care, and the fleeting thought moved through her that maybe she hadn't messed her up totally, after all.

Chapter forty-one

Simon

It had taken an age to get the statements done. He had been too late to prevent Ella's dad from terrifying them, not too late to lay his hands on him, though. He had wanted to punch the living daylights out of him, and probably would have if the police hadn't arrived. Mike told him later that he had been like a crazy man on the drive to the house, jumping out of the car while it was still moving at the sight of him ambling across the grass.

It was good to get it off his chest and to be listened to by the policeman – surprisingly so.

A knock on the door later revealed Mike holding a tray of food – food for meat eaters and for vegetarians, as well as pudding, cake, wine and chocolate. 'We didn't know how you were fixed so we put this together for you. I hope that's ok. Oh yes, and these.' He picked up a bunch of flowers off the path as Simon took the tray. 'Jane wanted to give these to Sophie, too.'

He was so shocked at their care that he was speechless. Only Sophie appearing over his shoulder, now dressed, albeit with wet hair, saved his embarrassment. 'Oh, Mike, thank you so much. You are so kind. Please thank Jane for us, too.'

The recollection of the journey from the station to the house hit him again as he recalled his terror and Mike and Jane's calm presence as Mike drove, probably well over the speed limit, to the house, with him shouting at the traffic to get out of the way. The last time he had seen him was as he ran up the path to the house.

'Dad, give me that,' Katie said as she took the tray.

Sophie stood with her arms around him as he told her what had happened. He slid down the door and sat on the mat, vaguely aware of the rough hessian sticking through his trousers, and sobbed.

Sophie

Food, that old enemy, now turned friend, did a good job this time in calming them all down. They had eaten in silence as it did its restorative work, and now, with the fire lit, the rapidly passed day was recalled together.

The church family had rallied too, and many messages had been left on the answerphone. The press had turned up wanting an interview, but Simon had managed to deal with them. Tash had also been in touch but they had closed ranks, and not even she was able to get past their defences.

Now they gathered and in muted tones began to unpick the day. Alfie, exhausted from the previous night, had fallen asleep on the sofa, and all of them, including Katie, sat with a glass of red wine in their hands.

Simon spoke first, telling them how terrible it had been to know that they were alone and in danger. He staggered through his words and finally landed with a comment that stunned them into silence: 'It was the same with Jakey. I couldn't save anyone.'

Katie moved to stand but Simon's hand on her outstretched leg prevented her. 'Please don't go, Kitty,' he said, staring into his glass. 'We must do this.'

'I don't want to.' Her voice shook with some untold feeling. Alfie stretched behind her and she lowered her voice. 'Dad, Daddy, please, don't.' Her young pleading whisper floated around looking for a place to land.

It was Sophie who responded to her cry. 'Come here, baby girl,' she soothed, and she came and curled up on her lap, her legs too long, splayed out like Bambi. Sophie heard herself mutter all the words she had held locked within for seven years. Unsure if they were words or tones, she continued to soothe her long-lost little girl as she cried silently.

Simon stood and scooped up Alfie into his arms. 'The windows and doors are locked. He'll be safe; he needs to sleep.' Taking control, he turned and left the room.

Simon

It had to be now. He couldn't let this torment go on any longer. They had to talk now, right now.

Alfie murmured as he lay him down, clutching Mr Bop, just like Jakey used to. If they didn't talk, how could they remember their son? For the last seven years he had called the funeral home annually to check that they still had his ashes, and now he wanted his son to be free, and his wife and daughter too.

He stood in the doorway and looked at them both, Sophie's legs laid out across the floor and Katie lying criss-crossed across her lap. They both turned to look at him as he entered the room. 'I don't know how to do this; I just know I need to do something.' He tested the air to see the temperature.

Every year I have to make a call to the funeral home. He practised the words inside his head. No, he couldn't do it.

'Ok, we need to make a plan for Alfie's birthday, don't we?' He spoke across the room. Just a few days earlier those words would have caused a meltdown, but now their faces displayed the calm of those who had survived worse. The relief that he had not mentioned Jakey was written invisibly across their expressions, too. He realised later that he had used the situation to full advantage, but he had to or he would have gone crazy.

Katie pulled herself to sitting. 'Yes, Dad,' she responded.

Simon started to speak about how he thought they should go back to Broomhill Sands and have a picnic, and maybe a barbecue. They slowly nodded their agreement. He insisted that they shop together for something for Alfie, and even though he was pushing his luck they acquiesced, obviously relieved that that was all that was required.

Kate

Kate and her mum agreed about the beach and going shopping. Dad definitely must have been asleep when I suggested it the other night, Kate thought with relief.

A text from Zara pinged on her phone, reminding her of her session tomorrow. It was a bit weird as it was so late, but then her battery had run out and loads of texts were arriving at the same time.

'Who is it, hon?' Mum asked

'Oh, it's Zara. I have an appointment tomorrow. Do you think I should go?' Kate asked.

Dad responded first. 'Oh yes, totally. It's probably just what you need. She can support you through all that's just happened, too.'

She knew what the 'too' meant and quickly texted back to say she would be there – anything rather than talk to Dad about it all. Mum relaxed next to her and flicked on the TV. The look between them did not escape her notice.

They caught the end of the local news: 'A 45-year-old man has been remanded in custody charged with assault. He was arrested after police were called to a house in Sevenoaks where a mother and child were being threatened with harm.'

'For goodness' sake, there's no escape. Can you turn over to the movie channel, Sophie?' Dad spoke over their heads.

Chapter forty-two

25th October
Friday

Zara smiled her welcome. She asked how things were and showed her shock as Kate told her about Ella's dad. Kate liked that about her – she didn't pretend and look at her with a blank face, which is what she had expected before she met her.

Zara asked her about her feelings, and Kate realised that she didn't need to protect her from how awful it had all been. It was hard to speak about her parents because she didn't want them to be judged – only she was allowed to do that! But she told her about her mum burning herself in the bath, and how afraid she had felt, even though she had only shown anger at the time.

Zara brought out her timeline and asked if Kate wanted to put what had happened on it. She was surprised, as she had thought it would just be for old memories, but it was good to mark it all down. Kate talked as she drew and slowly came to the realisation that in some strange way Ella's dad had done them a favour – he had helped to break the silence.

'The silence is broken?' Zara asked.

Kate's eyes met hers momentarily. 'Yes.' She cried and made the paper wet, and Zara let her. Kate felt relieved to talk, although she had no idea why. It was true – she was actually starting to feel safe, and maybe she could finally speak.

Later, as they sat in silence, she heard herself whisper, 'It was my fault.' Zara said nothing.

Sophie

She met Katie in town as arranged. Her session appeared to have gone well and they sat in silence drinking their hot chocolate. Sophie had

171

suggested they go to the supermarket so they could get toys and the birthday picnic things all together. She realised that they had reached a sort of truce whereby they wouldn't speak about Jakey and would use Alfie's birthday to distract them. It's all rather bizarre, Sophie thought, considering how we've tried for ages to get Katie to talk about it. Obviously it was the lesser of the two evils, and they both knew it. Simon was definitely on a mission to deal with it all. He had refused point blank to talk to her about it when they had gone to bed last night, though – not like him at all.

They finally agreed on a big yellow digger that would hold bricks and sand on the beach and which he could sit on while he was still small. It hadn't been as hard as she had thought it might be. They were so much alike, she realised, using the same distraction techniques. Have I done this to her? she wondered. They were conspiratorial in their actions – anything but go near that day. The past few days had succeeded in pulling them from poles apart to standing next to each other, she realised.

Simon

Work had been good already, allowing him to work with such flexibility. Being a consultant definitely held some perks that a normal nine-to-five job would not have allowed. The doctor had told him now that he was suffering from stress and exhaustion, which he thought was a bit rich considering he had taken hardly any time off before – but then maybe that was the problem. Mike had called and Simon had agreed that he could pop in for coffee as Sophie was out with Kate. Waiting for him to arrive, Simon realised that Mike was someone he had seen across the church many times after the morning service (on those occasions when he had actually gone), but just a smile and a nod did not help you to get to know someone. He couldn't remember whether or not he had been there before everything had happened. This should be interesting, he thought.

Mike was a big man, he realised, as he sat across the table from him. The edge of a tattoo poked out from under his sleeve. He caught Simon's look and spoke about his earlier years as a biker, and how he had found Jesus in a cell where he had been put for being drunk and disorderly. Simon's surprise was evident as he responded, saying that no one would believe he had lived in such a way. He knew he was unrecognisable now – not that he didn't struggle. He didn't drink alcohol any more, and added that he had been clean for more than 15 years.

'What about you, Simon? What about your faith?' he asked.

Simon thought for a moment about where it had gone, knowing that it had dissolved seven years ago. 'Well, I lost it really, I suppose,' he heard himself say.

No one had asked him that question for a long time, he realised. He had retreated from church life and believed that no one had pursued them, although he knew Sophie would disagree. He was aware that he had rejected them and God; they had not saved him, nor had his faith, so what was the point?

Mike was not to be undone. 'Do you want to talk?' he asked carefully.

Alfie banged his spoon on his tray, bringing order once again; he appeared to like Mike responding to his voice and smiles. 'What are you up to, Alfie? You're such a good boy, aren't you?' Mike reached out to tap on Alfie's high chair. 'I don't suppose you know that Jane and I can't have children; not the sort of thing to shout about, eh?' His eyes met Simon's momentarily.

Simon's mind started to freewheel as he considered what he was saying. He recognised an invitation to share but really didn't know if he could do it.

'We don't seem to be able to have babies that survive. The doctors don't know what the problem is, but after last time I don't think we'll try again,' he continued, much to Simon's discomfort.

'Oh, I'm so sorry,' was all he could think to say.

'Jane is amazing, putting up with me. She deserves better, and she definitely deserves a baby of her own. But when our son Samuel was born at 24 weeks and died, it nearly broke us both, so now we're hoping to adopt.'

He seemed to be offering him an exchange, his pain for Simon's. The deal was completed as Simon took the risk and spoke. 'It's awful to lose a child; we don't really know how to get past it.'

Chapter forty-three

26th October
Saturday

Simon

Sophie had called to see if he fancied fish and chips; she was going to collect Katie from work on her way home from walking the dogs. So he had laid the table with the required condiments and now Alfie and he sat in anticipation of their treat.

'Where are they, Alfie, eh? I'm starving.'

The back door banged open and Katie stormed through the kitchen, followed by her mum who stood shrugging her shoulders, bearing no evidence of dinner.

'What's the matter with Katie?'

Sophie shrugged in the doorway.

'Did you get the fish and chips?' he asked cautiously.

She shook her head, appearing to bring herself to, and answered him. 'Oh yes, I did. It's in the car, sorry.' And she disappeared outside again.

They sat, just the three of them, in the all-too-familiar situation of missing Katie. Things had been good between them all lately, in spite of recent events – or was it because of them? Simon wondered.

Katie had been grumpy when she had picked her up from work, Sophie explained, and she wondered if work was too much for her with everything that was going on. Still, he was not prepared to let things slip again; he really didn't think he could do another seven years of the same.

Alfie stuffed his fish in his mouth in total absorption. He was a happy boy, and Simon was determined to ensure he had the best life; he had to save him from this.

He looked across at Sophie: she had been talking. 'The thing is,' she emphasised, 'it's hard to go through therapy. She was ok yesterday but it will affect her; we don't know how much she's engaging with it. But if she is, then it will be terrible – I know.'

'I want her to face it, and you too,' he said as he looked at his wife. 'I can't do this again. Look at Alfie – we owe it to him.'

Kate

When Mum picked her up she felt exhausted. She didn't know why; she was alright when she left work. It was a distraction even if it was just a short shift, but when she saw Alfie she suddenly felt the pain all over again. Jakey was coming back. She had kept him away for so long. Hugging her baby cushion to her, she sat in her room. The smell of fish and chips wafted up the stairs and made her feel hungry in spite of herself. She knew Dad would be pleased if she went down, but still, could she do it and not cry? she wondered.

As she pushed open the door they all turned towards her, relief written over their faces – apart from Alfie's, which was covered in dinner. 'Kaka,' he chimed.

'Sorry, Mum. I felt really bad when I got out of work,' she said.

'It's ok,' Dad said, squeezing her hand.

They handed her the meal, still in its paper, and they ate on in silence. She knew they had been talking about her, and Mum seemed stressed about something, but she couldn't deal with it then so she kept silent.

Chapter forty-four

27th October
Sunday

Simon

The sun shone brilliantly; the beach, recently washed by the retreating sea, glowed in the afternoon light. Behind a windbreak the barbecue flared as sausage fat caught the flames. The girls sat on a rug with throws around them while Alfie played with his new toy. He grinned as he filled the digger with stones and sand under the ever-watchful eyes of his mother and sister.

'Are the plates ready?' Simon asked, and Katie scrambled to her feet, arms outstretched to take the sizzling bangers.

'Yum, Dad, these look great,' she smiled.

The rolls were split and buttered, ketchup drizzled down the length of each one and a sausage added. Alfie, ever ready for food, was up on hands and knees and gaining on the plates at speed.

'Come on, my son, sit with me.' Simon swung him up with one arm and released a seat from its cover with the other.

'Ooh, look at you, Dad,' Katie teased. 'So clever. Isn't Daddy clever, Alfie?'

He broke off a piece of the sausage and blew on it, wrestling with Alfie's determined grip. 'Wait, Alfie, it's too hot.'

Sophie, ever resourceful, handed him a roll – large, white and round. The sheer size of it made him grin.

Sophie

It was a miracle. Here were the four of them celebrating Alfie's birthday. She couldn't believe it. Alfie sat on his dad's lap, thrilled to bits. Clutching his oversized roll, he rammed it into his mouth. Katie sat next to her, calm and relaxed. Her sudden, 'Look, it's the Mexican!' took them all by surprise, as there, perfectly timed, he appeared in the water. The wreck from long ago joined them as they trod their precarious path down memory lane.

'I haven't seen him for years,' Katie whispered into her roll.

'No, hon, it's been a long time,' Sophie agreed. She looked up at Simon, who was transfixed, staring out to sea. She realised he had not been here since and, just like Katie, he had forgotten.

'Jakey loved the Mexican,' Simon said. He lifted Alfie from his lap onto his shoulders and strode down the beach towards it.

Kate

Dad walked really fast down the beach as she ran after him. Alfie twisted on his shoulders when she called his name, and finally Dad stopped. Standing still, he stared out towards the wreck.

Kate stood next to him and slipped her arm through his. He gave her a squeeze and then lowered Alfie to the ground. Squatting down, he pointed, 'Look, Alfie, look. It's Jakey's Mexican.'

He had said, 'Jakey's Mexican.'

Mum spoke, making them suddenly aware of her presence. 'Jakey loved it here, didn't he?'

She handed them each a spade and a bucket and in silence they built a sandcastle.

Chapter forty-five

28th October
Monday

Sophie

Sophie was pleased Katie had another free day as it meant she could try to spend some time with her, even if it meant she would not be studying. Sometimes life has to take priority, she thought.

Tracy had called after everything had happened but Sophie had found it difficult to talk to her. It was not her fault, but just speaking to her brought the memories crashing back. She had asked to meet up and Sophie had agreed, so now she had to face her and Ella, along with Katie.

'You ready, Mum?'

Katie stood there, shorts, tights and DMs topped with a leather jacket. She looked lovely, and Sophie felt old and dowdy in comparison.

'You look lovely, hon,' Sophie said as she grinned at her.

'Do you like my latest eBay purchase?' she twirled round for her to see.

'It's really nice. Will you keep an eye on Alfie? I need to put on something else, I think.'

As she passed her, Katie hugged her and told her she always looked good, which was a bit of a shock to say the least. She changed anyway.

The café was full but Ella and her mum had bagged a table and waved them over. No need for a high chair today – Simon was looking after Alfie, so they could relax. They all hugged each other, holding on for those extra 'it's good to be alive' seconds. Tracy insisted on buying, and now they sat looking across at each other.

'I'm so sorry, Sophie—' Tracy began.

Sophie stopped her in her tracks. 'It's not your fault. This is about him, not you. I'm just so glad to see you alive and well – both of you.' She reached across and held both their hands. They all welled up, and laughed off their relieved, unified tears with humour.

Tracy told them that because he would definitely be locked away they could move back home; they just needed to sort out a few things first. Katie asked what had happened to them that day, and so they all recounted their own separate experiences and thus were able to make sense of the turn of events.

Kate

Kate had been looking forward to seeing Ella. Mum had seemed relaxed, too, so that was good. They both looked really well. Tracy was clear of bruising and looked almost healthy, and Ella looked relaxed. She had missed her. They spoke about what had happened and then Ella and she were able to talk together while Mum and Tracy chatted.

'How are you really?' Ella asked her in hushed tones.

Kate was surprised at her question as she had thought she looked ok. 'Do I look bad, then?' she asked.

'No, it's just that you look a bit sad, somehow.'

Kate smiled, realising that her lovely friend could see beneath her make-up to the real her, and she made her decision. 'I've been having therapy,' she whispered.

'Because of my dad? I'm so sorry!' she gasped.

'No, not because of him.'

'What do you mean, then?'

'I can't talk here; later, maybe. I will tell you though, I promise.' And Kate meant it.

Simon

He was not really a sneaky person but he felt like one today as he made his way to Mike's house with Alfie. He had rung him after they had left, half expecting him to be at work. But Mike was working from home and glad, he said, of an excuse to stop. He had said he didn't mind if he brought Alfie as Jane would be pleased to look after him so they could talk.

Simon was surprised to discover that they lived fairly nearby. Their cottage was down a lane surrounded by trees, and it was beautiful.

They were welcomed warmly. Alfie was taken off with Jane in hunt of biscuits and a drink, while Mike led Simon into his office. He had a view out of his window 'to die for', as Sophie would say – fields and trees off into the distance.

'Great, isn't it?' Mike asked, as they stood and marvelled at it.

'It really is something,' Simon agreed. 'Where did you find this place?'

'It was a wreck when we found it, but the man who owns the big house up there took a shine to us and sold it to us providing we did it up, so we did. I suppose it became our baby.'

'Well, it's really great.'

Jane appeared with coffee and biscuits for them, and informed Simon that Alfie was happy playing with her saucepans and that he could relax. He realised that he actually did feel relaxed in the presence of this man.

They continued to stand looking out of the window, holding their mugs as he spoke. 'So how are things now, Simon?'

'Difficult actually, but it's not about last week. It's something else.' He turned to face him, unsure what to say.

'Let's sit, eh?' Mike moved towards one of the chairs.

'Mike, I don't know why I thought I could talk about this or why I have come to you. But when you spoke about Samuel I thought maybe you would understand.' Mike looked at him, appearing to be waiting for him to go on. In the silence he felt his old fear of losing it rise up again, and he couldn't keep his gaze.

Mike spoke then. 'When we found out we were finally having a baby and we saw him moving on the scan, we started to plan for the first time. We'd had so many treatments that had failed; I sometimes wondered if God was punishing me for all I had done before. So Samuel was a blessing beyond belief. We decorated a nursery and bought toys and clothes; we knew he was a boy. We would talk to him, and truly we were so happy. Then suddenly, for no apparent reason,

Jane went into labour. They tried to slow it down but nothing was going to stop him being born.'

Simon looked up as he paused; he was standing again looking out over the fields. As he continued, his voice was low with emotion. 'I was there as he entered the world. He was so tiny, so perfect; we couldn't believe God would take him from us. We were devastated. Jane was beyond despair, locked in her grief. It was the most terrible time. We blamed ourselves. Really Jane blamed herself – she had carried him, after all, she would say. So we looked to see what we might have done wrong. Had she eaten the wrong food, drunk alcohol, or something? Random thoughts would go through my mind, like my body was wrecked from my previous lifestyle so I caused it. It could have destroyed our marriage, but it didn't, thank goodness.'

He turned and came back to his seat. 'That was three years ago, and I still think about my son every day. I imagine him running down the fields and round the house. When we were on the train that day I saw your love for your family, and your terror at the thought that something might happen to them, and something weird happened. I realised that even when children live, they still bring with them pain and worry, and in that moment I determined that if I could support your family in any way, then I would. Something shifted in me, and now I feel different.'

Simon looked across at this man who had said so much, and saw peace in his eyes. He was shocked at his words, his honesty, and his offer of support. 'Mike, I don't know what to say.'

'Just know we're here if we can help in any way. Jane wants to ask you and Sophie round for dinner sometime, if you're up to it.'

Sophie

It was strange having Simon around all the time. He seemed to be quite content to spend time with Alfie, which freed her up – not that she had been writing again after everything. But he also had found someone to talk to, which surprised her even more.

As they sat together he told her what Mike had said. She couldn't imagine how hard it must have been for them to lose a baby and be without children. Now they were about to go to a panel to be approved as an adoptive family. They had jumped through many hoops to get there, including therapy. She was shocked at how open he had been with Simon; she thought men didn't talk like that, and she said so.

Simon agreed. He had been taken aback too, but when he spoke about Jakey and how he had gone to talk to Mike about him, she was finally stunned into silence.

'Sophie, the thing is, I can't keep on like this. I want it out in the open. I want his picture on the wall, our pictures, of all of us. I want Alfie to know all about him. I want my girls back.'

He looked at her like he was relieved to have finally spoken, and she realised again that she had silenced him, too, with her grief. She could feel her tears rising up and brushed them away with irritation. He was right, she supposed – it was the right time, but how?

Chapter forty-six

29th October
Tuesday

Tash was silent as Sophie brought her up to speed with everything, then she spoke. 'Is all this in the book?'

'Yes, but I need to put Jakey' (there, I said his name, she thought) 'into it too, and it's hard.'

'What about Katie? How's she doing with it all? I can't believe you did Alfie's birthday at Broomhill. How amazing is that!'

'Well, I think she's getting there too. We could actually arrive at the same place together.' She sat back, suddenly afraid as a memory flooded her mind.

'What is it, Sophie?' her lovely friend held her arm.

'I refused to bury Jakey's ashes and now I don't know where they are,' Sophie said between gasps.

'Don't worry; Simon will know, I'm sure.'

'I should have asked him, but I couldn't,' Sophie sobbed.

He had taken the dogs out so she couldn't ask him, and anyway, how would she say the words? How terrible that she didn't know where they were, where her boy was. Her thoughts ricocheted around her head.

Katie had returned from college in high spirits, which was good to see, and was off out to see a film, so that meant she and Simon would be alone, once Alfie was in bed. Sophie filled the kitchen sink with water and sat Alfie in it, much to his delight.

'No point in filling up a bath just for you, eh, Alfie? Jakey used to do this too.' She tried out the words to see if anything happened; no, she was still alright.

The kitchen door opened to reveal Simon, fresh out of the shower, standing there. 'Well, look at you, Alfie. Did I hear Mummy telling you about Jakey?'

He came to her then and wrapped her up in an embrace as they stood together.

'Simon, I don't know where the ashes are,' Sophie mumbled into his chest.

She felt him draw in oxygen deeply. 'They're safe, don't worry.'

As they stood there the evening light diminished and outside disappeared, revealing their reflections against the glass.

Chapter forty-seven

30th October
Wednesday

Why she had agreed to go to Jane and Mike's for dinner she had no idea. Simon had really wanted to; he wanted her to meet them properly, not just at church. She had seen them across the church for years – she even knew their names. It was strange how the two families had suffered greatly, but neither knew the story of the other.

Is that what church can be like? she wondered. Unless you spend time together out of church, you don't really get to know each other properly. Still, she was grateful to them already, as Simon was talking about going to church again, like his faith was being reawakened.

He was right: the cottage was beautiful, ablaze with light as they pulled up. I would never have thought they had a home like this, she thought, shamefaced. How could I be so judgemental? They looked totally different, too, to when she had first met them years back. It was only now that she realised why – they had come through their grief and were getting better.

They both stood in the open doorway, waiting for them as they got out the car. Mike had his arm around Jane, filling the door frame, she noticed.

'So good to see you both. Come in.' Mike's voiced echoed out. They led the way into their lovely home; it was so warm and inviting. The wood burner was red with fire, and glasses were set on a little table in front.

'Let me get you a drink. What would you like, Sophie – red or white, or something else? How about you, Simon?' Mike asked.

'What about you? What are you having?' Simon answered, remembering their previous conversation.

He smiled. 'I'm having alcohol-free beer. Do you want one?'

'Sure, I'll give it a go.'

The women had disappeared into the kitchen to find a vase for the flowers Sophie had brought, and they followed. They seemed at ease together, he noted with relief. Sophie had been a bit uptight before they got here; now she had a ready smile for him as she turned.

'Look outside, Simon.' She reached out for his hand and pulled him towards the kitchen window. Lights twinkled in the trees and were wound in and out of the trellises that surrounded a decked area. 'It's so beautiful,' she laughed with delight. 'It must be magical to live here.' They turned around to see the smiles of their hosts.

'It's really lovely to share it with you, Sophie,' Jane responded. 'Would you like to go outside? We have loads of wraps; we love to sit out there in all weathers.'

Cushions were pulled out of cupboards, and before long they were sitting around a table festooned with tea lights. 'This is amazing, Mike. Did you do all the work yourself?'

'Yes, it's taken the best part of three years but it's worth it now.'

Sophie was swivelling in her chair, trying to take in the rest of the garden.

'Do you want to walk around?' Jane offered.

'Oh yes, do you mind?'

'No, come on.'

Still wrapped up, they wandered off down the path, leaving Mike and him alone.

Mike leaned forward, speaking softly. 'Samuel's ashes are there by the big tree at the bottom. I'm going to put a swing there, and when our children arrive they'll play near him.'

They watched as the women neared the tree. They stood together and then moved closer as they merged. They were still for a long time and then Sophie turned and buried her head on her new friend's shoulder.

'Will she be ok?' Mike asked.

'I think so. It's time,' Simon replied.

Driving home later, Sophie leaned over to grasp Simon's hand as she recalled her tears. She had been surprised at the safety she felt with these new friends. Two children would be a shock for them; maybe they could support them, too.

Kate

Ella had come round to babysit with her again; she was pleased to see her. Once again they had eaten pizza and were ensconced in front of the fire. They talked together about all sorts of things until Ella suddenly pointed to the box. Kate had totally forgotten it was there, with everything that had been going on. 'Isn't that your box? What's in it?' Ella asked.

Kate felt sick rise up into her mouth and swallowed it down quickly. 'It was my brother's box.' She spoke with controlled caution.

'What, Alfie's?' Ella looked confused.

'No, my brother Jakey's.' There, she had said it. Now she knew.

Ella turned to face her and opened her mouth to speak. Kate had to stop what she knew was coming, so she spoke again. 'He died seven years ago, when I was ten.'

The weight of the words slid her further down onto the cushions and she curled on her side. Ella didn't hound her; she just lay facing her, stroking her hair.

They were asleep on the the cushions when Mum and Dad came back.

Chapter forty-eight

31st October
Thursday

Simon

By the following morning he had made his decision: he would talk to Mike about it all. Sophie needed to get some writing done so he arranged to meet him at the park with the dogs and Alfie.

It was freezing, and walking was only possible with scarves across their faces. Alfie was snug under the rain covers and would probably fall asleep.

'You sure you want to do this?' Simon asked him.

'Sure, if you're up to it.'

They trundled on up the hill, faces bent against the wind, as the dogs raced to and fro. His mind was full of words, but in the end he could only say one sentence. 'My son Jakey died on his fifth birthday. He was riding his new bike.'

He thought for one moment that Mike had not heard him. He turned to look at him to find he had stopped. He stood a few steps behind with his hands over his face. He had heard. 'Simon, I'm so sorry.'

Tears were running down his face as he moved to him and drew Simon into a bear hug, the like of which he had never experienced before.

They stood there for a while as the wind whipped around and until the dogs came and sat still beside them. No other words were necessary. The exchange was completed; they had trusted each other with their pain.

Sophie

The screen was open in front of her but the words would not come in the order she wanted. She had placed Jakey's picture in front of her once again, but she did not know how to start. She placed her lips to his image and whispered her 'sorrys' again and again, and then placed him back in her wallet.

She started to write random thoughts about her mum and stepdad, about their wedding that she had not attended. She felt guilt pursue her as she considered the decision she had made. She had still held her mother's relationship with Brian responsible for her last encounter with her dad, so she had voted with her feet and stayed away.

After Dad died, there was a funeral. I didn't want to go and so Mum let me stay with friends and went without me. I don't know what she was thinking. I couldn't go and say goodbye to the man I had once loved but who had petrified the love out of me. I was upset that she went, but she said it was the right thing to do.

Life slowly seemed to get better. Mum was calmer and we did some things together. We would go to the cinema and shopping, but I always thought she really wanted to be with Brian. How she ever thought I believed the lie that he was just her friend was beyond me.

Sitting back, she wondered how hard it had been for her mum. She had not kept her safe, that was for sure, but she did deserve another chance at love, didn't she? She had never looked at her and Brian with compassion before, and the thought took her by surprise.

Forgiveness. Now there's a word, she thought, as she left the table in search of solace. There wasn't much as she really needed to go shopping again; some fruit and crackers would have to do. Staring out of the window, eating absent-mindedly, she suddenly recalled the plaque on the tree in Mike and Jane's garden: 'Much-loved son Samuel'. Sophie wrapped her arms around herself. Where was Jakey? He needed to be safe, too.

It was impossible to write, she realised, and on the spur of the moment she drove round to Jane's house – she had said to pop in any

189

time. Simon had taken the big car and it took a while to locate the Fiat's key.

There was no car in the drive when she pulled up and she was about to drive away when she saw movement in the window. Jane appeared at the door before she had turned off the engine.

'It's so quiet here; we always hear cars arrive. Come in. It's lovely to see you.'

The coffee was frothy, just the way Sophie did it at home, and they sat at the kitchen table that Jane had rapidly cleared of papers and photographs.

'Are you ok, Sophie?' Jane asked.

'I wanted to talk to you, but I didn't know if it was alright.'

'You can talk about anything you like,' Jane reassured her.

The sound of the telephone interrupted their conversation. 'Do you mind if I get this? I've been waiting for it,' she asked as she moved across the room.

'Hello, Jane speaking. Oh, hello Monica. Do you have news? Really? Oh, that's so great, thank you so much. Yes, yes I'll tell him. When? Ooh, that soon?! Wow. Thank you, thank you.' She hung up the phone and turned, her eyes alight. 'They have approved us for adoption and now they want to move everything on quickly.'

Sophie stood, her own thoughts pushed to one side as she hugged her friend in delight. 'Is Mike at work?' she asked

'No, he's out with Simon, walking the dogs.'

Sophie's surprise was evident but it was skilfully brushed aside to focus on Jane again.

'His mobile is here so I can't call him,' Jane said.

'I can call Simon.' Sophie pulled out her phone and dialled.

Simon

Mike was delighted to hear the news and it was arranged that Simon would drop off the dogs and meet them at Mike's house. He was pretty surprised to realise that Sophie was there too – she was supposed to be writing.

They were all in the kitchen when Alfie and he arrived, glasses of bubbly at the ready. 'Here's to a faithful God who doesn't leave us abandoned,' Mike said as he lifted his beer bottle, and they cheered the good news. They gathered around the table. A high chair had been found for Alfie, much to Simon's surprise.

'So what happens now?' Sophie asked as she placed Alfie in the chair.

'Well, they've matched us already. It's all a bit back to front, but we still need to go to the matching panel. Do you want to see a picture?' Jane's joy was plain to see.

They lay their treasure on the table – three pictures; one with the two children together, and the other two of them individually.

Simon picked up the one of the two children together – a boy and a girl. 'How old are they?' he asked

'Kirsty is nearly two and Jake is four,' Mike replied.

Sophie gasped and covered her mouth. 'Did you say his name is Jake?'

'Yes.'

All eyes were on her now, and Simon wondered what she would do. To his shock, she said, 'Our son was called Jake, too.'

Mike and Jane looked at each other. Mike, well ahead of the game, spoke first. 'I'm so sorry about Jakey, Sophie.'

She looked across from him to Simon, her expression revealing that she knew he had spoken about him to Mike. 'I went for a walk with Mike and told him about Jakey, and that he died when he was five.' Simon spoke his words deliberately to ensure she knew all the facts.

'Our son-to-be, Jake, is blind. That's why he hasn't been placed yet, and his sister may also go blind – they don't know yet.' Jane's voice broke through.

There was silence for just a moment before Sophie came to. 'Oh my goodness, you are amazing to take them on.'

He watched as his lovely Sophie snapped herself out of her world.

'No, we're not really,' Mike responded. 'Have you any idea how many children get left in children's homes because no one wants them?'

They passed the pictures to each other, examining the faces of their soon-to-be son and daughter. Their joy was apparent as they explained about the lights in the garden and their plans to make it a sensory experience for them.

191

They stayed just long enough to finish their drinks, then Alfie's nappy and Simon's lack of forethought to bring a spare meant they had to leave.

As they left, he heard Sophie as she spoke to Jane. 'I came here to tell you about Jakey. Can I come another day?'

He couldn't hear her reply; he only saw the hug.

Chapter forty-nine

Kate

Mum and Dad were sitting in the front room when she came home. She had obviously interrupted them. 'Shall I go out?' she asked.

'No, silly, come here. We were just talking about Mike and Jane. They're adopting two children.' Dad patted the sofa next to him.

'Aren't they the couple you went to dinner with last night?'

'Yes. They're adopting a brother and sister. The boy is blind and his sister may go blind – they don't know yet. Don't you think they're amazing? The thing we were talking about is that the little boy is called Jake.'

She swung around to look at her father. 'Really? Oh, I don't know if that's good or bad.' Her voice once again held her emotions low in her tone.

Simon pulled her to him and murmured. 'I think it's good; it's time.'

Kate sat up straight and asked for a lift, one of the reasons she had come in in the first place. 'I have a session at six. Will one of you give me a lift, please? It's freezing.'

'Sure, Kitty,' Simon answered, as she moved across to retrieve the box from its hiding place.

Kate sat on her bed and stared. She still was unsure what was inside – blankets and toys, but were there pictures, too? She wanted to take one to therapy, but she felt frightened.

She knelt up quickly and pulled open the lid. Taking the blankets out carefully she was confronted by a red jumper with a fireman on it. She pulled it to her, smelling it for a trace of him. There was one picture stuffed down the side; the corner was bent over. Tenderly, she pulled it out and turned it over. There he was, and there she was. Together they sat, Jakey holding the book as she read it.

The knock was so quiet she almost missed it. Her father moved towards her and spoke from behind. 'Can I see it too?' Kate held it away from her body as her dad sucked in his breath and held her tight.

'There he is, our Jakey.' They sat together, father and daughter, for a time, until she came out of it with a jump, worried about being late. Simon moved to accommodate her and drove her to her appointment.

Sophie

Simon had gone to check on Katie after she had taken the box and not come back for ages, only for the both of them to appear and dash out to Zara's.

Alfie was still snoring. He definitely won't sleep tonight, she thought, as she pushed open Katie's door. The room was a total shambles but the box was within reach on the bed. Stepping with care, she sat down next to it. The lid was still off and a blanket and jumper were lying on the bed. She tenderly picked up the jumper and held it to her, rocking and keening once again in anguish. How was she meant to do this? How would she be able to bear having his pictures around?

Still rocking, she put her hand in the box and pulled out a folder. His school booklet. He had made it in his first and only term in school. He smiled at her in his school jumper – always cheeky, always funny – as she carefully turned the pages.

His teacher had written under the drawings entitled 'My family': Mummy and Daddy and my big sister Katie.

She shut it suddenly and examined his face and spoke aloud. 'Jakey, why didn't you stop? Mummy told you to be careful.'

And then she sobbed, loud enough to wake Alfie, who pulled her out of her torment.

Kate

'How was your week?' Zara began.

Kate recounted various events, finally grinding to a halt, almost breathless.

'You're in a hurry today, Kate.'

'It's just that I brought a picture of me and Jakey and I don't know what to do.'

'What would you like to do?' Zara enquired.

'I want to show it to you.' Kate quickly handed her the photograph.

'Do you want to tell me about it? Take it slow. Do you want to put it on your timeline as you talk?'

Kate nodded as Zara moved the surface and her timeline nearer. 'How about I put the picture on here?' Zara offered.

Kate found the place on the line where she thought it would go and started to talk. 'I think I was about seven and he was two. I loved to read to him; he loved me doing it too.' Her tears fell again as she remembered the feel of him on her lap, her baby boy. 'I used to think he was like my own baby. I would bath him and all sorts, and then as he got bigger he wouldn't do what I said.'

'He was starting to be naughty?'

'Yes, yes, that's right, he was.'

Kate sat back and surveyed the paper. She had written in big letters, *He was a naughty boy.* She was surprised at how young her writing looked.

'So Jakey was a lovely little boy, and then, like all children, he started to have a mind of his own?' Zara enquired.

'Yes.'

Chapter fifty

Later that night Mum came and laid on her bed in the darkness. She had not done that for a long time. 'Are you ok, Kate?' she asked.

'I suppose,' Kate replied. 'It was hard at Zara's.'

Sophie's response surprised her. 'I am sorry; it's hard to talk.' She paused and then continued. 'I came in your room earlier – I hope you don't mind – I just needed to look in the box.'

Katie stiffened and then relaxed. Why shouldn't she look? He was her baby, too, she thought. 'What did you find? Did you see the jumper?'

'Yes, and I found his school stuff, too. It made me cry. I had a thought, hon, about Dad looking through the entire box with us. He did put it together, after all. I think he could help, and we really need him to. What do you think?'

Kate was struck by how like her mother she was, how her words came out in a torrent when she was anxious. Sleepy now, she agreed.

Simon

Simon was surprised at the suggestion, but pleased too: he had been left out for too long; now it was his time. He was unsure as to the best way to do it and prayed aloud, asking God for wisdom. A random thought came into his mind, unbidden: Jakey died because he was so full of life.

He tried to stop his thoughts as he grappled with the words. Was this God whispering?

He had found it almost impossible to get past what had happened. He had read the police reports and witness statements, but the two closest to him felt responsible, and were struck dumb.

He had never spoken to Sophie about what had happened in the hospital. In fact, he had only spoken in therapy. But in an instant he could transport himself back into the room that had held Jake's body.

He had been told that an accident had happened and that his precious boy had died. The officer had tried to stop him from barging into the room – he supposed it was to prepare him. But he had to be there, to be by his side, to see him and hold him – to save him, for goodness' sake! There must have been a terrible mistake.

As soon as the door opened he had known the truth. Sophie's howls filled the air, and Jakey's absence was palpable. He lay there in silence. He looked perfect, his face unmarked – asleep, surely.

He had moved to the edge of the bed without looking at his wife, and reached down to take his precious boy's hand. He was neither cold nor warm. He lifted him up and laid his hand over the bandage on the back of his head, holding him against his chest.

Then and only then did he look at Sophie, over Jake's shoulder. Her screams and cries bounced off the wall: 'I'm sorry. I'm sorry.'

He had known she was a great mother, but for one solitary, split second, his look had questioned her. He had poured on her an intolerable burden, and she had collapsed. He knew later that his questioning was normal – of course, he needed to know – but it had tipped her over the edge. It was the last time they had been together with Jakey. His final farewell to his little boy had been alone; leaving him there had very nearly broken him. His little ten-year-old daughter Katie had been his only reason to carry on.

Jakey had been full of life, it was true, and so had Sophie, in the early stages of a pregnancy only he and she knew about. But it was not to be: she miscarried at four months and as the baby died, she seemed to too. The unborn child had forced her to carry on after Jakey's death, but in the face of the baby's death too she became emotionally unavailable, until now.

And so it was with great caution that he proceeded. He now had an opportunity to help them all, including himself, and thus rescue Alfie.

Simon sat with his back to the sofa; the box sat next to him. Katie had agreed to the plan and she and Sophie had gone to bed, leaving him alone with the task at hand – namely, he thought, saying goodbye to Jakey, finally. It was strange, he pondered, how looking again at Jakey's belongings would enable them all to say goodbye. It was almost like they had to say hello first, in order to face it fully. He was pleased and terrified at the thought; it had been a shock just looking at that one picture with Katie earlier.

He knew he had placed everything in the box, but he had no recollection of what was in there. He recalled that he had grabbed anything that had been touched, worn or played with. Anything that held his image or a memory of him, anything to not lose his boy, anything that would ensure he would not be forgotten.

Breathing in deeply, he started, all the while mumbling to Jakey. 'Come on, my lovely boy, it's time.'

His tears rained down as he also held the jumper to himself, as he held the school booklet that Sophie had spoken about. The baby book was placed next to him along with packets of photographs and framed images, all to be looked at later. Next came a giraffe – was its name Derek? he pondered as a smile rose unbidden through his tears. There were the clothes that he had worn home from hospital when he was born, along with his wristband and his first pair of shoes. He doubled over again, unsure if he could do this, but he owed it to Jakey and to the women in his life: he had to ensure that Kate was able to engage fully with the world again. So he continued.

There were cars, lots of cars; memories of them lined up around the house on make-believe roads, ready to trip up an unsuspecting sister or parent. He stopped. He had forgotten, and the memories now unleashed forced others up from secret hidden places – boat rides, trips to the pool, holidays. Flipping over a frame, a holiday picture slapped him in the face, father and son eating ice cream, one of Jakey's favourite things.

'My boy, my boy,' he whispered, and he cried.

Chapter fifty-one

1st November
Friday

Sophie and Simon sat together. Kate had gone off to college. Alfie played at their feet with the giraffe, whose name *was* Derek, it turned out.

Sophie

She had been anxious when Simon had suggested that they do some of the box when Katie was not around, but he said he thought it would be less overwhelming when they did it with her if she knew what was coming.

He had sat up until late, he told her, and had cried a lot and then fallen asleep before coming to bed. Now he laid out the contents in some sort of order: toys, photos, clothes and wellies. It was the wellies, blue with Fireman Sam on them, that caused her to sob – they were so small; he had so much growing still to do; he was too young. She let Simon hold her as she let her grief out. Alfie turned to her and gave her Derek, pulling himself to standing against her legs, once again rescuing her from being totally overwhelmed.

Simon

He knew he needed to tell her again, even though in the beginning after his initial response he had told her he did not blame her. 'It wasn't your fault, Sophie; he was too full of life,' he muttered against her hair.

There. He had said it, and she turned to look at him, her face awash with tears. Her eyes seemed to scan his for signs of truth. 'Sophie, you have to forgive yourself. You have to lead the way for Katie.'

She did not speak.

He continued, 'When I was in therapy she told me that I could not rush either you or Kate, so I didn't. But now I really want to do this. I want our boy back in our family. I want his things around – well, at least his pictures – and his box, our box of memories, mustn't be hidden any longer.'

Sophie looked at him silently, her face drained of colour. She seemed to shake herself a little and then she spoke in hushed tones. 'Since I started to write I have found out some things. I have lived in a shutdown state since I was a little girl. I couldn't stop my dad hurting me and Mum. Then when Jakey and then the baby died, I really thought I would die too. I was no use to anyone any more. I had let our son die, and our baby.'

Tears ran down both their faces. She had finally said it out loud, and now Simon had something he could help her with. His relief at her communication forced him to smile through his tears as his wife reappeared. He hugged her to him and told her how much he loved her and that it would be alright – he would find a way.

Kate

Kate was surprised to receive a text at college later that day. Her dad was suggesting that they all go out to dinner that night; he wanted to go early so that Alfie could come too. She felt suspicious as to what he may be planning. That morning she had taken her cereal into the front room to eat in front of the TV and had found the box on the floor by the sofa. Mum had mentioned Dad looking at it, but had he?

They appeared to be surprisingly calm when she came home. Dad told her he had booked a table in a restaurant in Whitstable, of all places, and asked her to hurry. She had tried to ask him what was happening, but he told her he just wanted to take them out.

'Come on, Dad, that's miles away! What's happening?'

'Kitty, just let me do this, please. It's a nice evening and if you hurry we'll miss the traffic.'

She had relented, and now they found themselves ahead of the evening rush, turning off the main road into the back lanes to park. Even in darkness she loved the smell and sound of the sea. The pub was ablaze with light, and as they neared, the sound of laughter and the chink of glasses filled the air.

'I wish we lived nearer the beach – then we could do this more often,' Dad said.

'Will they let Alfie in?' Mum asked.

'Yes, I checked when I booked the table,' Dad replied.

They had a table all ready and a high chair for Alfie. As they sat down, Dad asked for a bottle of champagne.

Simon

He had sat with Sophie pretty much the entire day, remembering and talking and crying about Jakey, interspersed with bouts of entertaining Alfie. He suddenly had the overwhelming urge to celebrate the fact that they had survived all that had happened. He wanted them to know how much they meant to him; he wanted them back fully in his life.

'Well,' Simon said as he poured everyone a drink, 'this is the deal. Today I realised again how close I came to losing you. I want to talk to you all about an idea I have, and I brought you here because I want you to hear me out.

'First I want to say how much I love you girls, how much I have always loved you. Nothing that has happened has *ever* changed how I feel about you both.' He emphasised the *ever* to ensure they got what he was saying.

He watched as they both stiffened and looked at each other, and he toasted. 'To my amazing family: Sophie, Kate, Alfie, and Jakey, who was so full of life we could not contain him.'

They looked aghast at him, but he cheered his glass with Alfie and then proffered it to both the girls.

'Dad?' Kate started.

'Chink my glass, Kitty. Come on, it's time. Ella's dad gave me a wake-up call, and I could have lost you all. You need to, I need to, and we all need to live life again and to bring Jakey with us… Please.' He could hear the pleading in his voice.

Sophie lifted hers and pressed it against Alfie's beaker, then turned to Kate. 'Dad's right, darling, it's time,' and she stretched out her glass towards Kate.

They watched as Kate's eyes filled up and overflowed down her beautiful face, and then slowly, very slowly, she wrapped her manicured fingers around the stem of the glass and lifted her arm.

Simon smiled at her. 'To you, Kitty. Brave, beautiful you.'

And they smiled through their tear-soaked eyes and touched glasses.

Kate

She couldn't believe what Dad said. She got it, but really, was he actually meaning the words? It was her fault – how could he seem to forget that? But his eyes had that look, like the time when he had broken down in the bedroom, and she couldn't say no.

Sophie

Simon toasted them all – and Jakey. What was he playing at? She knew it had been a difficult day, but really? She honestly thought Katie might lose it. But it was when they had both looked in shock at each other that she realised, for the first time, that they *both* felt responsible. How could she have been so stupid, not to have seen it before?

Simon

He was determined not to let them linger on what was written all over their faces. He needed this, and he thought they did too.

He gave them all permission to have whatever they wanted to eat. As they sat eating, with a caution that was visible, he started to share his thoughts. 'So, everyone, can I share my thoughts with you? Are you listening, Alfie?'

Alfie responded with, 'Dada.'

Sophie and Katie mutely nodded.

'We need a place to go to remember Jakey, don't we? Seven years ago the worst thing ever happened in our family, and we have nowhere to go where we can remember him.' Simon spoke with steady deliberation. His words moved forwards without pause. To stop, he realised, would permit them both to shut their emotional doors, and he was not going to allow that.

'At Mike and Jane's house they have laid the ashes of their baby boy, Samuel, under a tree so that they mark his life in some way, and have a place to go to remember him.'

They were starting to look concerned now. Raising his hands, he clarified: 'I don't mean we do the same, ok? But we do need somewhere. Well, I do – I can't have his ashes stored any longer in the funeral home.'

Sophie's breath could be heard across the table; she obviously hadn't realised or thought. 'Oh my boy, I'm so sorry,' she started.

Simon was still on a roll and determined to keep them focused. He reached across and held her hands, squeezing gently.

'Why would you? The both of you have walked devastated lives for seven years. It would be the last thing on your mind, especially as we did have a service.' He raised his hand again to stop either of them speaking. 'When we went to Broomhill Sands for Alfie's birthday, and I was sitting there and the wreck appeared, all I could think about were the times we went there with Jakey. All the sandcastles we built and how I swam out towards the wreck with him one day in the dinghy. He absolutely loved it; I could almost feel him there.'

He paused and looked intently at the faces of those he loved and continued, 'These are my thoughts: what if we sprinkle Jakey's ashes around the Mexican and along the beach? Then we would have a place to go.'

They were all silent.

'What do you think? Sophie? Kate?'

Simon sat back and picked up his drink. He could feel the pressure from holding everything in finally release.

Sophie

Sophie was so shocked when she realised where the ashes were that for a moment she didn't know what to do. She was so overcome with shame and guilt that she had not laid her boy to rest that she thought she would be sick or scream or something else, she didn't know what. But Katie's face as it drained of colour and filled up again in front of her, and the realisation that she was her little girl, and she owed her something as a parent, snapped her out of it.

'I think it's a good idea, Simon, 'she heard herself say. 'Don't you agree, Kate?'

Katie looked at her mother, her hands in her lap, her dinner getting cold on her plate, and she nodded almost imperceptibly, and then very quietly spoke. 'Yes, Mum.'

Kate

She was so shocked at what Dad said, and also so relieved, that she had no idea what to think any more. She had always thought it was her fault and that she was to blame, so when he included her and Mum in that toast, saying he had always loved them, it was weird. But then to say that about the ashes, that was even stranger. When they were at Alfie's birthday all she could think about was Jakey, too – they felt the same, she and Dad. So she agreed before she had time to do anything else.

Dad then stopped them all from talking about it any more. He looked much happier and told the waiter they were ready, and after the plates were cleared the waiter appeared with a cake with sparklers on it, much to Alfie's delight.

'Happy birthday, Alfie,' he sang and they joined in too.

Dad raised his glass and toasted, 'To Alfie, my precious second-born son.'

Chapter fifty-two

2nd November
Saturday

Zara had said she could text her any time, so she did. Dad had thrown her and she really didn't know what to do next. She wasn't due to see her for a week, but it was worth a try. She was surprised that she texted her back so quickly. She had a cancellation that day, so that was great.

'How are you doing, Kate?' Zara asked as she sat down. Her timeline was there ready if she wanted it. She picked it up, and Zara handed her her box of pens.

'I need to say something but I don't know how to say it.'

'Just take it slowly. You are in charge of how you say it, and how fast. Or you could write it, if that would be easier?' she offered.

'Can I ask you a question?'

She nodded.

'I know my dad spoke to you before I came to see you. But I don't know what he told you. Will you tell me?'

She seemed to consider for a moment and then replied, 'What he told me, Kate, was that your little brother died riding his bike in front of a car, and you witnessed it.'

Katie was shocked that she would say it out loud, but she had asked her, and Zara had told her right from the start that she would be open and honest with her, and she was. She pushed her further. 'Did he say it was my fault that Jakey died?'

'Katie, he did not, but he told me he thought you believed it was your fault.'

She couldn't help it, and burst into tears.

'Was he right, Kate?'

205

She had to say it out loud, but it was so hard. After all these years the day was stuck in her mind without words, just sounds. The screaming of Mum and the sound of the car and then silence; all she could do was nod.

They sat there in silence as she cried, and then slowly she drew the energy to say the dreaded words. 'I waved at him.'

'You waved at him?'

'Yes, that's why it happened.'

Zara stated quietly in response. 'You have believed for seven years that Jakey died because you waved at him. I cannot imagine how terrible that has been for you. I'm so sorry.'

'You don't understand. It was my fault. If I hadn't waved he would still be alive,' Kate clarified with determination.

'He was alone on his bike?'

'No, Mum was there, but it was my fault because I waved.'

'What does your mum think, Kate?'

'I don't know. We can't speak about it. We never have.'

'So let me check this with you. You and your mum were there and saw it all and you have never spoken about it, and you believe she blames you.' She paused and looked out the window before she spoke again. 'Kate, you were ten years old. You were her little girl then. What does she think? Does she blame herself for it, rather than you?'

Kate was shocked at what she was saying. 'I'm sure she blames me, or she would have said so, wouldn't she?'

'Maybe she was too distressed to speak.'

Sophie

The day had dawned bright and hopeful. Alfie was full of beans so a walk with the dogs was required before anything else. Also she needed to think, and sometimes thoughts became clearer if she was walking. Simon was on a roll: he wanted closure – that stupid word that she had heard bandied about. But was that possible, how could 'closure' occur when your son had died and you had caused it?

He had talked to her the night before, after that bizarre meal in Whitstable – what a crazy night. She had argued the point, and he had told her that closure meant closure on the constant shutting-down of the grief, not on Jakey. What he wanted was for Jakey to come with

206

them into the future; he wanted a place to go to remember him, and the box out somewhere for all to see. As she thought about it, her hand covered her mouth. How would she do this? He had told her she had to do it for Katie, and he was right. Katie had looked so shocked at the meal that something had shifted in her mind, something ridiculous, and something she should have known all those years ago.

'Come on, Alfie, how about you try and walk?' The dogs ran and she and Alfie started out after them. His little hand was enclosed in hers as he tottered next to her up the path, pointing and laughing at the dogs. 'You're so clever. What a big boy you are.'

Lost in the moment, she cast her eyes across the expanse and was transported back in time. An old fallen oak lay, a shadow of its former glory; it had shrunk so much over time that she had to look around to make sure it was the same one. She swung Alfie up onto it. 'This was Jakey and Katie's tree,' she told him.

It was, but time had rearranged itself, and now here she was with Jakey's little brother. He held both her hands and flung himself into the air, his expression the image of Jakey's, and in spite of herself, she laughed.

As they continued their wander, she continued her inward journey. Alfie shouted as another dog joined in the rumpus and she had to swing him up suddenly out of reach as they careered by. 'Oops-a-daisy – they nearly knocked you over.' He pushed his face into hers – his attempt at a kiss.

'You are the most gorgeous boy. Come on, dogs, let's go.' And they were off again.

Later, as Alfie napped, she continued to write.

> *Brian and Mum slowly became an item. She would say he had just popped over and was going to stay for dinner.*

From where she was now she realised that her mum had tried to gain her permission, but she wouldn't have any of it.

When she found out she was having Katie, she had thought it would heal it all, but it had appeared to be too late.

A sudden thought hit her: when Jakey died they had tried to help, she was sure. She had a memory of Katie spending time with them and of Brian trying to be nice. It occurred to her that they had lost a grandchild, too. She had the suspicion that her mum knew about her pregnancy as well, but she had never said anything. She determined that she would ask Simon later.

She knew that the next thing to write would be about the accident, but was she ready? And what about Katie? Did the look she had given her at the meal really mean that she believed she was to blame? She struggled not to slip back in time to the day; Joanna had taught her the 'running technique' to move her mentally away from the trauma to a safe place, so she used it. It was amazing that the mind could have its own safety net, a safe planned place to retreat to, a kind of shelter in the storm. She wondered later if Katie used it too, and decided to ask her.

Simon

He was pleased with himself; to have spoken aloud was a massive achievement, and so far everyone else appeared to be ok. Sophie had returned from her walk with a tired baby boy and had let him put him down for a nap. She had also let him make lunch, which to anyone else might not sound like much, but she prided herself in always providing food for everyone, like it was her job, her very profession, so it was a big deal. She had been typing away and had barely looked up when he put a coffee next to her.

Later, as they sat – he, Sophie and Alfie – eating the sandwiches he had made, she started to talk. He realised then that he would have to fill in the missing pieces, which might not go down well.

'Did you tell Mum about me losing the baby? Did they look after Katie around that time?' she asked.

He decided to just be totally honest and get it all over and done with. 'I'm going to tell you the truth, but I want you to stay calm, ok?'

Sophie nodded and, surprisingly, reached out to hold his hand. 'Sophie, your mum and Brian were devastated when Jakey died. They stepped in and took care of Katie. You were in no fit state to do it yourself, and neither was I. And so yes, I did tell them about you being pregnant, and when you went into hospital for the miscarriage they were there too. In fact, they were really great – supportive and kind.'

Sophie looked shocked, so he knew he had to explain. 'When Jakey died, you seemed to die too in some way. I couldn't reach you, and neither could Katie. Your mum stepped in to mother her. She was so lovely – that's probably why it's hard for Katie to hear that she didn't keep you safe when you were small. And also to realise that you have unresolved issues with her. She loves them both. And then, just days later when you had the miscarriage, you totally shut down and had to have all that therapy – I mean, you were in hospital for about three months, practically comatose. They had you sedated and on all kinds of medication. Slowly over the next few months you came out of yourself. You started meeting with friends like Tash again, and you started to take responsibility for the house and Katie. That's when you got Sid for her, remember?'

She did remember getting Sid, but the rest was a blur.

'The problem we faced was that you seemed to have shut down enough to shut out your mum and Brian again, but Katie still needed them. So she started to go round there without you knowing after school. It was what she needed, but it meant she continued not to talk to you about everything.'

Sophie looked so sad he wanted to hug her, but he knew she needed to process this. They all loved her, and she needed to let herself move through it all to receive the love that was waiting for her.

Kate

She found them in the kitchen. They weren't expecting her home, she knew, but the look on her mum's face told her that this was a conversation she should avoid. So she quickly explained her presence and went to leave.

'You went to see Zara today, didn't you? But you only saw her a few days back,' Mum asked.

'Well, yes, but that trip to Whitstable started me thinking, and she said I could always call, so I did.'

'Did you go and see Gran too?' she asked.

Kate knew then that she needed to fess up, but she wasn't sure how Mum would take it. But Dad smiled at her.

'Well, actually, I did go round afterwards. Look Mum, I know you had a terrible time but they've been really good to me. I'm so sorry about your dad and that Gran didn't keep you safe, but she did help me a real lot.' It was out finally.

Mum looked shocked and pushed her chair back from the table, but Dad stopped her. 'Sit down, Sophie, please. Hear us out.'

And then he did it. He told her all about how ill she had been and how Gran and Granddad had been so kind, not just to her but also to Dad, and also how understanding they had been when she still wanted nothing to do with them later on, right up until Alfie was born.

'Sophie, you need to know how much we all love you – your mum, Brian, me, Kate: all of us.'

The time had arrived to speak – Kate just knew it. She could feel a pulse in her eye start to flicker. 'Mum, I'm so sorry I made you ill. It was my fault Jakey died.' The words burst out louder than she meant to. Mum jumped and looked at her with horror, and burst into tears.

Sophie

She thought she was in some sort of waking dream, and now it turned into a nightmare as her baby girl told her she had caused Jakey's death.

'NO, you didn't, Katie. It was my fault. I was in charge, not you. I couldn't stop him. Oh, darling, I'm so sorry – I had no idea. I can't believe I was so ill.' She paused. 'I want you to know something else, too.'

She didn't know if she could do this, but she had to help her daughter make sense of her behaviour. She looked at Simon, and he nodded. 'Katie, I was pregnant when Jakey died – four months, and then I lost the baby. I think it must have unhinged me in some way. It was not your fault, any of it. I'm so sorry, darling, for everything.' And she cried some more.

Alfie banged one of Jakey's cars on his high chair and shouted.

Kate

She couldn't believe it – her mum had been pregnant! Two of her children had died, and she didn't know. Suddenly the silence ended. Just like Zara had said, they did not think it was her fault at all. Gran had always said it wasn't; why hadn't she believed her? She had said

Mum was ill and it was not because of her. A thought occurred to her. 'Did Gran know you were pregnant?'

Dad spoke then, amazingly calm. 'I did tell your gran at the time, Kate. You were too young to cope with anything else. I didn't tell your mum that I had, though. I've only just told her.'

She needed to ask him. She had to know, but she felt sick as her words came into her mouth. She breathed deeply, not holding her breath as Zara had said, and spoke slowly. 'Dad, do you think it was my fault that Jakey died? I waved at him across the road.' Her heart felt like it would burst out of her chest.

He wrapped her up in his arms like he used to. It felt good as she sunk into him. 'My lovely daughter. Kitty, you were a little ten-year-old girl, full of life and joy. You were funny and clever, bright and shining. You adored your little brother and would never, ever have done anything to harm him. It was not your fault.'

Mum moved in to join them as they hugged and rocked each other. 'I'm so sorry, Katie. I wish I'd been able to speak to you,' she murmured into her hair.

Their rescuing second-born son was silent as they hugged. Over Kate's head he smiled at his dad, Jakey's car in one hand, Mr Bop in the other.

Chapter fifty-three

3rd November
Sunday

Simon

Simon offered again to help. He would take Alfie to church so she would have some time. Her agreement and smile confirmed his plan.

She would try to write.

Katie was asleep, and the calm of the house, she told him, no longer held the pressure of silenced memories. Simon knew deep within himself that he could finally support her to move forward alongside him.

Sophie

Everything had changed. The pressure of silence had been lifted; they could all speak if they wanted to. Nothing needed to be hidden. She felt as if a huge weight had been lifted off her chest, and she could now breathe again. She remembered that somewhere in the Bible it said something about everything working together for good for those who loved the Lord. She realised that Ella's dad had woken them all up out of their stupor and reminded them of the value of family.

She sat, laptop primed to begin. Scanning the room, she started to thank God for her blessings – not just the material ones that cluttered the walls and floor, but the ones that filled the air again. The lost memories of laughter and fun; lost memories of games played and meals eaten; lost memories of holidays taken, and Christmases and Easters... She wrapped her arms around herself as she tried to reach her boy as he laughed and played. It was time to really remember, and time to say goodbye.

She thanked God that light was shone into the darkness and that truth was revealed.

Everything was suddenly moving very fast. She knew that it was beyond her to control it; she was unsure she even wanted to. So many people wanted to get involved, and they had all come up trumps. It's at times like this, she realised, that friends come into their own and rise to the occasion.

Simon was sorting out all the heavy things that needed to be taken to the beach, leaving the food and decorations to her. Tash had taken over the food organisation, along with Rebecca and Ruth and the girls from the group, leaving her free to sort out decorations and the special personal things.

Tracy and Ella had felt so bad about all that happened, and couldn't believe how it had been part of the process that enabled them to finally do this. They were shocked and sad to hear about Jakey, but honoured to be trusted with all of it, so they would be there too, along with the twins.

Mum and Brian had asked, via Simon, what they could do, and now it was becoming a rather big event – not the quiet occasion she had envisaged. Simon had said that it would reflect Jakey – big, loud and full of life – and that they needed to celebrate his life now. He was pleased, so she was going along with it. He was on a roll, making everything happen at speed; he needed it done now. She realised that she had been the cause of the delay and put aside her own fears to free him up as they moved forward. He is a good man, she thought.

And then there was the box: they had started their journey into there, too.

Jane and Mike, new friends though they were, had turned out to be amazing; even Katie was taken with them. Sophie had really wanted to help them get the bedrooms ready, now that the children had been matched with them. Simon was spending a great deal of time helping them too – time off work was coming in handy – and had called to say he was taking Alfie there after church to give her more space to face the final part of her writing. She was still not totally alone, though – Katie could wake at any time.

She leaned back and hooked an arm over her head, pushing her fingers into her hair. How do I do this? How do I put in black and white the day everything stopped? She had placed Jakey's picture in the corner of the screen and held in her hand his hospital wristband.

'Baby Pritchard grew into you, Jakey, full of life, full of adventure.' Her internal dialogue continued. Removing the picture, she clutched it in her hands, along with the wristband. Closing her eyes, she ran back in time, pondering how she had got to where she was.

The numbness had lifted finally when she had discovered she was pregnant with Alfie, allowing her to engage with her pregnancy and with her husband and daughter. The miracle of Alfie had not escaped her: sex had been the last thing on her mind for years. She was too cocooned in her grief to allow herself pleasure of any kind, and too guilt stricken to engage in any intimacy. Every now and then she had tried to be the wife Simon needed, but more out of obligation than desire. He had never pressured her, though, and it was amazing that he had stayed.

In her therapy sessions she had been finally able to face the horror, as Joanna provided her with a safe haven. But she was alone in it, separate to everyone else; she could only access it in isolation as she had no words to speak to her family.

Finally, as the therapy moved towards an ending, Joanna had suggested that she write about her past. She must have known that as Sophie continued to process it alone, she would continue to use the techniques she had learnt. And that finally she would become more aware that she had shut down. She was smiling to herself as she recognised her therapist's craft, when the door opened to reveal Katie.

'What are you doing, Mum?' she asked with the quizzical expression she was perfecting these days.

'Oh, I was just thinking how clever my counsellor was. She knew me so well.'

Katie came and plonked herself alongside her mother. 'Zara's like that too: she seems to really get me. I love her straight talking.'

'I'm so pleased you like her. It really makes all the difference, eh? Did she teach you the running technique? So you have a kind of escape route from trauma when it rises up?' Sophie suddenly realised that this was a perfect opportunity and wondered at the thought that surfaced in her mind.

'No, what do you mean? Are you going to write about it?'

'No.' Her decision made, she spoke. 'I'm actually meant to be writing about the day Jakey died. The thing is, because I've always run away from it to the safe place in my mind, it's hard to go there. What about you, hon, how did you manage it?'

Sophie turned to look at her child. Katie, her teenage daughter, suddenly looked so young and troubled again. She couldn't bear her to be hurt any more, so Sophie spoke to distract her. 'I was horrified that Gran had to take over looking after you. But since we have spoken – you, me and Dad – I'm so relieved she did. At some stage I need to talk to her, to thank her. She'll be coming to the beach, Dad said, so maybe I can talk then? Or maybe I need to see her before. What do you think?'

Katie's face regained its colour as she answered. 'I think Gran would be so pleased to see you. Maybe she's very different to the person she was when you were little. She always told me it wasn't my fault, but I never believed her. She never said anything bad about you, you know – she just wanted you to get better.'

It was strange for Sophie to hear her little girl talk in such adult terms about her mum, the mum who hadn't kept her safe, but had managed it with her granddaughter. She knew she would have to deal with it at some stage, and with Brian too, but now she wanted to ask Katie something: 'Have you spoken about when Jakey died with Zara at all?'

'A bit, but it's so hard. Really it's been about how I've felt all these years, and we're doing a timeline too. She thinks you were too upset to talk to me when it happened.'

She's learning things rapidly in therapy, Sophie thought, recognising the invitation to respond. This had to be done now. 'She's right, hon. I really should have talked to you. I should have told you it wasn't your fault, but I couldn't face anything to do with it, and then everything seemed to collapse inside me when I lost the baby.'

Katie's nose stud caught the light as she nodded, her eyes wide with amazement. Sophie could hear her breathing, slow and laboured.

'Are you ok, Kate?'

Her response came, along with her exhalation of air. 'You *really* don't think he died because of me? I did wave at him.'

Sophie pulled her to her and they sat, her daughter's head on her shoulder, the laptop redundant beside them. The picture of Jakey was still clutched in her hand as she soothed his big sister.

Tea made, they continued their time together. She knew that they needed to deal with the two versions of events – Katie's and hers: it was the only way. 'Shall I tell you what I remember of that day?' Sophie asked.

Katie nodded mutely.

'Kate, it's very important that you know this was in no way your fault.' She took her daughter's face in her hands and looked deep into her eyes. 'I mean it, Kate. It was in no way your fault.'

Sophie gathered herself and began. She did it for her daughter, whom she had abandoned in her grief; she did it so she could engage in her role as a mother, for Kate, and not just for Jakey.

'Jakey and I had been up to the park so he could ride without restrictions. Do you remember how he would climb everything and learnt to ride a two-wheeler when he was only four?'

She nodded again, and Sophie steadied herself. She owed this to her daughter. Holding her close and wrapping her arms around her, she spoke the words she had practised in her head. 'We were on our way home to have a birthday tea. I had told him to stay near me and away from the roadside, but when we came around the corner by the shops he swapped to the outside and moved suddenly to avoid a post, but he lost his balance. I didn't even realise you were across the road until I heard your screams.'

There. She had said it, and now Katie wrapped her up in her arms, and they both sobbed.

Kate

All these years she had believed that Jakey had seen her, and ridden in front of the car, when in fact he had lost his balance. She was stunned into relief, silence and shock. Mum sat with her head on her and cried and cried. She had blamed herself and only now was able to speak the words to her. They finally cried together.

'Will you forgive me, Kate?' she heard her mumble. 'I have failed you as well as Jakey.'

'Oh Mum… Mum. I don't have anything to forgive you for. You lost Jakey and my other sister or brother. Honestly, there's nothing to forgive.'

She hugged her tight, as memories of her lying ill in hospital suddenly flooded her mind. She used her breathing to steady herself as her mother pulled back and looked at her.

Sophie

'You ok, hon?' she asked through her tears. 'What are you thinking about?'

Sophie realised that it was going to be ok, as the mother within her overrode her grief to meet the needs of her daughter, finally. She was so relieved that she burst into tears again.

'Oh, Kate, it will be ok, I promise.'

And she knew she was right.

Chapter fifty-four

4th November
Monday

Simon

It was a lovely sunny day at Jane and Mike's. The bedrooms were nearly finished. Kirsty's was pretty and pink, full of lights and mobiles, and Jake's had a clear and simple layout and was also full of lights. The shelves of toys were in easy-to-reach positions and both of the rooms had murals, which Katie was helping to paint. Jane and Mike's excitement was tangible and knew no bounds. It was only as they listened to and supported Sophie and Simon in their plans for Jakey's ceremony that it was put to one side.

They sat together, talking through ideas for the day, drinking coffee as Alfie moved from chair to chair, suddenly really mobile, as if turning one had released him to move more freely.

'Jakey was just like him,' Simon told them, 'full of life, an explorer. But Alfie has a calm centre that Jakey didn't have, and he seems to be able to read others' feelings even at this young age. Don't you, baby boy?' Alfie moved towards him, smiling his widest grin.

'Simon, we want to talk to you about something, but we want you to know you can say no, too.' Jane spoke quietly.

'Ok.'

'We know that you won't have a place near here to place some of Jakey's ashes, and wanted to say that if you'd like to put some under our tree with Samuel's we'd be honoured. You could mark it however you wanted. I know it's a bit strange as it's our garden, but we would love to share our trees with you. They are accessible from the common, too. It's just a thought.' Jane smiled at him gently as they continued to sip their coffee.

He was really taken aback by their kindness and generosity; it was so lovely of them. 'I'll talk to Sophie. You are so kind to us. Thank you.'

The girls were sitting together, the box on the floor between them, when they got back. Jakey's clothes sat on Sophie's lap while toys lay on the floor, and photographs were laid out to form a sort of collage.

'Hi darling,' Sophie said as they came in the room. 'Can you hold on to Alfie a minute while we move these pictures? We're making a collage for the ceremony and to keep on the wall here. What do you think?'

'Wow, that's so brilliant. I hadn't thought of that. How come you're doing it?' Simon was so surprised to find them doing Jakey things together.

It was Kate who spoke. 'Dad, Mum and I have done it – we've talked about what happened. We now both know what the other has been thinking all these years.' She got up, then, and came to him, wrapping her arms around both him and Alfie. 'It wasn't my fault, like you told me. Jakey didn't even know I was there.'

They stood there, the three of them, as Sophie looked on. She looked younger than he had seen her look for an age. Her make-up was smeared and her hair was a mess, but something was gone – the haunted eyes – and he wasn't going to miss them.

Kate

Mum had asked her to arrange a meeting with Gran for coffee, away from home so she could just turn up with Alfie and surprise her. Kate had decided that she needed to ask Granddad too. He had been amazing to her, and she just loved him.

Kate saw her first because she could see down the street. She looked lovely – all smiles as she walked. It was only as she saw her spy the back of Granddad's head that her expression changed, and for one moment Kate thought she might change her mind. As she came in, Kate stood up and waved her over. 'Mum, we're over here. There's a high chair if you want for Alfie, too.'

219

Kate smiled at Gran and Granddad as she manoeuvred her way over. 'Did you plan this?' Gran asked quietly.

'No, Mum did. Didn't you, Mum?'

'What?'

'You planned this, didn't you? It was your idea.'

'Yes it was. Hope that's ok. Hi Mum. Hi Brian.'

'It's lovely to see you and Alfie. Hello, Alfie. You're getting so big now, aren't you?' Gran said, her voice the spit of her mum's, Kate realised.

Alfie performed beautifully, laughing and waving his legs as Mum tried to get him in the chair. Gran was up in an instant.

'Let me help you, Sophie.' She gently directed Alfie's legs into position. Sophie leaned across and hugged her, saying her thanks. Gran looked overwhelmed for a minute and sat down, quickly picking up her tea.

'Did you order a drink, Sophie?' It was Granddad's turn to speak.

'Err, no, not yet.'

'What would you like? Let me get it for you.'

'Oh, thanks. I'd love a cappuccino, please.'

As Granddad went to get the drinks, the two women looked at each other. Gran appeared to be speechless for a moment. 'It's so lovely to see you, Sophie. You look really well.'

Mum smiled at Gran, and Kate suddenly felt really emotional. She couldn't remember the last time she had seen them together like this.

Sophie

It had seemed like a really good idea until she saw the back of Brian's head. Katie had set her up. She had only planned on speaking to Mum, but Katie obviously had other ideas.

Their expressions had moved from troubled to pleased, as they gauged how she was feeling. She felt so guilty that she had put them through so much. Brian went to get her a coffee and she reached across and took her mum's hand.

'I'm sorry, Mum, for everything. Thank you so much for taking care of Katie for me.'

Mum sat there in shock as she listened, and then her eyes filled up with tears which then ran down her now more papery skin and made her blouse dark. She said nothing, just reached out and took her other hand.

Brian stood alongside the table, coffee in hand, unsure of what to do. 'It's ok, love. Sit down. Me and Sophie are having a really nice chat,' Mum soothed.

'Here you go, Granddad,' Kate spoke and reached out for the coffee.

Sophie had a strange moment, sitting there watching them dote on their grandson. The far past had been outstripped by the more recent past. Ella's dad had pushed the four of them together, and now, speaking about Jakey's death had enabled a way back to her mum too. It may not have been achievable without it. It had taken the worst event in her life to enable her to let her mum back in. She realised that her mother had stepped up to the mark with Katie, her own daughter, in her absence, and that realisation, that discovery, had forged a way.

Chapter fifty-five

5th November
Tuesday

The wind had finally dropped and everything and everyone was in place. The weather was due to change and so some friends had taken days off work, but all had come to say goodbye.

The gazebos, surrounded by screens, were festooned with lights, balloons and pictures. Under one, the table groaned with food and drink, under another a barbecue blazed, and under the final one the chairs were gathered.

The winter sun hung low in the sky as the sunset began its show. Reds and oranges battled with the purples and blues for supremacy. The result was a riot of colour.

They all gathered – those too young to have known him along with the ones who had watched him grow. Simon had donned his wetsuit and the dinghy was ready. At the water's edge they watched as he placed the ashes into the boat. He had stood before his friends and spoken, with his arms around her and Katie, about his firstborn son, Jakey. He told of times gone by and thanked them all for their part in the journey. They had all raised a glass to their boy.

Now he stood, ready to take this final journey. The Mexican had surfaced and the waves were unusually still. Their plan to coincide with the tide had been timed to perfection, and God had been generous with the weather. The four of them gathered around the dinghy and said their farewells, and then Simon turned and pushed the dinghy out onto the water.

As he neared the wreck he turned and raised his hand as arranged. As Jakey's ashes spread out across the water, they stood together ready, and raised their arms to release the balloons – a cacophony of colour from Postman Pat blue to Fireman Sam red, and every colour in between.

She found herself held by her mother and her daughter, their faces wet with tears, yet smiling. They had managed this terrible day that brought honour and remembrance to the little boy too full of life to be held back, and now they stood, ready for the future together.

Epilogue

Simon

As darkness started to fall, the lights really came alive. Each path had it contours marked out in colours. The trees sparkled with soft glowing orbs. The heady aroma of mulled wine hung around them as they clasped their steaming glasses.

Jake sat on the swing while Katie pushed him back and forth, his laughter light and high. Kirsty and Alfie had ride-on cars and were following each other as though an invisible string linked them. Mike and Jane, arms around each other, glowed with the unexpected gift of parenthood as they watched the children play together.

Slowly they came back together and he gave Katie the plaque that she had designed:

Jakey
We love you and miss you still

The ground had been prepared and some of the ashes had been placed together with the scan picture of the baby. They stood and watched as Katie placed the plaque alongside Samuel's.

Simon spoke: 'Jakey, we will always miss you and the brother or sister we never got to meet, and we will wonder what life would have been like if you had stayed with us. Now, today, we all start a new journey. It will be a journey when times will be hard, and a journey where joy is now allowed. We will never forget you, my son.'

Back home, Sophie's mum stood in the kitchen, a pile of ironing completed by her side.

'Did it go ok?' she asked, moving across the room to hug her.

Brian came in from the lounge. 'There's a fire in here if you need to warm up.'

'Thanks, Brian, that's lovely.' Sophie moved nearer to him, still unable to hug him, but touched his arm instead. Katie stood, arms linked with him, and plonked a big kiss on his cheek.

Simon filled the kettle and turned to look at Sophie with that look she knew so well. She nodded. He moved across the kitchen to put his arm around his wife, and smiled at his daughter. 'Do you want to share our news, Kitty?'

'Mum is pregnant!' she laughed, and hugged her grandparents in delight.

For help and advice

Care for the Family's Bereaved Parent Support

Support for any parent facing the death of their son or daughter at any age, in any circumstance and at any stage along their journey of grieving.

We run day and weekend events around the UK to enable bereaved parents to meet together and find comfort, strength and hope amongst others who understand and care.

We provide a free telephone befriender service from trained befrienders, all of whom have themselves lost children. This is available to those whose child was aged 35 or under. We aim to link with situations of a similar age or circumstance.

We produce a regular email newsletter and a growing bank of helpful resources for bereaved parents and those supporting them. See http://www.careforthefamily.org.uk/family-life/bereavement-support/bereaved-parent-support

Contact us by email at mail@cff.org.uk or call 029 2081 0800.

Find us on facebook at www.facebook.com/bpscff

Women's Aid

For women: www.womensaid.org.uk

For children and young people: www.thehideout.org.uk

Helpline: Freephone 24-hour national domestic violence helpline run in partnership between Women's Aid and Refuge: **0808 2000 247** www.thehideout.org.uk

For more information about Susie Flashman Jarvis and her speaking and writing ministry, see www.daughter-of-the-king.com

Page Three model, serially unfaithful, heroin addict.

Loving mother, honourable wife, daughter of God.

Two lives. One woman. One God.

Susie was a rising star of the modelling world. Her image graced TV screens, billboards and magazine covers across the globe. But she was a private failure, addicted to Class A drugs and promiscuously jumping from one broken relationship to another.

Then God...

A life transformed; a loving Father nurturing and disciplining a wilful, frightened daughter towards healing and reconciliation. A story of God invading the everyday joys and pains of family life.

Once a body exposed to shame and lust.

Now a life laid bare to tell of the Father's love.

'Joyous and heart-breaking. Shocking but inspirational. The ruthlessly honest, movingly written, self-penned story of Susie, our lifelong friend, and her journey of struggle, redemption and hope.'
Steve Chalke, MBE, Oasis UK, and Cornelia Chalke

'This is a real story of a real woman with real issues arising from a wounded inner child, but one who is determined to hold on to the Lord and face the issues, one by one, with courage and dedication.'
Jennifer Rees Larcombe, Beauty from Ashes

'You will hear elsewhere many tales of a radical change, but this one is told from the hindsight of several decades and offers hope and encouragement to readers who will persevere as she has done.'
Anne Coles, New Wine

Instant Apostle is a new way of getting ideas flowing, between followers of Jesus, and between those who would like to know more about His Kingdom.

It's not just about books and it's not about a one-way information flow. It's about building a community where ideas are exchanged. Ideas will be expressed at an appropriate length. Some will take the form of books. But in many cases ideas can be expressed more briefly than in a book. Short books, or pamphlets, will be an important part of what we provide. As with pamphlets of old, these are likely to be opinionated, and produced quickly so that the community can discuss them.

Well-known authors are welcome, but we also welcome new writers. We are looking for prophetic voices, authentic and original ideas, produced at any length; quick and relevant, insightful and opinionated. And as the name implies, these will be released very quickly, either as Kindle books or printed texts or both.

Join the community. Get reading, get writing and get discussing!

instant apostle